KILL THE RAVEN
A THRILLER

KURT B. DOWDLE

Black Feather Press
Salt Lake City, Utah

for Kamp

"Bring me an axe and spade,
Bring me a winding sheet"
—William Blake

1

"It's going to explode, isn't it?"

Nyx Bauer stared at Aodh Blackall's face and awaited the answer. The corner of his mouth turned up, but he said nothing.

They reached the spot where they'd remembered digging the seventh hole in a string of charges intended to break up the coal seam.

Aodh said, "Musta been eight."

Nyx caught a faint whiff of smoke and turned to look up at the spot near the ceiling where they'd dug the eighth hole.

A breeze blew into the room, and the fuse that led to the eighth charge, which had nearly but not entirely gone out, sparked to life and raced the short distance to the blasting cap.

Aodh had only enough time to say, "Ah, Jaysus" before shoving Nyx to the floor and catching the brunt of the explosion in his back.

SIX HOURS EARLIER MEN SHUFFLED FORWARD and loaded themselves into the car as it emerged from the mouth of the mine. As she joined the procession, Nyx caught a fragment of a distant memory.

She'd just come home from picking raspberries with her sisters, who'd run ahead of her into the house to show their mother their haul for the day. Nyx heard the hoof beats and wagon creaks that meant her father was coming home. She'd stood in the front yard, waiting for him to come into view, that exquisite instant before she laid eyes on him.

She'd met the wagon at the road and looked into her father's eyes, searching for reassurance that wasn't there.

"Daddy?"

"Yah."

"Are you all right?"

That night, after her sisters had fallen asleep, Nyx had lain next to the stovepipe hole in the floor that led to the kitchen. She heard him tell her mother that his good friend Roy Kunkle had died that day in an explosion and that only Kunkle's body had saved him from the same fate. She'd heard him say he'd carried Kunkle's head out of the mine and given it to the undertaker, already on the scene.

NYX SWALLOWED HARD AND STEPPED into the mine car. She stared straight ahead into the maw, not looking at any of the men who made no attempt not to stare.

The car passed under the thick, rough-hewn lintel onto which someone had scrawled in charcoal the words "*Sic Transit*."

Candlelight from the mouth of the mine lit the way, and Nyx saw an immense wooden door straight ahead. The door had words and pictures painted on it, including a form Nyx recognized as the double *distelfink*, the good luck goldfinches. The door seemed to creak open of its own accord, and when it did, she felt a blast of foul air, as if the whole earth exhaled smoke and sulfur.

Once they passed through, Nyx saw a small person, probably a kid, standing next to a wooden bench. The kid closed the door after they went through, and all went black.

She felt the rough canvas cuffs of her jacket sleeves against her hands and smelled the breath of the men riding with her in the car, felt the pressure of their bodies pressed together and shaken down the iron tracks.

Friction thrummed up through the soles of her boots, and Nyx felt her throat constrict, fought the urge to grab the man next to her for comfort. She clenched her jaw and prayed for the car to stop moving, stop plunging into the black, stop going down.

When it did, by the light of the men's candles, Nyx saw a room to her left, supported by heavy timbers, floor-to-ceiling, wedged hard. The men gathered their gear and walked through the room which led to another and another, and so on. The only sounds were their boots crunching on the floor and the clinking of their gear.

Nyx wished someone would say something to her, to welcome her or simply to acknowledge her presence. But no one spoke. She'd never worked with men and didn't know this was often typical.

She felt the absence of her own set of tools, the *Gezähe*, they called it. She lacked the equipment to mark her as a member of the group, not that she would have known how to use it. Nyx felt the heat that met them the further down they went and felt, too, her breasts and ribcage pressing against the bandage Angus had wrapped around her torso before sunrise.

She recalled another moment long past, the ghost of a sensation, the feeling of her father's embrace when he left for work.

When they reached what looked like a dead end, a jagged wall of coal and slate, the men set their gear on the floor. Two of them took off their shirts.

A man said to Nyx, "Get down."

The man's voice snapped Nyx from her reverie. Coal dust filled the lines in his face which otherwise looked to her like a red mustache and greasy smudge under the candle flame.

She said, "Why?"

The silence held for a long moment, and then a low ripple of laughter passed through the men.

The man pointed to the dark, far corner of the room and said, "There."

Nyx said, "All right, I'll play along."

"Yah, you better would. Though this ain't no game."

More laughter.

She crossed the room, belly tight, fingernails pressing into her palms. Nyx got down on one knee and faced the man who handed her an iron spike. He pointed to a spot on the floor.

"Put it there."

A man stepped forward, holding a sledgehammer. He took up his place a few feet from where she knelt. The man raised his shoulders to his ears and then relaxed.

Nyx said, "What should I do?"

The first man said, "Ach, you don't do *nussing*."

She held the spike with her left hand, arm fully extended.

"Use both hands. And don't move, not even a whisker." No one laughed this time. "An' fear not, lad. This big Irish don't miss."

The man with the sledgehammer, Aodh Blackall, stepped closer. He wore no helmet, shirtsleeves rolled up his forearms. Aodh stood a little sideways, waiting for Nyx to do her part. She inched closer to the spike, wrapped her right hand around her left and closed her eyes.

The sledgehammer came down with force, landing square on the spike and driving it in. Nyx held it fast, and the man hit it again, then once more.

The first man said, "You can open your eyes now. And step away."

Nyx said to the first man, "What are we doing?"

"Round of holes."

"What?"

He pointed to a point three feet up on the wall. "There."

Nyx placed the spike, and Aodh gave a mighty swing from the side. As with the previous blows, this one was true, transferring the energy from the hammer to the spike and straight into the seam.

They repeated the process a dozen times with Nyx placing the spike and Aodh driving it home.

When they finished, the first man, whom Nyx learned was the fire boss, said, "Now back around."

They returned to the first hole, and the fire boss handed Nyx another implement, this one a three-foot long rod. They repeated the entire sequence with Nyx holding the rod and Aodh hammering it in. Blisters formed on Nyx's palms and her ears rang with every strike.

Sometimes the hole would fill with coal dust, and another miner would remove it with a long, thin spoon. By the time they finished the second round, she felt as if she'd collapse. But she steadied herself and stood among the men, who made room for a small, thin man to move forward. He produced an iron cylinder from one pocket and a spool of fuse from the other. From yet another pocket, the man pulled a pair of pliers.

Nyx leaned over to Aodh and said, "What's his name?" Aodh shrugged without acknowledging her. "Well, what's he doing?"

Aodh looked down at her. "Crimping the caps."

"What does that mean?"

The fire boss said to her, "Don't mean nix to you."

The man with the pliers squeezed the top of the cylinder, then unspooled the fuse as he moved to the next hole. Nyx noticed that the other miners shuffling farther and farther back until they'd exited the room. In short order the man had filled every hole with a cylinder, and all were connected by the same line.

The man walked backward from the room still unspooling the fuse.

"Everybody back," the fire boss said, though none of the men needed to be told. They'd already retreated into the shadows. "How many?"

"Twelve."

"Remember to count 'em off, boys."

The explosives man struck a match and touched it to the end of the fuse. Everyone plugged their ears with their fingers.

The first charge went off, shaking the ground all around them and showering them with dust. Then the second charge exploded and the next and the next as the flame raced along the fuse. When the thundering ceased, the group stood up straight, took their fingers from their ears, and listened.

The fire boss said to the explosives man. "How many?"

"Eleven," he said.

He turned to Aodh. "What was your count?"

"Eleven."

The fire boss turned to Nyx. "There's one hole missed."

"So?"

There was an eruption of laughter, and the fire boss said, "So, go find it."

"Find what?"

"Ach, the one that missed."

"And then what?"

Aodh said, "I think it was seven."

He walked back into the room with Nyx following. She tried to remember where they'd put the seventh hole and guessed it was close to the floor, meaning she'd have to dig to find it. Aodh got on his hands and knees and removed large chunks of coal and rock. Nyx fell in next to him, tossing pieces left and right.

He grabbed her wrist hard and said, "Careful."

The fire boss called into the room, "Come on outta there, Blackall. You done your bit already."

AFTER THE EXPLOSION AODH STAGGERED forward but didn't fall, as the fire boss looked him over. Aodh put his hands to his ears.

"Don't worry, they're still there," the fire boss said.

"What?" Aodh pointed to his ear. "I can't hear."

The fire boss faced him and held him by both shoulders. "I said, get back to work."

Nyx toiled alongside the rest of the team, working by the light of their candles, carrying coal and dumping it into the mine car. Each full car was rolled away by two children, one pulling and one pushing.

No sooner did a full car disappear than an empty one took its place. In this way the team filled the hours in the day. Nyx couldn't discern the time, and as the day wore on, her senses dulled and she stopped imagining the world above ground. She focused mostly on the pain in her shredded hands until that, too, seemed far away.

At a moment well past any kind of exhaustion Nyx had known before, the fire boss blew a brass whistle, and the work ceased. The men gathered up their tools and trudged out the way they'd ridden in. She noticed Aodh walking with his back straight and arms barely swinging.

She discerned by the fire boss's candle the dim outline of the kid, still sitting at the heavy wooden door. He stood up and eased it open, and Nyx felt the rush of foul air escaping to meet the night.

2

Kamp rapped knuckles on the door just below the brass sign that read "Strictly No Admittance" and listened for sounds inside the room. Kamp hadn't been there in a long time and didn't want to be there now. He heard nothing and knocked one more time just to make himself feel better about having tried to find the Big Judge Tate Cain.

But as he turned to leave, Kamp caught a whiff of blended tobacco, heard the creaking of floorboards and then a voice.

"What is it, Wendell?"

"Open the door."

"Are you armed?"

Kamp felt his gut go tight. The Judge was goading him already. He didn't bother answering the question and instead waited for the Judge to unlock the door.

When he did, Kamp entered while the Judge took his seat in an ornate chair by the window. He wore his customary black silk dress and high lace-up boots in the Victorian style.

The Judge put his pipe to his lips and took a long, thoughtful pull, then let the smoke cascade over his bottom lip while he gazed out the window. Kamp waited for the Judge to turn back around. He didn't.

"What's on your mind, Judge?"

The Judge banged the dead ashes from his pipe on the arm of his chair, then repacked it with tobacco from a tin emblazoned with the words "Turtle Island Smoking Tobacco." He struck a match on the windowsill and held it to the bowl, sucking the flame down on the inhale and letting it bob back out. Once sufficiently lit, he let it burn.

The Judge said, "It's you who called on me. How may I be of assistance?"

"I have some questions."

"Proceed, Wendell. Time is short."

The Judge gave no indication that he had anything else to do and certainly nothing pressing.

Before Kamp could speak, the Judge said, "Whatever became of your friend, the little fugitive?"

"Who?"

"The boy, Becket Hinsdale. Where is he now?"

"Gone."

The Judge took a pull on the pipe, fashioned from briarwood. "All for the best, wouldn't you say?"

"Judge, listen—"

"Wendell, in your studies at the college, you spent considerable time on philosophy, pre-Socratic. And natural science, is that correct?"

"Yes."

"So, perhaps better than anyone, you appreciate—"

"I need—"

"You can appreciate the shift taking place in our world, man's massive move from the dark into the light. I mean that ironically, of course."

"I thought you said time was short."

"Well, in spite of technical advancements and fantastic inventions, the rise of industry, the Heraclitean fire, nature's conflagration, the Darwinian struggle for existence rages without ceasing, and without remorse."

"Judge, a soldier came to my front door with a letter. Official business. What do you know about it?"

The Judge took another long pull on the pipe and exhaled slowly.

He said, "I take issue with those who say society is progressing, don't you? What progress?"

"Why did a soldier deliver a letter to me?"

"Probably because it had your name on it." The Judge looked out the window to the tall stacks pumping black smoke into a grey sky and said, "Society functions only for the sake of keeping secrets. Wouldn't you agree?"

"What's the letter about?"

The Judge turned back around to face Kamp. "Did you sign for it?"

"What?"

"Were you required to sign for the letter?"

Kamp felt a flicker of irritation at the base of his skull.

"Yes, I did. But why did I get it in the first place?"

"I don't know. Perhaps the contents of the letter told you."

"Tell me—"

"You did read it, the letter? You didn't? Oh, Wendell, at least learn the facts first."

Kamp rubbed his eyes with his thumb and forefinger.

"Judge, they sent someone after me."

"Who did?"

"Black Feather."

The Judge pursed his lips and shook his head, then stood up and produced a bottle from a desk drawer, along with two shot glasses. He poured the whiskey and slid a glass toward Kamp.

The Judge sighed, then raised his glass and said, "To divine mysteries."

The Judge tossed back the shot, but Kamp left his glass on the table.

Kamp said, "Her name is Adams. Do you know her?"

"Of course I know Adams."

"How?"

The Judge leaned back in his chair. "Her father and I were colleagues in Philadelphia. I knew her when she was a little girl. She doted on her father."

Kamp downed the shot and said, "You know what she does now."

"Not as such."

Kamp felt the whiskey quiet the roaring in his mind, felt his thoughts slowing. "Where is she?"

"I don't know."

"When was the last time you saw her?"

"I don't like your tone." The Judge sat straighter in his chair.

"Where is Nyx Bauer?"

The Judge rolled his eyes. "I don't know."

"Where does Black Feather think she is?"

"Wendell, you're not well. You're disturbed. It's time for you to go."

"Maybe it's time for you to go."

Kamp let the words hang and stood staring at the Judge, who interlaced his fingers in front of him, and smiled.

"Wendell, when you were a boy, many times I'd come to your family's farm to visit with your father. And more than once I saw you talking back to him, arguing with him. Your brothers were much more respectful, I can assure you. But you, Wendell, you antagonized that man, much like you're antagonizing me now. And on more than one occasion, your father removed his leather belt and put an end to the argument. There you were, squirming on the ground, clutching your little red bottom. Sad."

"What did you and my father talk about?"

"You made him hit you, Wendell. You realize that."

"Sounds like you enjoyed watching."

"Oh, I did, I did. You were a willful boy who needed constant correction."

"I guess it didn't work."

"On the contrary, Wendell, you became a war hero. The state you're in now is due to your injuries.

It's not your fault that your mind doesn't function properly anymore."

"Don't bother, Judge."

"Then again, perhaps your father was right. When he finished, he used to say that you're an ungrateful bastard. That's the source of your weakness, Wendell. Ingratitude. And disobedience."

"What about Wyles, Judge?"

"Who?"

"Emma Wyles. Did you make peace with her?"

The Judge stood up, crossed the room, and said, "I adjudicate the cases that come before me. I don't make war, and I don't make peace." He leveled his gaze at Kamp. "But for what it's worth, that bitch can rot."

"Leave her alone."

The Judge put his hand on the doorknob. "You're lost, Wendell. Go home."

Kamp pressed his forearm against the Judge's throat, pinning him to the door.

"What is the letter about? Who sent it?"

"I don't have a fucking clue. Read it yourself and find out."

Kamp eased his grip.

The Judge stood up straight and smoothed his long beard.

"How is Shaw?"

"She's fine."

"And Autumn?"

"Have you prepared for them, Wendell? Will they be ready?"

"Ready for what?"

"Your leave taking."

3

Nyx could tell by the way Aodh walked from the mine that the blast had done its damage.

She called after him. "I'm sorry I got you hurt." He kept shuffling and didn't speak. "I said, I'm sor—"

"You dinna do anything wrong."

"It's my fault."

"If you'da gone in by yourself, we wouldn't be talking."

"That's my point. You saved—"

Aodh stopped walking and looked at Nyx.

"There's a black river flows out of the hole. Your only concern is that it keeps flowing."

He tilted his head back to look at the stars and began walking again.

She said, "Well, are you going to be all right?"

Aodh said, "See you *amárach*" and shuffled down the mountain.

Nyx looked at her hands, ripped and raw, in the moonlight and said, "Yah, tomorrow."

KAMP WALKED THE MILES from town alone. He looked up into the black expanse and listened to his feet crunching the gravel and in so doing created a barrier against the ruminations that would have swooped in otherwise.

He'd stayed in Bethlehem longer than he expected to and longer than he should have. Maybe he wanted to get home after they'd gone to bed, though he didn't know why.

Are they ready for your leave taking?

Leave taking. Farewell. Kamp felt as if he'd been preparing Shaw for it since the day she found him. Truth be told, he felt himself leaving a little every day, with each forgotten remnant of a memory, with every new and desperate delusion. Every waking nightmare and tortured night of sleep dragging him away, piece by piece.

That's not what the Judge meant, though, or seemed to mean. He was just responding to a threat with a threat.

Rounding the last bend, Kamp saw the candle in the window and as he approached his house, he saw Shaw in the front room. Kamp stepped onto the porch, put his hand to the knob on the front door. Locked.

Before he could knock, the door swung open. Shaw saw the look of irritation on Kamp's face.

"We agreed to keep it locked."

"I know, I know."

"And I didn't know where you'd gone, love."

"I talked to the Judge." Shaw put her hand on Kamp's shoulder, and he shrugged it off. "It didn't go well, naturally."

"Meaning what?"

"Meaning he wouldn't answer my questions. Wouldn't tell me what he knew about Adams, said he didn't know whether Black Feather knows where Nyx is."

Shaw faced him and took him by both shoulders.

"He can't help you, and he never has."

Kamp pressed his palms to his eyes. "He's the only person who knows how it all fits together."

"But, love, he'll never tell you."

He pulled in a breath. "I asked him what he knows about that letter."

She smiled. "I can tell you that."

"You opened it?"

Shaw nodded.

"What did it say?"

"You sure you want to know?"

Kamp nodded.

"It says that there are some of your things—"

"What things?"

"Things from the war are in a warehouse or something. And that you can go pick them up."

"Do you have it? The letter?"

"It's upstairs. Why?" She saw the color rising in his face. "What's wrong?"

"Nothing."

AFTER SHAW WENT TO BED, Kamp stood next to the fireplace, holding the envelope. He focused on the three-cent stamp picturing a man in profile—Jefferson, probably. He couldn't be certain, because the image was mostly obscured by the cancellation mark, a fancy cancel, in the pattern of a grooved five-pointed star. The star was centered exactly at Jefferson's left temple. Kamp tossed it in the fire.

UPON HER ARRIVAL at the cabin, Nyx felt the anger and fear she'd pushed down all day rumbling in her chest. With the skeleton key she wore on the rawhide string around her neck, Nyx unlocked both padlocks on the front door.

Just below the surface of her consciousness, Nyx perceived that a single misplaced word or even a sideways glance from Angus would set off an eruption. After all, in matters of another person's suffering, Angus could appear indifferent, if not entirely oblivious.

Nyx expected to see Angus at his workbench, hunched over a rifle, effectively blocking out all sensation. But when Nyx went in, she saw the metal bathtub in the center of the floor, filled with water and steaming. Angus appeared from the bedroom and focused on her.

Nyx said, "I know, I know. You don't even need to say it. Where was I? Why didn't I come home until now?"

Angus didn't speak and instead held Nyx by both wrists and turned them so that her palms faced up. He saw the ripped blisters, covered in coal dust, the stump where her little finger had been.

Nyx said, "And, yes, I know you didn't want me to go there in the first place."

Angus looked at Nyx's miner's hat, sooty and sitting lop-sided atop her head. He removed it and set it on the workbench.

Nyx's voice hit a higher pitch. "You're not going to ask me how it went? You're not going to say I told you so? You're not going to say *anything*?"

Angus slid Nyx's heavy coat from her shoulders, then unbuttoned her shirt and tossed it to the floor.

He unwrapped the bandage around Nyx's torso and let that fall, too. Nyx pulled in a deep breath, feeling her ribcage expand. Angus knelt and pulled off her boots, then removed Nyx's wool socks. By the time Nyx was fully naked, she'd begun to shake with sobs.

And as she stepped into the hot, clean water, Nyx said, "It's too hard, Angus. It was all too hard."

Angus said, "Tilt your head back."

Nyx followed the instruction, as Angus took a bar of soap, worked it into a lather and began washing Nyx's hair.

"Now tell me about it."

She explained the day's events and the people she'd met: the agent, the fire boss, Aodh Blackall and the rest of the crew.

"Sounds like Irish," Angus said.

"So what?"

"That's trouble. They're not going to like you."

"They were fine. No one gave me any trouble at all."

"Except for when they sent you in to catch that *ferburstung.*"

"They didn't want me to get blown up. They just needed me to find the charge that didn't go off."

"Ach, maybe they set it up that way."

"As a trap? Well, if they did, they got the wrong person."

"Who? That fella Aodh? Yah, well, if that's so, *he's* the problem for them."

Angus finished washing her hair and rinsed his hands before drying them on his pants. Nyx swung her head to look at him and said, "You just don't want me to be there in the first place."

"Not exactly."

"And, anyway, if Aodh wasn't supposed to help me, why did he do what he did?"

"I don't know. Ask him."

KAMP WAITED UP LATE, waited for quiet to descend on the house. He waited for his thoughts to slow and for the knots in his neck and shoulders to loosen. They didn't.

When he heard the great horned owl in the tree behind his house, Kamp laced up his boots, put on his heavy coat and went to the back door. As he turned the knob, he heard soft footfalls on the stairs.

He turned to see his daughter Autumn in a white nightgown and with a doll in each hand, a boy and a girl, held by their ankles. She set the dolls on the kitchen table, went to Kamp and hugged him hard.

"You can't go," she said.

"I'm not going anywhere."

"That's not true."

Kamp stroked her hair. "Well, I was just going for a walk. I wanted to say hello to the owl before he goes to bed."

The girl let go, took a step back and stared up at Kamp. Her eyes, one brown and one blue, brimmed with tears.

"That's not true. You were going away for good."

Kamp knelt so that he was at eye level with his daughter. "What do you mean, sweetheart?"

"I had a dream."

Tears streamed down her cheeks, and Kamp brushed them away with his thumb.

"I'm not leaving, Autumn. I promise."

She wiped her nose with the back of her hand. As she headed back up the stairs, she said, "Well, anyway, before you go, you should marry mommy."

Kamp looked at the dolls on the table. He took off his coat, unlaced his boots and turned out the lantern.

The figure in the forest, the one that had watched through the window and waited for him to emerge, saw the light go out and disappeared back over the mountain.

4

Nyx readied herself in the pitch darkness. She checked the mutton cloth that Angus had wrapped around her hands to make sure it was tight before putting on her gloves, boots and miner's hat. She picked her way down the mile-long trail under bare branches that swayed and creaked in the hard wind.

She remembered a morning like this years ago when, lying warm and awake in her bed, she'd heard her father and Danny Knecht talking at the back-door. She'd jumped out of bed to say goodbye before they headed off to the mine. For an instant she felt an old combination of excitement and love before it was replaced by a pang of sadness.

She shut her eyes against the memory and against the urge to run back to the cabin. Nyx waited for the emotion to wash over her, then started marching again.

When she saw the glow of the fire at the top of Sleeping Bear Mountain, Nyx remembered all the gear, the *Gezähe* she needed: the *dicka Hamma*, *sheesa* kit, and *Schachthut.*

I don't even know what that shit is, she thought. She knew she had to buy it all at the Black Feather Company Store. Nyx didn't know where she'd get the money, let alone the time to go shopping. And she knew she wouldn't be allowed to borrow anything.

The fire glow grew brighter as Nyx neared the top, and she discerned still another peak, to the left of the entrance to the mine, the spoil heap.

People—old men and women, and children— picked through the spoil, even in the pre-dawn. They searched with bent backs, black fingers rooting for smooth crow coal, eyes searching for its luster in a moonbeam. The wretches on the spoil heap, exposed to the elements, didn't even have tools.

Nyx saw the agent, ledger in hand, checking boxes with a pencil by the candle light from miner's hat he wore. She approached him empty-handed and ready to plead with him to let her go back underground. As Nyx put her head down and trudged to the agent, a voice called to her from behind.

"Hey, hey. Slow up."

She turned and saw Aodh.

The agent cleared his throat and said, "Ach, I told you, no *Gezähe,* no *Arwet.*"

"I couldn't go to the—"

"It's here. I have his kit here."

Aodh pushed in front of her and held out a haversack full of gear. In his other hand, he held a pick and shovel.

The agent sneered. "Ach, you know you daresn't use another man's *Gezähe.*"

"Casey don't need it no more, Butcher."

"That's the rules." The agent looked back down at his ledger, dismissing Aodh. "And don't call me that."

Aodh pushed the sack into Nyx's hands.

He said to her, "Get going."

She took it, walked past the agent and climbed into the mine car. Aodh waited for the agent to look up.

When he did, Aodh said, "You want your number for the day, you gotta let that black river flow. Otherwise, daddy won't be happy. Butcher."

THEY ROLLED INTO THE MAW with the purple pre-dawn vanishing behind them. Nyx rode in the mine car next to Aodh. They stood silent and heard the creaking of the beams, the click-clack rhythm of the wheels and the low, shifting rumbles of the earth.

Soon enough, Nyx was on hands and knees again, crawling with pick in hand into the space they'd blasted out the day before.

She still didn't have a candle for her hat and so she had to work by the flicker of Aodh's light. They settled into a working rhythm, hacking out the pieces, filling the bucket and dumping it into a car.

"Aodh?"

He worked lying on his side, facing away from her and hacking at the seam and saying nothing.

"Aodh? I have a question."

"Yah."

"How do you know when you're finished for the day?"

"When you hit the number, you're finished." He kept working while he talked.

"What number?"

"Seven."

"Seven what?" Nyx perceived his irritation by the way he shifted.

"Cars. We hafta fill seven cars with coal. Every day."

"Well, with all ten of us working, that shouldn't be too hard."

Aodh stopped working the pick. "It's not ten. It's two. The two of us have to hit seven. Otherwise, we donna get no pay. Not for six, not for six and a half. Nothing. Unless we hit seven. That man above ground, the man with the pencil and the glasses. He has a number, too. If we donna get our number, he can't get his."

"Why did you call him Butcher?"

"Tha's enough."

"Whose tools did you give me? Who's Casey?"

"Work."

Aodh raised his pick and tore into the seam. Nyx saw splotches of blood blooming through the back of his shirt. She backed out of the crawl space, stood up, and dumped the contents of her coal bucket into the mine car.

Nyx guessed they'd been working over an hour already. The mine car, the first of the day, wasn't even half-full.

Aodh more than made up for the work Nyx couldn't do. He didn't slow for the remainder of the day, hacking and hauling coal without pause and without comment.

As soon as they'd filled a car, he'd yell, "Done."

A pair of figures, children, would soon appear and take their places, one in front of the car and one behind. They'd roll the car from the room and within minutes, an empty car would appear, guided by two more children.

Nyx spent equal time hewing and watching Aodh in order to learn his methods. She knew she wouldn't be able to keep up, not at first. And she discerned, too, that she'd have to conserve strength, lest her body fail before the end of the day. Not that it seemed like a day.

Their world extended only to the edge of the candle's glow. Beyond that was unending night, the sky replaced by the crushing tons above their heads. Whenever Nyx allowed herself to think about the darkness and danger, she felt panic in her throat.

So she focused on Aodh, his movements and techniques. She noticed that he appeared to have entered a trance, a mode in which there was only movement and labor, stripped of thought.

Aodh topped off the seventh car with the contents of the last bucket. He shouted "done" and stood to his full height. Nyx gathered up her tools and started out of the room.

"Behind it," he said.

Nyx stopped. "What?"

"The car. If we want the credit, we walk out behind the car."

Soon enough, the children appeared, filthy and bent and rolled the cart ahead. Nyx felt an urge to help them, but the fire in her joints instructed her otherwise.

When they reached the heavy wooden door, the boy stood up from his small bench and swung it open, releasing the mine's last breath of the day. Once outside, Aodh settled up with the agent and started down the mountain. Nyx felt herself weighed down by her tools and doubted she had the strength to carry them home. She thought about stashing them somewhere, then thought better of it and shuffled after Aodh.

"Where can I put my tools?"

"Store."

"Where is it?"

"Where I'm going."

At the base of the mountain, she saw a string of kerosene lanterns hanging from the roof of the wide porch with more burning inside. Nyx caught a whiff of supper and felt a powerful twist in her guts. She'd finished her lunch by eight in the morning and hadn't allowed herself to think of food since.

Aodh went in first, boots sounding off the wooden floor planks. He walked to the counter at the back of the room and laid down his tools. When he did, a small man emerged from the back room.

"You're lucky," the man said, "I was about to close."

"For that I'm eternally grateful."

The clerk lifted a large iron ring and slid each tool onto it via the hole at the end of every handle. Once finished, he hung the ring on a hook on the wall.

The clerk looked past Aodh and saw Nyx, glassy-eyed and slump-shouldered.

"Ah. New guy."

Aodh took Nyx's tools and handed them to the clerk who repeated the process of putting them on the ring and hanging them on the wall. Finally, he placed two brass tokens on the counter. Aodh picked them up, tipped his miner's hat and turned to go.

Nyx mumbled, "Can I have something to eat?"

The clerk said, "Have you money?"

"No. Can I pay you later?"

"Can I extend you credit? Why, sure."

Aodh took Nyx by the elbow and guided her toward the door.

The clerk said, "*Gut nacht.* See yous tomorrow."

"CHRIST, I JUST WANT SOMETHING TO EAT."

"And you'll get it once we get back." Aodh turned onto a trail that led to Mauch Chunk.

"Back where?"

"The patch."

"I have to get home. I told Angus—"

"You can't get back tonight, lad. Yer on the other side of the mountain now."

They saw lights flickering ahead. Nyx knew the patch town was there and had avoided it for fear of being recognized. But no one was out now. And when she followed Aodh into a shack on the outskirts of town, she heard only snoring loud enough to rattle the windowpanes.

Aodh lit a candle in the kitchen and motioned for Nyx to enter. When she did, he said, "Two things."

"Yah."

He handed her a circular brass tag the size of a half dollar. She held it next to the candle flame and inspected it. In the center of the tag was a large number "5."

"Tha's your number. Donna lose it."

"Or else what?"

"Or else your tools is lost to some other poor bastard. You need that for to get yer *gay-hizzle*."

Around the periphery of the tag it read, "Property of B. F. E."

"What's B. F. E.?"

"Black Feather Extraction." Aodh handed Nyx two apples and a slice of bread. "And donna take nothin' from Black Feather on credit. Never. They'll kill ya on the vigorish."

"Why'd you call that man Butcher?"

"Donna matter."

He led her into the main room, pointed to an open space on the floor, and handed her a wool blanket.

"Thank you."

"Welcome."

She sat cross-legged on the floor and watched Aodh in the kitchen while she devoured the food. He started a fire in the stove and removed his shirt. Nyx saw his back, black and purple, encrusted with blood.

He washed his shirt in the water he heated and used it to clean his wounds, as best he could. She felt a surge of emotion for the man, the likes of which she hadn't felt in years, or ever. Nyx thought to help him as she tilted sideways and fell asleep.

5

"By order of the Office of the Secretary, U.S. Army and the Honorable Tate Cain, I order you to open this door!"

When the they arrived, Kamp was still awake, savoring the feeling of relaxation that had just begun to seep into his bones.

But then he'd heard one man's voice and then another, angry whispers outside the window. And then the pounding began, along with the shouting.

Kamp crouched low, hustled to the kitchen and retrieved the Sharps rifle from the closet. He loaded it and moved to the front window of the house.

Blue uniforms—he counted six—circled the house. A seventh man in a great coat strode to the front door.

Kamp slipped onto the porch, raised the rifle and sighted the man, who beat his fist on the door again.

"Open this door, or we shall be forced to enter."

The man in the great coat motioned for two uniformed men to come forward. They carried a battering ram. The man stepped aside as the uniformed men prepared to destroy the front door.

Kamp said, "Don't."

The man turned to look at Kamp, saw the rifle barrel pointed at him and raised his hand for the men with the battering ram to stop.

The man said, "Ah, there you are."

The soldiers who'd encircled the house now came running, pistols drawn.

He called to them, "Put those down, put those down. He's right here."

With the rifle still raised, Kamp approached the man in the great coat who said, "I'm certain you can see you're at a grave disadvantage. I advise you to lower your weapon, lest your family have to witness your execution."

Kamp said, "Who are you?"

The man smiled and said, "The real question is, who are *you*?"

"You're not taking me anywhere."

"Nor do I intend to. I simply wish to inform you of where things stand. Let us talk."

"Things?"

"Indeed, the process, and your impending trial."

Kamp heard the upstairs window open and looked to see Shaw's face there, and he heard Autumn starting to wail. He looked back at the man in the great coat, lowered his rifle and said, "All right. But they're staying outside."

THE MAN PRODUCED a leather-bound portfolio, set it on the kitchen table, then removed his coat.

Kamp started a fire in the stove and turned to the man. "Coffee?"

"Yes, thank you. I must say, you appear quite calm, considering.

"Uh huh."

"I always admired that about you."

Kamp put the kettle on the stove and said, "You're in my house, and you're upsetting my family. I don't want to make it worse."

"Fair enough. May I?" The man gestured to the portfolio. Kamp nodded.

Shaw appeared in the doorway with Autumn clutching her leg.

"What's going on, love?"

"A half dozen assholes and two cups of coffee."

The man stood and said, "Ma'am."

"Go back upstairs," Kamp said.

He finished making the coffee and handed a mug to the man, then took a sip from his own.

Shaw said to the man, "What's your name?"

The man opened the portfolio and said. "Reid, A. R., Colonel, U.S. Army, retired. I was Wendell W. Kamp's commanding officer in the war."

Kamp said, "I've never seen him before."

"Precisely. That's because you're not Kamp."

"Come again?"

"You're not Wendell W. Kamp. You've assumed his identity."

"You're insane."

A.R. Reid said, "Ma'am, I'm afraid your husband is an impostor."

Autumn, still clutching Shaw's leg, said, "What does *that* mean?"

"It means that it's time for this nice man to leave," Shaw said.

Reid shook his head. "I'm afraid it won't be that easy. Wendell Kamp served his country with distinction. He did nothing wrong. But this man has committed a crime. Many crimes in fact."

Shaw said, "Who has?"

Reid gestured to Kamp. "This man. His name is Nickel Glock."

"Bullshit."

Reid pulled two sheets of paper from the portfolio and slid them across the table.

"Please look carefully. This one is a form, signed by Wendell W. Kamp when he first mustered in, 1861. The second is a form you signed several days ago to confirm the receipt of a certified letter. Notice the signatures."

Kamp and Shaw leaned over the table and examined the papers. The first signature was written in cursive with large, swooping W's. The second was printed in crude, blocky letters.

"Means nothing," Kamp said.

"Alas, it does. We've known about you for a good while, but we lacked proof. This means you're not who you say you are. And that's a problem. For the government, and for you."

Kamp studied Reid. He had a bald head, ruddy face and thick, red sideburns that extended below his chin and cradled his jowls. Reid wore a tailored, grey three-piece suit with a pocket watch and chain. Kamp was certain he'd never seen the man before.

"Tell them to leave us alone," Kamp said.

Reid smiled. "Mr. Glock, we've come straight from the courthouse on the orders of the Honorable Tate Cain."

"Leave." Kamp pounded his fist on the table.

Reid's face turned serious. "I'd like to show you something else. But the child must not see this."

Shaw walked upstairs with Autumn, who said, "No, no."

Shaw came back down alone and took a seat at the table.

Reid slid a photograph from the portfolio. It depicted a man's head in profile, supine, eyes open. At the temple, there was a ragged hole roughly the size of a silver dollar. At the bottom right corner, it read, "Patient: W.W. Kamp."

Reid looked at Shaw and said, "That's the real Kamp."

Shaw pointed to the large, star-shaped scar at Kamp's left temple and said, "Yes, so is that."

Reid unclipped a note from the back of the photograph and read it aloud, "December 15, 1862. Fractures of temporal, sphenoid. Removal of bullet fragments. Surgery unsuccessful. Deceased."

Kamp said, "Who wrote that?"

Reid produced another photograph of the same scene but with a wider angle that showed the entire body laid flat on a wooden table in front of an open tent and a man standing next to it.

"That man, the surgeon." Reid pointed to the man in the photograph.

"Do you know him?"

"Of course."

"What's his name?"

"He died, too." Reid looked directly at Kamp. "Tragically."

Shaw picked up the first photograph, studied it, then looked at Kamp and back at Reid.

"You're lying."

Reid put the materials back in the portfolio, stood up and put on his great coat.

He looked at Kamp and said, "Nickel, it's time you told your wife the truth. Not only will this matter not drop, it will go forward. You've a hearing tomorrow morning at eight o' clock sharp with the Judge. Be certain to attend."

6

Aodh pulled Nyx from a dream. She was picking raspberries with her sisters on the slope behind their old house. In the dream she ran with a full bucket, eager to share the bounty with her father. They were on the road well before dawn.

She and Aodh had been the last miners at the company store the previous night and now were the first to show up. Nyx handed her brass tag to the clerk who fetched her *Gezähe*, then did the same for Aodh.

Aodh said to the clerk, "It's today, ain't it?"

The clerk shrugged. "*Mebbe, mebbe* not."

Aodh left the store and hurried in the direction of the glow at the summit, the mouth of the mine.

Nyx said, "What's the rush?"

"Trouble."

"What trouble?"

"An' I donna want no part of it."

Nyx labored to keep up with him as he ascended Gravity Road. The sounds of the approaching day—the murmur of birds and the clank of the gravity car hooking into the track—spurred him.

She caught him as he reached the top and grabbed the hem of his coat. He spun to face her and winced when he did.

"Not *now.*"

They passed the spoil heap and the wraiths who scoured it, then reached the agent who conducted a brief inspection of their gear and waved them on.

They rode an otherwise empty car into the mine, past the kid who swung the door open and then shut it behind them and then down to their room and finally to the tiny space where they hewed the coal. Not long after they'd begun, they heard noise above them in adjoining rooms, excited shouting and a series of loud *whumps*.

"Ah, Jaysus."

Nyx said, "What is it?"

"Dis Padgett called for an action."

"Meaning what?"

The commotion grew louder, more shouting and men banging shovels against the sides of the mine cars. Then they smelled smoke, and Aodh backed out of the space and stood up.

"Let's go."

They hustled back out through the maze of subterranean rooms, found the track and joined the stream of men flowing toward the surface. At the heavy door they passed the trapper kid who, instead of opening and closing it as each group passed, propped the door open and let the flood of men pour out into the morning sunshine.

She thought the miners looked like demonic, shambling foot soldiers. Some carried coal axes, but most were empty-handed. A knot of men formed fifty feet from the mouth of the mine.

Nyx saw that they'd surrounded the agent, the man Aodh called Butcher, slapping his face and jeering. One of the men knocked the agent to the ground with a clout on the ear, and the rest set to, kicking and spitting on him.

The agent pulled his knees to his chest and covered his head with his hands. The men didn't relent but rather redoubled the attack.

A HIGH WHISTLE PIERCED THE AIR, and all heads swung around to see a man emerging from the mine, not far from where Nyx stood. She'd never seen him before but had heard his name. Dis Padgett.

He stood well over six feet, and unlike most miners, was unbent. His face was grimy, even dirtier than the rest, with hard blue eyes staring out from it.

The miners waited in silence as Padgett strode toward them with a sledgehammer slung across his shoulders. They made way when he reached them, and he stepped to the agent, still curled in a ball on the ground.

Padgett said, "Butcher, you paid for your number with another man's blood. That you cannot do."

The agent peered up at him through the broken lenses of his glasses and said, "I don't make the rules. And I didn't hurt your man."

Padgett turned away from the agent and scanned the crowd. When he saw Aodh, Padgett held out the sledgehammer, offering it.

Aodh gave him a flat expression and shook his head. In one motion Dis Padgett spun on his heel, raised the hammer and brought it down on the agent's thigh, smashing his femur.

"Flip him over," Padgett said.

The attackers rolled the agent onto his back. Again Padgett raised the hammer and again he brought it down, destroying the agent's other leg as well.

"Now give him a ride."

A cheer went up as a pair of miners dragged the agent by his arms to a mine car poised at the top of Gravity Road. The men loaded him into the car and stepped aside. Dis Padgett walked to the car and looked at the agent, whose head and face showed bright red lumps and a trickle of blood from one eye. Padgett leaned in and gently cradled the agent's head.

He said, "Well done good and faithful servant."

Then Dis Padgett stood up and brought the hammer down one more time, smashing the brake that held the mine car in place. It began its descent, rolling down the track and picking up speed.

The men watched the car screaming down Sleeping Bear Mountain. The agent, benumbed by shock, made no attempt to slow the car. It departed the tracks when it reached at the curve at the bottom and slammed into a concrete wall. Momentum ejected the agent from the car, hurling him face first into the wall.

The crowd atop the mountain saw the impact and heard the thud a second later. They watched the agent's body crumple to the earth next to the mangled mine car. They waited a beat and then another to see if he would move. When he didn't, a calm settled on the scene.

Dis Padgett clapped one of the attackers on the shoulder and addressed the miners, "Before they was wondering. Now they'll know. The above-world belongs to them, but the world below is ours."

A mighty cheer arose.

"Go, men. Take your rest today, and come back t'morra."

Most of the miners started down the mountain, laughing and hooting.

Dis Padgett called after them, "And for the sake of Jaysus, donna burn down the company store."

More laughter and then Padgett turned to Aodh and extended his hand.

"We did a necessary thing, lad. For Casey and for our kind." He squeezed Aodh's hand as he said it. Padgett let go and said, "Well, god bless you, lad. And god bless Casey." Then he vanished down the slope.

Aodh turned and walked into the mine, and Nyx followed. Nyx noticed that some of the other miners did the same, heads down and shuffling back down the hole.

When they reached the kid at the heavy door, Aodh said to him, "An extra dollar if you stay the day."

"*Ach*, I don't need no extra," the kid said, "but that don't mean I'll turn it down."

AODH FELL TO WORK STRAIGHTAWAY. He and Nyx filled a car, had it hauled off, then began filling another. Aodh took off his shirt and tossed it to the ground.

Nyx said, "What happens now?"

Without stopping, he said, "You're lookin' at it."

"What about that man?"

"Who?"

"Butcher."

"What about him?"

"How can they just do that?"

Aodh scratched the red whiskers of his beard. "What's your name, lad?"

"Nef."

"Nef what?"

She hadn't thought of a last name, and she wasn't ready for the question.

"Bahr," she said.

He cocked his head to the side and studied her. "Nef Bahr, you look young to me, but you sure donna look stupid."

She felt her legs starting to shake and had to look away.

She said, "Why did that man offer you the hammer?"

Aodh started hewing again.

He said, "Because of Casey. Me an' my cousin Casey worked down here for a year. But Butcher sent him to his last dark an' lonely."

"How?"

"Put us in a room that exploded. Casey got the worst of it. Some think Butcher done it to pay him back."

"Casey?"

"No. Padgett. Padgett and Butcher had a runnin' agro."

"A what?"

"Feud. Irish against German. Padgett was settling a score with the Germans. He knew me an' Casey worked together an' that we was kin. Thought maybe I'd want to do the honors myself."

"Why didn't you?"

"I din' approve of what Butcher did, but I din' wanna kill him neither. I got no time for that can o' piss. Padgett had his own reasons besides."

"Like what?"

"Jaysus, nephew, but you got all the questions."

"Like what."

"Maybe he was in love with Casey."

"Oh."

"But don't tell that to Mrs. Padgett." Aodh hefted his coal axe. "Or Mrs. Casey."

"I won't."

"Jus' remember, Nef Bahr, if you have to wonder whether a body down here is for or against you, that body is against."

Nyx shifted her gaze to Aodh, who'd turned away from her and begun hacking the seam above his head. His bare back was crisscrossed with scars, some healed, most not.

She said, "You're not against me."

"You got Casey's number, got his place. That's good luck for you."

"I'm German, and you're Irish. How come you're helping me?"

He paused with the coal axe above his head and said, "There's work, and there's bullshit." Aodh brought down the axe with all his power and sprayed coal in all directions. "See if you can figure which I prefer."

7

When Kamp reached the wide lawn of the Judge's property, slowed his breathing and crouched low. He scanned the Judge's residence, a mansion in the Jigsaw Gothic style. All the windows were dark, save one on the second floor that he knew was the study.

Kamp couldn't wait for the hearing the next morning in order to make his case. He thought he remembered a time when he understood his place in the world, remembered the feeling of solid ground beneath his feet. He recalled, too, the moment he lost his footing. He tried to concentrate on casing the house but found himself slipping backward into fragmented memories.

In his mind's eye he sighted a grey uniform by a low wall across the field and raised the Sharps. Staring down the barrel, he saw his foe and pinpointed the exact spot where the bullet would enter the man's forehead.

In the gap between the flash of the muzzle and when the bullet did its work, Kamp saw his enemy fire as well. He felt the impact at his temple and in that flash wondered why he felt it at the side of his head rather than straight on.

Before that, he never wondered about his place or purpose in the world, and after that, he couldn't remember ever having known.

KAMP CIRCLED THE PROPERTY, searching for guards and seeing no one. He went to the stone patio behind the house and waited at the edge of the lawn, listening. He waited another minute, then went to the door and tried the knob. Unlocked.

He made his way to the foot of the staircase and listened again. He heard the floorboards creaking above him and then nothing. Kamp ascended the stairs and made it half way before the first shot rang out, splintering the wood panel just above his head.

He looked up and saw the Judge's gun.

"Judge, it's me." The Judge fired again and missed. Kamp scrambled down the stairs. "It's Kamp."

The Judge emptied the pistol, and when he did, Kamp went running back up. He tackled the Judge by the legs and pinned him to the floor.

"Unhand me, you son of a bitch."

"Why?"

"Why what?" The Judge's face went purple.

"This Nickel Glock story. Why are you going along with it?"

When the Judge didn't answer, Kamp pressed his forearm hard into the Judge's throat, cutting off the flow of blood. As the Judge's eyes rolled up in their sockets, Kamp felt the tip of a cold gun barrel at the base of his skull, then heard a man's voice.

"Ach, I know you and the Judge is well-acquainted, but this here just ain't, well, it ain't *freindlich*."

The barrel bit into Kamp's neck, and he heard the cocking of the pistol. Kamp pressed his forearm even harder until the Judge's eyelids began to flutter.

The man behind him said, "Hell, I knew you was a stupid bastard, but who do you think you are anyhow, breaking into this fine adjuticator's house, middle of the goddamn night?"

Kamp had heard that voice before but couldn't place it. The man flicked the tip Kamp's earlobe with the gun barrel.

Kamp eased up on the Judge, who clutched his throat, rolled onto his belly and took in great gulps of air. The Judge hauled himself to his feet and sat in a chair.

He said, "Anton, that's enough."

Anton?

Kamp swiveled his head around and saw the familiar, unpleasant face of Anton "Duny" Kunkle.

"This man is a lion, Anton." The Judge leaned his head back and rubbed his neck.

"Ach, Judge, that's the Scotch talking."

"Oh, that very well may be." He produced the tin of Turtle Island Smoking Tobacco, packed the bowl of his pipe and lit it. "But you can't talk to a lion."

Kamp said, "Judge, what was it you called Duny? A flea? A worthless little flea."

"Wendell, you've caused enough trouble already this evening, don't you think?"

"Yah, Wendell, you don't hafta get all sore-ass, 'specially when I could still put one in your head."

With his free hand, Duny tapped Kamp's left temple.

"Oh, Duny," the Judge said, "he's just confused. Come, Wendell, sit down and have a smoke." He gestured to an empty chair.

"Why are you doing this to me?"

"Doing what?"

"The hearing tomorrow. This Nickel Glock horse-shit."

The Judge took a pull from his pipe and let the smoke cascade over his bottom lip. "It's probably nothing. A piffle."

"Then tell them to drop it."

"I can't. And remember, Nickel Glock was your invention."

"Invention?"

The Judge struck a match and re-lit the bowl. "Of course. Wendell Kamp invented Nickel Glock. Or was it the other way around? I suppose it doesn't matter."

"You mean the Order of the Raven invented a story."

"Why would they do that?"

"To harass me, to punish me. Drive me insane."

The Judge let out a heavy sigh, shook his head and said, "Oh, Wendell, if only it were that simple. And, besides, even if the Fraternal Order of the Raven existed, they wouldn't care about you. No, this is the U.S. Army's concern, apparently." He banged the dead ashes from the pipe and onto the rug. "In any case would you pass along my regards to your dear wife. I've always—"

"She's not my wife."

The Judge pursed his lips and pulled in a breath. "I've always admired that woman. So smart, so willful, so strong. And savage, too. Am I right?"

"Tell them to drop it. I have no interest in explaining myself to the army. I don't want to—"

"I, I, I. I am not I if there be such an I." The Judge settled into his chair. "Wendell, this rigmarole is based on actions you took, crimes you committed, and on your vain attempts to escape the truth. It's finally caught up with you."

Duny cleared his throat and said, "Ach, I told you, Judge."

"Told me what?"

"Told you this bastard was crazy an' stupid an' difficult."

"Alas, he's had a difficult life, Anton. That's all. Now, if you'll show him to the door. He has an appointment in my chambers tomorrow. And I don't want him to miss it."

8

Angus swung the door open to let in Nyx. He looked at her filthy boots and rough jacket and at the dented tin hat sitting cockeyed atop her head.

"When I didn't hear nothing from you, I started to wonder. Jesus, but you been through the wringer."

"Yah."

As she walked in the cabin, Angus tried to close the door behind her, but the man following Nyx held up his hand to stop her.

"Ach, who's this?"

"This is Aodh Blackall." Nyx turned to Aodh and said, "And Aodh, this is Angus Kamp."

Aodh extended his hand, but Angus didn't take it.

Angus said, "You must be hungry."

"That I am. And pleased to meet you as well."

61

"Yah." Angus turned and went to the kitchen. "Just relax. I'll have yous some supper. And take your boots off once."

Aodh took a seat at the table, unlaced his boots and let out a long sigh. Angus brought steaming bowls to the table and set one in front of Aodh.

"What's this?"

"*Karnickeleintopf*,"

"Say again."

"Rabbit stew."

He handed a spoon to Aodh, who began wolfing down the food. When he'd finished the first bowl, he looked at Angus with raised eyebrows. "May I have another?"

"Why, sure."

Aodh scanned the room and looked at Angus's workbench and at the long rack of rifles along the back wall.

"Gearing up for a war?"

Angus came back with the second helping and said, "Not exactly."

Nyx broke in, "Angus is a gunsmith. The best."

Aodh dove into the second bowl. Between bites he said, "Where're you from?" Angus ignored the question, but Aodh persisted. "I say, where are you from?"

Without looking at him, Angus said, "Oh, down the line."

"And where'd you learn to smith a gun?"

"Here and there. Nyx, could you pass the pepper?"

Nyx said, "Are you good with guns, Aodh?"

He shook his head. "Never had occasion to shoot one."

"You should learn," Angus said.

WHEN SHE'D HAD HER FILL, Nyx fixed a bedroll on the floor, then heated a pot of water. She doused a washcloth and handed it to Aodh, who held it on his face for a long moment, then wiped the grime from his cheeks and forehead.

When he took the cloth away, Nyx said, "So that's what you look like."

He turned to Angus. "Thank you for the food and the accommodations."

"*Gern gschehne.*"

Aodh walked to the bedroll and sank into it. Within seconds, his body became still, apart from deep, regular breaths.

Nyx cleared the dishes and returned to the table, where Angus had begun assembling a percussion lock for a rifle. He didn't look up from his work.

Nyx said, "Is something wrong?" When she didn't get an answer, she put her hand on his. "What is it?"

Angus looked in Nyx's eyes, then at her hand, then back at her eyes. Nyx took her hand away, and Angus resumed working.

"It'll be the death of us," he said.

"What will?"

"No one can know we're here. You know that."

"I trust him." Angus shook his head. "And besides, maybe he can help us. We can't do everything alone."

Angus looked up once more, parted his lips and drew in a breath as if preparing to speak, then went back to his work.

"We can't just hide forever," Nyx said.

SHAW HEARD KAMP COME BACK as the last solemn notes of the great horned owl faded before dawn. She assumed he wouldn't come to bed, and he didn't.

Shaw checked in on Autumn and saw the girl still sound asleep, then walked down stairs to find Kamp seated at the kitchen table, staring out the front window with a steaming mug of coffee in his hand.

She went to him and stroked the back of his head.

"Good morning, love."

"Morning."

"Long night?"

"Yah. Judge sends his regards."

He turned his head to look up at her, then looked back down at the coffee. She waited to see if an explanation would follow. When it didn't, she stood up and started cooking breakfast.

Kamp said, "Don't you want to know what I'm going to do?"

"About what?"

"The hearing, this morning. I'm not going." She sat back down across the table from him and took his hands in hers. "I won't go. It's just a—"

"You don't have a choice."

He squeezed her hands and hardened his gaze. "You know they're lying."

"Of course, but—"

"You know who I am, don't you?" He watched Shaw pull in a breath and waited for her to answer. "Don't you?"

They both heard the knock at the front door. Kamp stood up and went to the fireplace. He picked up the Sharps, then motioned for Shaw to go upstairs. He stepped to the window and saw no one on the porch, but the knocking continued.

"Who's there?"

Through the door, he heard a girl's voice.

"Message for you."

Kamp swung the door open and saw a girl, maybe seventeen years old with wide-set pale blue eyes and long, straight hair with the color and texture of corn silk, tied back with a red silk ribbon.

"What is it?"

9

Nyx tensed her belly in expectation of punishment. If any rule governed the miners' motions, if any law held sway above or below ground, there would have to be swift justice meted out and counted in cracked skulls and jailed bodies.

But when they reached the store in the pre-dawn, all appeared as it had the day before. Same lanterns lit, same *Gezähe* hanging on the wall, and the same churlish clerk standing behind the counter. The clerk gave Aodh what could have been a knowing glance, but that was all.

Nyx and Aodh headed up Gravity Road toward the fire glow, alongside the track that Butcher had traveled in the opposite direction the day before. By now Nyx knew better than to ask questions above ground, out in the open.

They were the first miners to arrive, beaten to the summit only by the wraiths who scoured the spoil heap and the man standing on the spot where the previous agent had stood. He wore a miner's hat with the candle burning to illuminate the ledger he held.

When they reached the man, Nyx recognized the greasy red mustache of the fire boss. He checked off their names in the ledger, as his doomed predecessor had.

Aodh said, "Same number, I take it."

"Lucky sevens all the way."

"Expecting trouble today, are ya?"

The fire boss sniffed, "Not as such." Then he jerked his thumb in the direction of the hole, signaling the end of the conversation.

Nyx held her tongue until they'd ridden down to the room, past the trapper kid at his post and past the ruin and rubble of explosions past and the ghosts they blasted into the ether.

She waited until they'd established their working rhythm, hewing, hauling, shouting "Done!" and starting again.

They were three cars in before Nyx said, "What's going to happen now?"

Aodh talked between swings of his coal axe. "With what?"

"With the man who was killed. What will the company do?"

"Dunno."

"They have to punish someone, don't they?"

"Depends."

"On what?"

Aodh backed out of his crawl space and stood to his full height.

"Jaysus, Nef Bahr. Enough."

"Well, I want to know."

His eyes flared with anger. "Yes, well, your wanting to know is costing us. Wondering anything down here donna get us no closer to the number. And wondering donna change what happens, or will happen, above."

"Well if you—"

"There's only below."

"That's what you think."

"Ya, tha's what I think. Once you get down here, you donna come back up. Not all the way, never."

He pulled in a breath through his nostrils, cleared his throat, and spat on the floor.

Nyx looked straight at him. "What are you afraid of up there?"

"Leave me be."

"What makes you want to hide down here?"

Aodh stared back at her and cocked his head to the side. "I could ask the same of you."

THE AGENT SAID THE TWO WORDS to the trapper kid when the first uniformed man appeared, brass buttons gleaming in the afternoon sun.

The agent shielded his eyes from the light and strained to see the first man and all those following him, a single file column marching straight for the mouth of the mine.

The trapper kid ran down the track and said the two words to the first person he saw, a helper-up kid everyone called Little Black. Little Black turned on his heel and did the same.

In this way the alarm was raised, each miner finding the next and sounding the alarm with the two words.

Nyx and Aodh heard footfalls behind them and wiggled out of their space. Nyx got to her knees and twisted around and saw the rough clothes and grimy face of a putter girl named Haas.

"What is it?"

Without expression the girl said, "They're coming."

NYX AND AODH JOINED the river of miners flowing toward the surface. They fell in line with their comrades, lamps bobbing and dancing like fireflies.

They imagined the scene above and wondered whether they'd be met with hammer blows, or bullets. None thought that the murder of the agent would go unpunished, and yet any single day's labor in the mine seemed punishment enough.

When the mine mouth came into view, Nyx squinted against the sunlight and looked for gun barrels. She saw none and heard nothing either, save the typical clank and grind of the machines. The miners emerged from the mouth in a crouch, bracing themselves.

But as their eyes adjusted to daylight and the scene came into clear focus, they saw the guards, each in a black wool uniform and peaked hat. Every guard held a Sharps rifle across his chest and wore a patch on the left shoulder bearing the Black Feather insignia. They stood in rows atop the mountain and beside the spoil heap. Nyx counted sixty in all.

She pulled her hat low and peered out from under the brim. She scanned the group of miners, now numbering in the hundreds, and looked for Dis Padgett. She didn't see him.

The guards held their positions, and the miners shifted and swayed, nervous above ground, exposed.

One of the men picked up a stone next to his foot, while others took up broken bricks that lay strewn beside the mine mouth. The silence held until the last man ascended the trail. They heard his boots crunching the gravel.

All eyes focused on the man, who wore a bespoke grey wool suit that included a close-fitting jacket with narrow lapels and a vest and watch chain underneath. The man was clean shaven, and he carried nothing.

And though the day was hot and the walk from the base of the mountain steep, the man was neither out of breath nor perspiring. When he removed his hat, the miners saw his wavy, flaxen hair, lightly oiled, combed back.

He made his way purposefully but without hurry past the guards, then took his place in front of them. He surveyed the crowd of restive miners end to end before speaking in a loud, clear voice.

"MY APOLOGIES FOR INTERRUPTING your work day. An intrusion such as this is always unwanted and unproductive."

Nyx took the man's measure while he talked. She noticed no extraneous movements, nothing to indicate that he was nervous, or unduly concerned.

"So you'll forgive the interruption, and I appreciate and esteem your willingness to pause, and to listen."

A voice boomed from the back of the group. "Yah, well then go the hell home, and leave us to work."

A laugh rippled through the miners, though none dared to speak openly. The man showed no reaction and waited for the silence to descend again.

When it did, he said, "As you are well aware, a grievous wrong was committed here yesterday. All of you know of what I speak, and most of you saw it happen. Be certain that as employees of this firm, your safety and security is our utmost priority. Furthermore, we must not and will not allow such a grave injustice to stand. As such, the responsible party must come forward."

An old hewer named Bruno at the edge of the group said, "Or else what?"

The man turned to face him. "Or else every man's pay will be reduced by five per cent each day."

The miners erupted.

"Ach, you goddamned louse."

"Yah, and I'll reduce your mother's pay, too."

"Who is this goddamned guy anyway?"

Someone hurled half a brick from behind where Nyx stood. Without flinching the man let the brick sail past, inches from his face. The guard nearest the man raised a rifle and pointed it at the miners. Nyx felt the urge to run but stifled it.

Again, the man waited for quiet, then said, "I appreciate your cooperation in this sad matter."

As he said it, he let his gaze settle on Nyx.

More bricks flew, and now there was loud jeering. The crowd of miners was transforming into a mob.

The guard behind the man said, "Fix bayonets."

"Enough!"

The shout silenced the miners. Nyx heard a shuffling of feet, as the group parted in the middle, starting from the back.

Dis Padgett made his way to the front and stepped out into the bright sunlight. He stared at the man in the suit.

"Tha's what you say, lad, that you can steal our pay. An' that may even be what you think. But tha's not what's gonna happen."

"While I respect your opinion, Mr. Padgett, you are mistaken."

Another round of jeers and whistles went up, and Padgett waited for them to subside.

"Well, you know who I am. But I donna know who you are, and I sure as hell donna respect your opinion."

The miners cheered in unison, and some spat on the ground. Nyx stole a glance at Aodh's face. His expression was flat, as he twisted a lock of his beard between his thumb and first finger.

The man said, "My name is Thaler. Joachim S. Thaler. I'm the managing director for your employer, Black Feather Extraction. Mr. Padgett, you work for me."

Padgett raised his eyebrows slightly and winced. "You donna have authority to take what's ours, mister director. An' you donna have the balls."

Joachim S. Thaler scanned the miners once more, then focused on Padgett and said, "Good day."

He set his hat back on his head, turned on his heel and left the way he'd come, black leather boots crunching the gravel down Sleeping Bear Mountain.

Once Thaler had disappeared, all eyes turned to Padgett, who spat on the ground and hissed, "Feckin' Germans."

10

K amp opened the envelope and read the message, written in a precise hand that he recognized. He would have asked the strange girl for a ride to Bethlehem on her horse, but she was already long gone. So Kamp put on his thin work jacket and slouch hat and hit the road.

The sign over the door read, "Pure Drugs & Chemicals," and the little brass bell jingled when Kamp entered. The pharmacist, Emma Wyles, stood behind the counter, finishing the preparation of a compound that she measured and then deposited in a vial.

She didn't look up until she was finished, and when she did, Kamp said, "*Wie bischt*, Emma?"

E. Wyles brushed a few strands of hair from her forehead with the back of her hand. "As I said in my note, you have to go, Kamp. Immediately."

"I just got here."

"There's nothing funny, and this isn't a joke."

"What isn't?"

She wiped her hands with a clean towel and said, "They're still after you."

"Who is?"

"Black Feather. They've concocted a story about you, about your real identity."

"Yah, I'm aware of that. They sent someone to my house and he—"

"Who was it?"

"Said his name's Reid, A. R. Reid. Said he was my commanding officer in the war, said I have to go to a hearing this morning with the Judge."

"You mustn't."

"Don't worry. I wasn't planning—"

"They mean to hurt you, Kamp. You and your family."

He pulled in a long breath. "Is that all you wanted to tell me?"

"Isn't that enough?"

"Well, sending that girl with the message. Kind of, you know, dramatic."

"Think of Shaw and Autumn. Take care of them."

He leveled his gaze at Wyles. "What else did you want to tell me?"

Wyles laid her hands flat, palms down, on the counter and let out a sigh.

She said, "I know where Nyx Bauer is."

"And?"

"But you can't go there, Kamp."

"Then don't tell me where."

"Well, I thought you should know, considering you and I are the only ones who—"

"But if I say I'm going there, you'll say I can't save her, right?"

Rarely, if ever, did Kamp bring Wyles up short, but it appeared he'd done so now. He watched his words register on her, and instead of plowing him under as she typically did, Wyles looked at him and then back down at her hands.

Kamp looked around the pharmacy. Everything was in order, bottles neatly lined along four shelves, but E. Wyles wasn't right.

"Emma, what does this have to do with you?"

"She's working in a mine. Mount Yakweha. Sleeping Bear Mountain. Are you familiar with it?"

"Yah, that's where—"

"They know she's there already, or they soon will. It's remarkable that she's been able to evade capture for as long as—"

"You sent that girl to come fetch me. You said it's urgent."

"It *is* urgent. They intend to harm you."

He rubbed his left temple with his first two fingers and said, "I appreciate your concern, but that doesn't exactly qualify as news."

She gripped the edge of the counter until the blood drained from her knuckles.

"You can be flippant and cynical, but you might show some actual gratitude, or at least some grace."

"What do you need from me, Emma?"

"To warn you."

He stepped forward and placed his hands on hers, and when he did, she looked straight at him.

He said slowly, "What do you need from me?" As he said it, a memory, long submerged, burst into his consciousness, and he felt a stab of grief in his throat.

Kamp saw the faintest quiver of Wyles' bottom lip.

She let out a long sigh and tilted her head to the side and said, "They want to shut me down."

"Who does?"

"The men who run this town."

"Including the Judge?"

One corner of her mouth turned up. "What do you think?" E. Wyles came out from behind the counter and locked the front door.

"What are they doing?"

"It's what they're doing, and what they're not doing. The shop has been vandalized, as you know. Bricks through the window. And they've harassed me. Young toughs coming in, miscreants bothering me, trying to frighten me. And no help from the police, of course."

"You've told them?"

"I told Druckenmiller."

"And?"

"And he laughed."

"What did he say?"

"Boys will be boys."

"But you think it's more than that."

Her eyes flared. "I'm accustomed to the obnoxiousness. I expect it. I'm very good at my job, I'm outspoken, and I'm a woman. But what's happening now—"

"Is different."

"That's right. It's been unrelenting."

"Why now?"

Wyles walked to the front window and pointed. "Because of that."

He looked across the street and saw a sign on a storefront window that read, "Native Plants & Medicine."

"Competition," he said.

"There's nothing wrong with another pharmacy. Bethlehem is growing. There's a need."

Wyles walked to the back of the shop, boot heels clicking off the wood floor, and came back carrying two green bottles.

"I have no problem with competition, as you know."

"Then what *is* the problem?"

"Two, actually. The first is that because of me, they can't get any business. People know and trust me."

As she spoke, Wyles began mixing a new compound in a mortar fashioned from a maple burl with the pattern in the wood that looked, to him, like an explosion. The burl had been polished so that it blazed.

He gestured to the bowl and said, "I remember where that comes from." He waited for her to glance at it. "From that tree you cut down."

She pulled in a breath through her nostrils and said, "The second problem is Black Feather. They own Native Plants. See?"

Wyles pointed to the upper right corner of the store's window, and he saw the unmistakable symbol painted there.

"They want control of everything, every business, every facet of people's lives. What they say and do, eat and drink, what medicines they take."

"Cradle to grave."

"And then some." She finished grinding the compound and put her fists on her hips. "And I'm in their way."

Kamp put on his slouch hat and said, "I'll take care of it."

Wyles' expression hardened. "Meaning what?"

He tipped his hat and headed for the door. "That's why you told me, right? You want me to take care of it."

"I want you to help Nyx Bauer, if that's possible. As for me, I can handle my own—"

As he left, he said, "*Machs gute*, Emma," and he closed the door behind him.

KAMP REMEMBERED THE LAST TIME he'd seen that expression on E. Wyles' face, the only other time he'd seen her frightened, and now the memory returned in its entirety.

She'd stared up into the branches and said, "You first."

He knew that this was her tree, the maple tree she'd climbed every day in the summer when they were nine years old.

Kamp had accepted her challenge to see which of them could climb higher, and he leapt to grasp the first sturdy bough with both hands and then swinging his torso onto it. He climbed as quickly and as high as he could, at least seventy-five feet off the ground.

Before he could even steady himself and call down to taunt his friend, she was already past him. Wyles sprang from branch to branch, barefoot in a blue and white gingham dress and climbing as if on stairs.

Kamp's belly, already tight from fear, churned as he watched her moving closer to the canopy where the branches might not support a person, even a slender kid like Wyles.

She paused to look back at him, smiled and said, "Eat shit, Wendell."

"Fine, you win. Come down." He felt afraid for her.

"Hell, no. I'm doing it." She turned, looked up and continued her climb.

They'd talked all summer about going to the very top, and the person who made it all the way, who actually stuck their head all the way out of the canopy would be the winner, once and for all. Kamp himself had never actually considered trying.

Wyles knew that if she waited much longer, the leaves would begin to fall, and the challenge would be null and void. If she waited until next year, she'd definitely be too big to even try.

And Kamp knew she wouldn't be persuaded to stop and that if he spoke now he might break her concentration. He watched, unable to help and unable to look away. She went higher, moving slowly now, testing every branch, taking her time.

Nearing the top, each bough bent under her weight, but she only had a few feet to go. She stepped up, then again, staying as close as possible to the trunk. But in order to get all the way to the top, she'd have to depart the trunk and shin out on a limb.

Wyles paused but soon made her move out onto the branch and then seconds later popped her head out of the canopy. Kamp expected her to start crowing in triumph, but instead, she went silent. He waited a minute, then another, and there was no movement from his friend.

"Emma?"

Nothing.

"Emma, hey."

"Yah."

Her voice sounded thin and far away.

"Are you all right?"

"Um."

He knew she wouldn't admit to being afraid, would never ask for help. But she was frozen now, treed. He worked his way as high as he could, much higher than he wanted.

He said, "I'm right here. Don't look down. Just follow my voice. Reach back with your right foot."

She followed his instructions, and he caught a glimpse of her face, tight with panic and stained with tears.

"Now, slide back. Good. One more and—"

"Fine, but I don't need your—"

When she snapped her head around and down to scold him, the branch gave a loud crack, and Wyles tumbled past him, cartwheeling through the branches, bouncing down through the boughs until she hit the ground with a thud.

He climbed down, heart pounding and eyes fixed on his friend who lay face down and motionless next to the large burl at the base of the trunk. He knelt beside her and placed his hand on her back.

"Emma, wake up."

Just as he tensed to start his run to get help, she rolled onto her back with a groan, eyes closed.

"Kamp? Is, is that you?"

"Yes, I'm here, I'm here."

She let the ruse play out a moment longer, then opened her eyes and grinned.

E. Wyles said, "I win."

THE BROKEN RIBS AND THE BLACK EYE had only made Wyles prouder of the accomplishment. But Kamp had seen her face the instant before the fall, the moment she knew she'd gone well past the limit and that the reckoning was certain.

He reflected on that look on her face. And he still wished he could have kept her from falling. The relief he'd felt upon realizing she would be okay didn't erase the terror he'd felt when he watched her tumble through the branches, when he felt certain he'd lost his friend. He couldn't save her that day from the weakness of those upper boughs or from the strength of her will.

11

Kamp made a fist and cocked it back, but before he could rap knuckles on the door with the brass sign that read "Strictly No Admittance," it swung open. He saw the unsmiling face of the High Constable, Samuel Druckenmiller.

Kamp said, "It's here, isn't it?"

"Is what here?"

"The hearing."

Druckenmiller screwed up his face, tilted his head to the side and said, "Who are you?"

He felt the flames of anger spring to life at the base of his skull.

"Sam, knock it off."

"I don't know you, and I don't like your tone."

"Christ, Sam, it's me. Kamp."

Druckenmiller's hand went to the pistol at his side.

"No...no, you ain't. You ain't Kamp. You must be that son of a bitch Nickel Glock."

With his hand still on the gun, Druckenmiller gestured for Kamp to enter the Judge's chambers. Kamp saw the Judge, seated behind his desk and wearing traditional court dress.

Next to him sat the man who called himself A. R. Reid. When Druckenmiller closed the door, Kamp realized another man stood behind him. The man wore a bespoke suit in brown wool. At a glance, he recognized him as the prosecutor, Grigg.

The Big Judge said, "You recall the district attorney."

"District attorney?"

Grigg said, "Indeed. Good to see you again."

The Judge turned to Reid and said, "Last year, Glock tried to lead Mr. Grigg, among others, to the conclusion that one of the leading figures in the Commonwealth of Pennsylvania, a captain of industry named Raymond Hinsdale, was guilty of a most heinous murder."

A.R. Reid said, "Good lord."

The Judge let the sentiment hang as he packed the bowl of his cherry pipe with Turtle Island Smoking Tobacco and lit up.

Exhaling a great cloud of smoke, the Judge said, "Indeed. Shameful. But that's not what brings us here this morning. High Constable, before we proceed, would you kindly inspect Mr. Glock?"

Druckenmiller stood facing Kamp and said, "Arms out."

Kamp stared at the Judge, then turned to look at Grigg who gave a small nod. Kamp raised his arms to shoulder height.

The Judge said, "Boots, too."

Druckenmiller knelt and reached inside Kamp's left boot, then the right before his hands traveled up Kamp's leg. When he reached the crotch, Kamp gave Druckenmiller a hard slap on the side of his face.

The High Constable cried out in pain and said, "Ach, why ya hafta be so ugly?"

The Judge said, "Mr. Glock, do that again and you'll be remanded to the city jail posthaste. Kamp raised his arms again and let Druckenmiller finish.

"He don't have no gun." The High Constable stood up, rubbing his jaw and muttering under his breath. "Goddamn louse."

The Judge cleared his throat. "Yes, well, Mr. Glock, if you'll have a seat." He gestured to an open chair, and Kamp sat down. "As you know, we're of the belief that you are one Nickel Glock and that for the past nine years you've been pretending to be Wendell W. Kamp."

Kamp raised his eyebrows and shook his head.

The Judge said, "Naturally, you'll continue to perpetuate this charade unless and until it no longer suits your nefarious purposes."

Kamp said, "Where are we going with this?"

The Judge took another pull on his pipe. "We're not going anywhere. It's you who's going."

"That so."

"Indeed."

Kamp turned in his chair to address Grigg, who stood behind him, arms folded.

"Are you following this? Do you believe any of it?"

Grigg took in a sharp breath. "Alas, there's a case."

"What's the charge?"

The Judge cut in, "Well, in addition to the crime of impersonating another man, there's breaking and entering, assault, obstruction of justice, and of course, corrupting the morals of minors, and possibly kidnapping."

"What?"

"The boy, Becket Hinsdale, you took him down a path that led to his disappearance, and to the destruction of his family. Incidentally, what do you know about where he is?"

"Nothing."

A.R. Reid shook his head in disgust.

"The real Kamp was the finest soldier I ever commanded. You're nothing but a fiend, a most foul fiend."

The Judge said, "And that's not even the worst of it. You took a young girl in her moment of greatest distress, a girl who'd lost both her parents at the hands of a killer, and you put murderous ideas into her very mind."

As the Judge said it, another man strode theatrically into the room. He had flowing hair, wireframe glasses and a beard in the Van Dyke style. He wore a bespoke three-piece suit with watch and chain, shiny black brogans, and he carried a leather-bound folio under his arm. The man went directly to the Judge and extended his hand.

"Your honor, please accept my most humble apology for my tardiness. There was a problem with one of the horses and—"

The Judge banged the dead ashes from his pipe on the edge of his wide, mahogany desk. "It's quite all right, doctor. Thank you for coming. Mr. Glock, may I introduce you to Dr. Alastair MacBride."

Kamp took in the man—the suit, the tidy beard, the sheen. He said, "Doctor."

MacBride's gaze hardened. "Much obliged, Mr. Glock."

The Judge said, "Dr. MacBride is the head of the Pennsylvania Hospital for the Insane, though I don't believe the two of you have ever met."

Kamp said, "I've enjoyed getting acquainted and everything, but I don't have time for this bullshit."

He stood up and put on his hat.

The Judge said to MacBride, "Show him."

ALISTAIR MACBRIDE WENT TO THE DESK and opened the folio. He removed several 8x10 photographs and arranged them on the table.

The Judge gestured to Kamp, "Come see."

Kamp said, "Yah, I've seen these already."

MacBride removed the handwritten note clipped to the back of the photograph and said, "What about this? It proves W.W. Kamp perished in the war."

Kamp looked at the Judge.

"What's your point?"

The Judge packed the bowl of his cherry pipe again and struck the match on the desktop.

"Kamp is deceased. You're here. That's the point."

He dipped the flame into the bowl then let it dance back out.

"So what."

Druckenmiller cut in, "So, that there is Wendell Kamp. He was my friend, and he died right there."

"No, Sam, that's a picture. No one died right there."

Druckenmiller took his pistol from the holster and raised it over his head. He said, "Ach, I oughtta clout you one."

Grigg picked up the photograph, gave it a closer look and said to Kamp, "What do you make of it?"

"I don't make anything."

"Meaning what."

Kamp sat back down in his chair and rubbed his eyes with his thumb and forefinger. "Who's to say who those men in the photograph are? And who's to say who wrote that note. Or why."

Grigg said, "Are you claiming these are forgeries?"

Kamp let out a sigh. "I'm not claiming anything. I'm just saying no one knows."

A.R. Reid cleared his throat and said, "Yes, well, I know."

"You do?"

Reid pulled on his lapels and straightened in his chair.

"Yes, I was there. I remember the day. Sad day."

Kamp said, "What was sad about it?"

Reid's tone turned somber. "The bloodshed, the carnage. Terrible loss of life in that battle."

"What battle?"

Reid's face twisted. "Is this some sort of inquisition? I'll certainly brook none of your skepticism, you, you—"

"What battle?"

Grigg said, "Yes, colonel, what battle?"

Reid focused on Grigg, "Why, Fredericksburg! And how dare this man besmirch the memory of that sacred killing field. God will not be mocked, gentlemen. He will not be—"

"I didn't besmirch anything," Kamp said, "I asked a question."

Druckenmiller said, "Yah, a question and another question and another. Until you go nuts from the questions. That's how he does it."

The color rose in Reid's face as he turned to address the Judge.

"Your honor, this man is a fraud and a disgrace."

"So he is," the Judge said.

Kamp looked at Reid. "You were there?"

"I was."

"And you saw that soldier, Kamp—"

"Finest soldier I ever commanded."

"You saw him dead on that table."

"Yes, I saw W. W. Kamp on the table. I saw the surgery, saw its grim conclusion, and I saw them take the body away." At this point, Reid's gaze drifted to the ceiling, as if he were lost in the memory.

"What was the surgeon's name?"

"The surgeon?"

"Yes, you were there. You know all about it. What was the surgeon's name?"

Reid's face turned purple. "I've had quite enough with this, this—"

Kamp said in a flat tone, "He's lying, Judge. You know he's lying, and you know this is a farce."

MacBride, who'd been watching the proceedings and thoughtfully stroking his chin beard now spoke.

"I assure you all that this is nothing of the sort. The colonel's description is not only true, it's verifiable."

Reid sniffed, "Indeed."

"And furthermore," MacBride stood with a flourish, "I've seen many connivers and manipulators in my work as an expert psychiatrist, and this man, this Nickel Glock, is a master of the dark arts. He'll do anything to keep us from getting to the heart of the matter."

Grigg said, "And what *is* the heart of the matter?"

MacBride's hard expression turned soft. He furrowed his brow and said, "Why, there's a girl out there."

"A girl."

"Indeed, a young, frightened girl. Lost and alone. In desperate need of shelter and warmth. But even more than that, in need of love and understanding."

Kamp said, "What are you talking about?"

MacBride's lips curled into a snarl, and he said, "Pardon my language. You know damn well, sir, what I'm talking about. That girl, that precious flower you plucked. The girl whose face you turned toward evil, whose foot you put on that path of mendacity and malice."

"Who?"

"Nadine Bauer!" MacBride's voice thundered. "She needs help. She needs succor."

"Succor?"

The Judge took a long pull on his pipe, then said, "I've often wondered, these past two years, what had become of the Kamp I knew before. I couldn't believe the stories I was hearing. Of course, now I know the truth. Wendell Kamp was a fine young man, an even better soldier, and a hero of the War Between the States. That his identity has been co-opted and his legacy befouled speaks to the depravity into which our society is descending. What the doctor is saying, sir, is that we believe you know the whereabouts of Nadine Bauer and that it is your responsibility to return her to the custody of the Commonwealth."

"Nyx? This is all about you forcing me to tell you where she is?"

"Hardly."

"Jesus Christ."

MacBride slammed his fist on the desk.

"Dammit, man, redeem yourself. Find her, bring her back." He took a dramatic pause and glowered at Kamp. "Nadine Bauer needs help."

The Judge cleared his throat and said, "Mr. Glock, you have thirty days to find Nadine Bauer and return her to the custody of the Commonwealth, where she'll be safe. If you fail to do so, you'll be captured and remanded to the Pennsylvania Hospital for the Insane, where you'll live out the remainder of your days."

12

Nyx picked up the note on the kitchen table, written in pencil scrawl.

It read, "For you."

Beside the note was a gun, a pepperbox pistol, and a box of bullets. She picked up the gun and stared into the swirling pattern on the Damascus steel barrels that reminded her of turgid grey river water. She hefted the gun in her shooting hand, and it felt cold and mean.

The weapon appeared to be well-used but had been expertly maintained. Nyx assumed Angus had spent untold hours restoring it.

Of all the secrets she kept, the one she cherished the most was that she was alone and needed help from no one. She held this belief so closely she couldn't see it, and it was only at moments such as this—when someone tried to help her—that Nyx felt its presence.

Rather than gratitude or relief, Nyx felt resentment. It was up to her to help other people, if necessary, if that's what she decided. She didn't want charity. And if she needed something, she'd take it.

That's how it went with the Hinsdale kid. She hadn't needed him to break her out of jail, but since he did anyway, she'd returned the favor when the time came, setting the scales back to balance thereby.

Nyx didn't mind that the Angus wanted to help. When the men from the city had seen her parents' ruined bodies, they wanted to help. But they didn't know that in the moment she learned of their fate— the moment she ran to her father's corpse and clutched his cold, cloven chest—they didn't know that the notion that she could be helped was absurd and rendered forever meaningless.

All of these memories and the feelings that accompanied them erupted when Nyx looked at the pistol and the note beside it. Angus meant well, and she left it at that.

That's what she liked about Aodh. He never tried to help her. They worked side by side, and more often than not she was able to do him a good turn without him complaining. She didn't feel his weight.

And if Nyx couldn't admit to herself that his presence was all that enabled her to keep going in the mine in those moments she felt small and abandoned, that denial was necessary for the time being, too.

KAMP BECAME AWARE of the shouting and commotion that trailed after him as he exited the Judge's chambers. When he hit the granite steps leading down to the street that flowed with the mid-morning mass of souls, he saw Shaw hurrying toward him with Autumn in tow.

Her expression, typically placid, now showed distress and irritation. Kamp hustled down the steps and put his arms around them. She put her hand over her eyes, the tears spilling down her cheeks.

"They threw us out," she said.

"Who did?"

"The police. A group of them came. One of them had a paper that said we're not allowed back in our home."

He turned and raced back up the stairs and into the courthouse. He went straight for the door to the

Judge's chambers and hurled himself against it. The door didn't give. He pounded the door with his fist.

"Let me in."

No response.

Kamp kept pounding until two large, uniformed police officers grabbed him and hauled him out of the building.

He went to a side door and ran up three flights of stairs and down the hallway to an office door with freshly painted lettering on the window that read, "B.H. Grigg, District Attorney."

He twisted the doorknob and went in before Grigg could look up from his desk. When he did, the district attorney said, "You can't be here."

Kamp put his palms on Grigg's desk and leaned forward.

"Tell me what they're doing."

Grigg stood up and closed the blinds. He turned back to look at Kamp and said, "You already know."

"How's that?"

Grigg produced a silver snuff tin engraved with the letters "BHG" from the watch pocket of his vest, flipped open the lid and offered it to Kamp, who declined.

He then took a sizable pinch, placed it on the back of his right hand and gave it a powerful sniff.

"As you know, they need you gone. You're an irritant, an impediment and a living testament to their misdeeds. But you're also a war hero. Disposing of you would create problems for them. I'm afraid I can't speak with you further. It would be most—"

"They want to throw us out of our house."

"Correction, they threw you out."

"You knew?"

Grigg took his seat behind his desk. "I saw the eviction notice, signed by the Judge."

"And you did nothing."

"It was a fait accompli."

Kamp shook his head gripped the edge of the desk.

"Don't you think it's wrong?"

"It's legal."

"I understand you're a lawyer, but Jesus, man."

"Your judgment is clouded."

"You're goddamned right it's clouded. They just—"

"Settle. Down. If they have to remove you from the building again, you'll be taken to the jail. That won't help your family."

Kamp closed his eyes and waited for the flames to subside, then said, "Can you help me or not?"

Grigg shifted in his leather chair.

"As I said, you can see the case they've made against you. That you're not who you claim to be. That you're an impostor, that you've perpetrated a fraud."

"What do you believe?"

Grigg raised his eyebrows and said, "I traffic in facts and in rationality. If you can't prove who you are, it hardly matters what I believe."

"In other words, you think this bullshit is wrong, but you don't care. Is that it?"

"That's not what I said. If you can't prove your identity, you can't win."

"And they'll make certain I can't prove it."

"Correct."

Kamp stood up and let his shoulders relax. He went to the window that overlooked the steps, checking to make sure Shaw and Autumn were still there before turning back to look at Grigg.

"You still want to destroy Black Feather, though, right?"

"Of course."

"And now that you're the district attorney, you have more power."

"In theory."

"But you need facts. And if they know you're building a case against them, they'll destroy you first."

Grigg nodded slowly.

"And if I provide you with facts, you'll help me."

"Behind the scenes, of course." Grigg stood up and extended his hand. "Good luck to you, whoever the hell you are."

"Kamp." He shook Grigg's hand.

"Good day, Kamp."

KAMP HUSTLED OUT to the steps, where Shaw and Autumn waited. He put his arm around them and started moving in the direction of the Third Street Station. Looking back over his shoulder, he saw a uniformed officer following them.

When they reached the ticket window, Kamp said, "Two, please."

He paid, and the three of them walked to the platform.

Kamp handed Shaw the tickets and said, "I'll tell you everything when I get there."

OFFICER FALKO STIER NEVER LIKED that asshole Kamp. He didn't like him from the first time he'd heard the rumor of what Kamp had done to a fellow officer of the law, a hardworking and upright deputy chief, no less.

Stier hadn't met the deputy chief. He'd only heard stories and seen a photograph. But every time he passed the brass plaque in the station that read, "In honor of the fallen Markus Lenz," Stier felt a sense of duty mixed with disgust for the murderer. Knowing that this fiend Kamp—or what was his name now—Glock? Knowing this fiend had murdered the upright Lenz sickened him.

That the whole shameful episode had been covered up and hidden from public view, well, that made it nearly unbearable.

Falko Stier had tangled with him before, when he found him aiding and abetting the fugitive Nadine Bauer at the pharmacy of one Emma Wyles.

Bauer had assaulted him when he arrested her in the commission of a crime. She was lucky he didn't give her the bullet to the brain she deserved. Same with Kamp. He was fortunate that he was only roughed up and doused with kerosene.

Stier watched Kamp climbing aboard the train with his family, that Indian and their half-breed daughter. It turned Stier's stomach. Kamp, Bauer, Wyles—the list of degenerates kept getting longer.

No wonder Bethlehem's going down the shitter.

Officer Falko Stier intended to stand his ground until the train left the station. He wanted to make sure that Kamp and his lot were well and truly gone.

KAMP GUIDED Shaw and Autumn onto the passenger train and then climbed in himself.

"You have to get going."

She said, "Get going where? What are you doing?"

He peeked out a window and saw Officer Falko Stier on the platform.

"Go to your father's house. I'll be there soon."

The train lurched forward and started to roll as the conductor approached.

"Tickets."

Autumn, who'd been silent until now, began to cry. Between sobs, she said, "Daddy, come with us," and she hugged Kamp around both legs.

Shaw looked into his eyes.

"Yes, come with us."

Kamp gently peeled Autumn from his legs, picked her up and handed her to Shaw. He kissed them both, then jumped out the other side of the train, ran across the yard and stood behind a steel beam. When the train left the yard, Kamp saw the officer watch the train depart and then turn and leave as well.

13

Kamp pulled his slouch hat low and fired a penny at the toll collector on the New Street Bridge. He didn't need to look across the river to know that Native Iron had grown even since the last time he'd crossed the bridge with the kid who'd called steel works a fire-breathing abomination.

But he didn't have time to ruminate on the ruination of his fair city, didn't bother to wonder what it might look like in a year, or in fifty. Even though Shaw and Autumn were already gone, half way up the line to Lehighton, Kamp wanted to go home, if for no other reason than to collect a couple things he'd need.

He figured he could talk his way past whoever they'd stationed at his front door. Arguing wouldn't work. It might spark conflict that would lead to violence, and ultimately reward Black Feather with their desired end. He'd be shot on the doorstep for trespassing.

So, he walked the miles back to his small farm, eyes on the ground, boots crunching the gravel and coming up with the words he'd need to talk his way into his own house.

NYX HEARD THE COMMOTION before she saw it. She'd been lost in a reverie on her way to the mine, a powerful memory of swimming in Shawnee Creek with the doomed Daniel Knecht.

She remembered the way she'd felt that summer day. Clean and cold. And she remembered climbing out of the water, how the sun reflected its light in the water drops on her bare chest.

Nyx rarely allowed herself these memories, because they had the power to pull her into the past but more importantly because they took her focus from the detection of threats in the here and now. And so it was with alarm mixed with some irritation that she snapped from her reverie and focused on the knot of men on the porch of the Black Feather Extraction Company Store.

Permanently begrimed miners crowded in, shoving and elbowing each other to get a better look at something affixed at eye level next to the doorpost. Nyx heard them before she could see what they were talking about.

"Ach, but she's a wild one."

"They say she killed a man with her bare hands."

"Yah, well, I'd put her on the straight and narrow. Believe me."

"Better to slit her throat first and then give it to her. Just to be safe."

Nyx felt the blood drain from her face, felt dread in her belly and numbness in the tips of her fingers. Her heart began to thud. Head down, she moved as close as she dared before shooting a glance. It was a poster that read:

$1000 REWARD
Will be paid in gold coin for the apprehension
DEAD OR ALIVE
of
the **MURDERER NADINE BAUER**
aka NYX BAUER aka NADJA KNEFF
aka BIX NEUER aka NOX VOLK

Above the text was a hand-drawn picture, and Nyx felt relief when she studied it. The artist must have worked from a family photograph taken seven or eight years before. Her face had changed in the intervening years, details the artist didn't know and failed to guess. Combined with her everyday disguise, which included close-cropped hair and several layers of coal dust, she looked nothing like the face on the poster.

Still, Nyx fought the urge to run. She walked into the company store with a straight back, wondering whether her fellow miners had an inkling of her real identity. But given that she hadn't been shot or bludgeoned as yet, the answer had to be no.

The pepperbox pistol, which she'd sworn to herself she wouldn't use, was tucked in her right boot.

BIX NEUER? NOX VOLK? Kamp realized Nyx had probably made up a number of aliases in order to avoid detection. But looking at the wanted poster and reading the fake names, he wondered how many lies had been told and how many facts invented about her since the murders of her parents three years before.

The creation and dissemination of a wanted poster was itself a powerful form of myth-making, he knew.

He'd first seen it when his march home took him past Grace Lutheran Church. A group of congregants had assembled around the poster, which had been nailed to a lamppost. They clucked and muttered.

"What her parents suffered, and now this."

"She was always a wild one. You just knew it."

"The shame."

The Reverend A.R. Eberstark, resplendent in a purple silk chasuble strode down the walk to where the group stood. They parted for him, and he took his place next to the lamppost.

Eberstark surveyed the group lovingly, then said, "Our lord and master said, 'Suffer the children and forbid them not to come unto me.' "

There was nervous murmuring in the crowd, and then someone said, "But she's a killer, a fiend!"

"Indeed, but she's been led astray, and deserves mercy."

"Yah, well, she'll have no mercy on you, reverend."

Eberstark looked up as if a fly had just buzzed past his ear.

Another congregant said, "That's right, she never showed you no mercy."

Eberstark lowered his eyes and let the comment hang, then tilted his chin up and said, "It's not this little one who's committed these crimes. She means me no ill-will, and she's done nothing wrong."

Anger rippled through the crowd.

Eberstark let the moment build and then roared, "It's the spirit of the Jezebel. The Jezebel spirit has invaded this girl's very soul!"

At the back of the crowd, a woman shouted, "He's right!"

He continued, "It's the Jezebel spirit sent by Satan himself. And it must be cast out, however harsh the trials may be." Flecks of spittle flew from the corners of his mouth, and his face matched the color of his chasuble. "We must hope that Nadine Bauer can survive the enemy's onslaught, not to mention the exorcism."

"Bless you, reverend."

Eberstark daubed his forehead with a silk handkerchief.

"Yes, well, first she must be found."

Kamp got close enough to inspect the poster, and he smiled when he saw that the picture didn't look like Nyx. He turned and walked away, confident that no one would recognize her. And he knew she would never allow herself to be discovered.

Still, a reward of that size would entice men to act even on the slightest suspicion. He wondered who could pay a bounty of that size until he saw the small letters at the foot of the poster, "Offered by Black Feather Consolidated."

Black Feather was behind the search for Nyx. And it was Black Feather who'd manufactured the scheme to disgrace him.

Behind Black Feather was the Fraternal Order of the Raven, not the Judge or MacBride the doctor. Ultimately, it was the Order who demanded that he find her.

After seeing that first wanted poster, Kamp saw it again and again on fences, storefronts, and trees on his march out of town. Black Feather offered no explanation as to why they, not the county and not the police, were offering a reward. It didn't matter.

And they provided no evidence to back up the claim that Nyx was a murderer. Given the notoriety she'd achieved, the absence of facts wouldn't matter. What mattered was that the Order wanted Nyx Bauer, and they wanted Kamp and everyone else to find her.

NYX MADE SURE that she and Aodh worked farther down in the mine that day than ever before. They stooped low under the last supporting timbers and then crawled another fifty yards to get at a fresh anthracite seam that glinted by the light of her candle.

Holding her hewing shovel in both hands, she moved on knees and elbows to her starting point, a crevice fifteen inches high.

Aodh Blackall watched her disappear into the dark. In the months since this young lad Nef Bahr had started working with him, he'd grown so accustomed to his questions that Nef Bahr's voice had become as much a part of the underground symphony as the creaking of timbers and the groaning of rough lovers that often emanated from the dark.

Bahr's voice had become a comfort to him, he now realized, because the lad hadn't spoken a word today. But Aodh knew that every man, young or old, had secrets and stored up inside him that demanded attention and sometimes silence.

And many a time, the deeper he wanted to go into the mine, the deeper he wanted to go in himself. Still, he sensed something amiss in Nef Bahr, and he wanted to hear him speak.

Aodh called out, "Upon thy belly shalt thou go, and dust shalt thou eat all the days of thy life. Ainna that right, Nef Bahr?"

Nyx heard him, but the words didn't register, as she'd already begun to hew the coal. She paused when she realized he was talking to her.

"What?"

"You know where tha's from? Upon thy belly shalt thou go, and dust shalt thou eat all the days of thy life?"

"Yah, I do," she called over her shoulder, "though I didn't peg you for a churchgoer."

"I'm not, not unless you fancy this black hole a cathedral. Not that I'll be lookin' for deliverance down here. And I certainly donna have anythin' t'confess."

He wanted to draw out Nef Bahr, and get him talking, but the lad starting hewing again, and soon Aodh did, too.

THE FLICKER OF FEAR NYX FELT above ground now became a raging fire. Only by dint of hard labor could she keep the flames at bay.

Nyx wanted to tell Aodh, tell him about her parents and about Daniel Knecht and how they all met their end. She wanted to tell him about a real murderer, Hugh Arndt, and what she'd done with his corpse, about how they'd hunted her with dogs and then nearly killed her and Angus in a storm of bullets.

Nyx wanted Aodh to know that she still had plans and hope for a future but that she had other matters to tend to first. She pushed down the impulse and made no sound, save the *chunk* of the coal axe sinking into anthracite and black diamonds hitting the floor.

KAMP'S HEART STARTED TO THUMP when his house came into view. He noticed smoke twisting from the chimney. Shaw would never have left a fire burning.

As he got closer and looked through the front window, he saw people inside. He slowed his walk when he reached the bottom stair to the porch, and he crouched as he made his way up and got a closer look. He thought maybe the men who'd evicted his family had stayed there, for what reason he couldn't fathom. But when he got a good look inside, he saw a woman, roughly Shaw's height, with straight black hair that reached the middle of her back.

Perhaps sensing that she was being watched, the woman spun around to face him, and when she did, he saw a face like Shaw's, except pale.

When she saw Kamp, the woman said, "There's someone here."

He heard footfalls thudding down the stairs, then saw a man cross the room. The door swung open, and he stood face to face with a man who looked like him.

The man's complexion and coloring, his height and build, the shape of his countenance: all were nearly the same as Kamp.

The man said, "May I help you?"

In an instant Kamp grasped the nature and scope of the deception, and he said, "Yes, you can."

The man stood straight, chin out.

"How might I do that?"

Kamp took a step closer, forgetting every word of the speech he'd rehearsed.

"By getting the fuck out of my house."

The woman, who'd been standing quietly behind the man, gasped and covered her mouth with her hand.

"Sir, I'll ask you not to use foul language."

Kamp felt the spark at the base of his skull burst into flame. "Do you have a kid, too?"

"Sir? I'm afraid I—"

"A child. Did you scare up a child who looks like my daughter?"

The woman put her head down and began to cry softly.

"Jesus, enough with the act," Kamp said.

The man's gaze hardened as he stepped onto the porch and closed the door behind him.

The man said, "Two years ago a house on this very site burned to the ground. Our infant daughter perished in that fire. I'll ask you to leave the premises now, sir."

"Tell me your name, your real name."

"I don't have to tell you—"

"Tell me!"

"All right, it's Wendell W—"

The sound of a pump action interrupted the man, and Kamp turned his head to see the barrel of an 8-gauge shotgun and behind that, a face he recognized.

Officer Falko Stier said, "You're trespassing. Leave."

Kamp didn't comply, and in a single motion Stier flipped the weapon around and with the butt of the gun, and cracked him in the jaw, knocking him back two steps. Kamp righted himself but then doubled over, a rope of bloody saliva stretching from his lips to the wooden planks of the porch.

Falko Stier turned to the man in the doorway and said, "Mr. Kamp, we're sorry for this intrusion. We'll not allow it again."

14

After fourteen hours in a space fifteen inches high, Nyx was ready to get aboveground, no matter the risk. Aodh had long since given up trying to talk to her, and she'd been able to work in solitude, allowing the successive waves of panic to wash over her and eventually ebb.

The fear of being caught was now outweighed by the need to pull fresh air into her lungs and to see natural light on her skin. When she backed out of her spot on bloody knees and elbows, she stood up slowly, allowing her body to adjust to moving upright.

Immediately, a hand clapped her on the right shoulder.

Nyx went rigid, and she waited for what she thought was coming next, the killing blow.

"Jaysus, Nef, but you're a squirrel today."

Aodh's fingers began to knead, coaxing the soreness from the muscles. Then he put both hands on her shoulders and pressed his thumbs into the back of her neck, and when he did, Nyx felt a powerful and not at all unpleasant shiver travel down and then back up her spine.

She let her head tip forward and let him work his hands. At the moment relaxation and pleasure began to spread through her body, Aodh stopped massaging her shoulders, picked up his axe and shovel.

On his way out, Aodh said, "Sometimes a man needs a friendly squeeze. But now it's time for a beer. Let's go."

When they reached the road out of the mine and began marching with their fellow miners, Nyx's fear took hold once more. She thought again about the pepperbox pistol tucked in her boot.

KAMP HELD HIS JAW as he shambled down the path from his home, and the pain clouded his thinking. He knew that seeking help wasn't an option and seeking revenge would be pointless. That two people had been installed in his house in order to assume his and Shaw's identities suggested the scope and complexity of an extensive plot, already well in motion.

When he reached the road, he tilted his head back and squinted at the sun. It was late afternoon, and he needed to find food and then a place to sleep.

Working his way through the woods and crouching low, he ran for the house of Sam Druckenmiller. Once he was convinced the High Constable wasn't there, Kamp hustled to the back door where he found a new brass lock. Then he went to Druckenmiller's shed, where he found a new lock on that door as well.

Kamp picked up a stone and swung it hard into the doorknob, smashing it open. He went straight to the cellar and found a ringwurst hanging on a hook. Then he hurried back up the stairs to the kitchen and took a loaf of sourdough from the counter. In the cold chest he discovered a bottle of ale. He put it all in a burlap sack, yanked the blanket off Druckenmiller's bed and stuffed that in the sack, too.

His only option for sleeping with a roof over his head was the one he liked the least. Kamp made his way along the familiar path beside Shawnee Creek, and when he reached the spreading chestnut tree from which the body of Daniel Knecht had once dangled, he turned toward the road.

The red house, the former home of Jonas and Rachel Bauer and their daughters, looked much the
same as the last time he'd seen it, hopeless and lorn.
The windows, which had been covered with boards,
were now open, the glass long gone. He walked to
the front step and found that while the door was still
there, the knob was missing. The door swung freely
when he pushed it.

Darkness followed him inside, and he became
aware that he had no candle and no matches but figured it was just as well. Seeing the interior of the
house clearly could let loose a torrent of images and
overload his senses.

Kamp went to the main room, spread out the
blanket and sat on it with his back to the wall. The
growling in his stomach grew louder and more persistent, but as soon as he fished the ringwurst out of
the bag, he realized he couldn't take a bite. The pain
in his jaw was too intense.

He stared at the food he couldn't eat, and the deep
anger and frustration he'd been keeping at bay burst
into his consciousness. Scenes from the past several
weeks—the letter arriving at his door, the guns
pointed at his head, the accusations and lies—all of
it spun and whirled before his mind's eye.

And then memories from farther back appeared,
the mutilated faces of Jonas and Rachel Bauer and

the charred ruins of his own house, followed by battle scenes and butchered men in heaps behind a canvas army tent. He stifled the urge to scream and allowed his body to shake, though it brought fresh pain.

As the anger and agony worked their way toward a crescendo, Kamp heard a thud upstairs. He sat up, listened and heard nothing more. Perhaps the wind had knocked something over. Another thud, and then shuffling. Someone there. He took a defensive crouch and waited in the pitch darkness.

He heard soft footfalls on the stairs, then saw the glow of a candle and the small hand that held it. A girl, maybe ten years old, reached the bottom step and stopped.

She wore a tattered dress and no shoes, and she was followed by another girl who looked like a little sister. The girls stared at him with frightened expressions that shifted to bemusement. The moment passed, and someone else came rushing downstairs.

It was the mother, looking shocked and dazed and then finally the father, who rubbed the sleep from his eyes. He regarded Kamp with a furrowed brow and talked in a harsh tone.

Kamp didn't understand the language but recognized it as Hungarian. Rather than try to talk, he pointed at his jaw, made a punching motion and then pointed at the food and shook his head. They understood. He pulled the beer bottle from the sack and offered it to the father, who nodded.

The mother retrieved a bottle opener, and the men took turns drinking from it. She also brought a plate and a knife and began cutting the ringwurst into tiny pieces.

The father pointed to the mother and said, "Tematea." He gestured to his older daughter who said, "Charani" and the younger, "Jeta." The man pointed his thumb at his chest and said, "Patrin."

"Kamp."

Tematea handed the plate to Kamp, who found he could eat without having to chew. Patrin motioned to Kamp's boots, suggesting that he take them off. Kamp unlaced them and wiggled his toes.

Patrin sat on the floor, and both girls sat cross-legged next to him, one on each side. Patrin began telling a tale that was sprinkled with enough recognizable words and hand gestures that he came to understand that they'd come from Hungary and hadn't yet found a home.

Patrin finished his story with a rueful nod, stood up and instructed his family to go back upstairs. They smiled at him once more and one by one filed up the stairs.

KAMP AWOKE ON THE FLOOR in the same position in which he'd fallen asleep, and he listened. He thought he heard what may have been a far-off voice.

He laced up his boots and heard another, louder shout, then baying hounds approaching. And beyond those sounds, he heard the Black Diamond Unlimited shrieking ahead of the dawn. He looked out the window and down the road and saw lanterns bobbing toward the house. Kamp ran upstairs to the bedroom once occupied by Nyx and her sisters and found the family sleeping there.

He yelled, "Wake up. They're coming." No one stirred. "You have to get out."

The father rolled onto his back, muttered, "*So kere*" and went back to sleep. Kamp hustled down the stairs and hit the back door just as the first man came in through the front, followed by another and another.

Running from the house, Kamp heard Druckenmiller say, "Ach, I knew it. Goddamned gypsies stole my ringwurst. And my blanket, too!"

B.H. GRIGG LIKED TO START working after washing his face and hands and before sun up. He'd had a fine sleep, so deep that he couldn't remember any of his dreams. He walked now to his mahogany cylinder desk. The wood blazed red by the light of his lantern.

It was once owned by a man named Philander Crow, his disgraced predecessor, whom he'd never met.

Grigg rolled back the top, set the lantern on the desk and slid out the leather writing slope. When he focused on the object placed there, Grigg felt his hands go cold as the blood drained from his face. His time on the planet was short.

KAMP DIDN'T WAIT TO SEE what became of the Hungarian family in the red house. He gained speed as he crossed the road and dropped onto the trail that led to the train tracks, slowing only to step from dry stone to dry stone across Shawnee Creek and then charging up the bank on the other side.

The Unlimited's engine had already passed, and Kamp scanned the box cars. When he saw the first car with an open door, he accelerated and made his leap. He caught the hand rail, put his foot in the iron stirrup and let momentum swing his body in a kind of pirouette that landed him on the hard boards of the box car.

He crawled across the floor, vertigo already overtaking him. He propped himself against the back of the car and watched the breaking dawn.

GRIGG INSPECTED THE OBJECT by the first rays of morning sun. It was exactly as it had been described to him by Kamp, an eight-sided silver coin. One side pictured a steaming locomotive engine. The obverse depicted the bust of a smiling figure wearing a cap in the Phrygian style, and behind the figure, a crossed pickaxe and shovel, enclosed in a circle. Inside the edge of the circle were the words "*Ex Fratrum Ordine, Et in Corvo.*"

Grigg locked the door and closed all the blinds, but that gave him no comfort. They'd already invaded his sanctum and could easily have killed him while he slept. He didn't pause further to reflect. He pulled on his coat, picked up his briefcase and ran for the train station.

15

Ada Farmer hadn't seen the wanted poster, and even if she had, she never would have thought she looked at all like the person depicted on it. She'd heard of Nyx Bauer, but only because she knew the famous story of how her parents died at the hands of a madman. She'd heard rumors that Nyx had gone insane as a result, or that she was possessed by a demon.

Ada Farmer didn't know that anyone who caught Nyx Bauer would be a thousand dollars richer.

On a bright, warm afternoon in early autumn the sixteen-year old Ada Farmer wasn't thinking about crime or money. She was thinking about a seventeen-year old boy named Klaus Vogel and looking at the red handkerchief in her hand.

They'd arranged a meeting in the woods about a mile from her home in Bethlehem. The plan was that when they got close enough to see each other, she'd wave the handkerchief and know she'd kept their date. Who else would it be? But for her the red handkerchief made it more exciting, much more romantic.

She walked beneath the cover of maple trees and stared at the blue sky looking back at her through the leaves. Ada Farmer felt a powerful tingle at the base of her spine and a twinge of guilt in her throat. Her father would disapprove, because she was going to meet a boy and because the boy was German, not Hungarian.

But the thought of Klaus Vogel's blue-grey eyes, the curls in his chestnut brown hair and his strong shoulders propelled her forward. She didn't know what the two of them would do when they met, but the possibilities thrilled her. And so she started running.

THE TWO HUNTERS IN THE WOODS that day had seen the wanted poster. They'd seen it on a lamppost outside their church and had talked about it, about the shame of Nadine Bauer's misdeeds and how she deserved punishment. They talked about how far a thousand dollars would go. The first hunter had taken down the poster, folded it and put it in his pants pocket.

Each man now carried a long rifle in his hands and a clip point knife on his belt. They shared sips of whiskey from a tin flask. When they came to a meadow, they paused to take a break and finish the liquor.

The men had first heard her when she stepped on a fallen branch at the edge of the meadow. If they hadn't stopped and knelt in the grass, Ada Farmer probably would have seen them. But instead she went running right past. They saw her dress and the silk ribbon in her hair.

The first hunter whispered, "*Gut im himmel.* It's her."

"Who?"

"Ach, Nadine Bauer."

"Who?"

"The *murderer.*"

"It is?"

The second hunter felt a flicker of doubt. This girl could be anyone. And a stone criminal like Bauer wouldn't be caught out like this in broad daylight. But this misgiving wasn't nearly enough to quell the building excitement, and he ignored it. Their euphoria, mixed with fear and alcohol, easily overpowered rational thought.

The first man shouted, "Stop!"

Ada Farmer heard the man's voice and knew that if she stopped, they'd ask questions. They'd figure out who she was and where she was going. And then they would tell her father.

Even if she didn't stop, they'd probably recognized her and would tell him all the same. *This is my last chance to be with Klaus Vogel*, she thought, as she put her head down and ran faster.

The second man would have been happy to tell the story of the day he'd seen Nyx Bauer in the flesh, running through the forest, and how she'd barely gotten away. The first man wasn't satisfied with the prospect of nothing but a tall tale.

He raised his Sharps and fired. The bullet entered the back of Ada Farmer's right arm, causing her to spin and fall in the meadow.

"Got her."

When they reached Ada Farmer, she was gasping for air, clutching her ruined arm and going into shock.

She looked up at the men standing over her and said, "Help me."

They stared down at her, transfixed by the sight of their wounded quarry and dumbfounded by the sudden, exhilarating turn of events. They'd found and captured a most wanted fugitive. The hunters also knew that this fugitive existed outside the law and that they wouldn't be held accountable for anything they did to her.

They didn't know that in addition to destroying the bone in her upper arm, the bullet had also severed an artery. So, by the time each man had had his turn, Ada Farmer had bled to death.

With the bloodlust draining away and with sobriety returning, the men stood up and began to assess the situation.

The first man rubbed his chin and said, "Dead or alive."

"What?"

"That's what the sign said."

"So?"

"So we still get the money."

The second man said, "There's a problem, Abner."

"What's that?"

"It ain't her."

"Ach, it *is*." He pulled the wanted poster from his pocket and unfolded it and pointed to the girl in the picture. "See?"

"No, I recognize *this* girl." He pointed at the corpse on the ground. "I seen her before."

"Then how come she was running?"

The second man stroked the orange and brown whiskers in his long beard to calm himself.

"I know who her father is, Abner. We done a terrible thing here."

The first man took off his straw hat with the black band. He saw a red handkerchief in the girl's open palm. He picked it up, wiped the sweat from his brow with it and said, "We didn't know that when we done it."

"I guess."

The first man said, "Well, then there's just one thing to do now."

"What's that?"

"Go in them woods and start digging."

KLAUS VOGEL WAITED AN HOUR before giving up and going home. He figured maybe the gunshot he'd heard had scared her off, or maybe she'd just changed her mind.

When it became clear to all that Ada Farmer was missing, rumors swirled. Some said it was Nyx Bauer herself who'd led the girl astray. Within weeks, the gossip faded away, and Ada Farmer's body would never be found. Her father assumed she'd run off with a boy.

NYX BAUER KNEW NOTHING of the many cases of mistaken identity, of which Ada Farmer's was the first. She sensed the bloodlust all around her, of course, borne out of the explicit permission to hunt any girl who looked remotely like her. Or, rather, what she used to look like.

No one recognized her the day the wanted poster appeared. No one even gave her a second look. By the time she went with Aodh to the tavern in the patch town, Nyx felt emboldened, believing that her ability to walk among these men without them recognizing her made her safe.

Nyx stood elbow to elbow with the other miners, detecting no threat, apart from Dis Padgett, who walked in just as she was leaving. He looked straight at her, giving her a long stare before turning his attention to the crowd and announcing he'd buy every man in the tavern a beer.

She parted ways with Aodh, and by nightfall she was back on the front steps of the cabin. Before going in, Nyx turned to scan the small clearing and then the tree line. She heard nothing, save the low croak of a raven.

When Nyx went in, she saw Angus hunched over his workbench. He always paused to say hello when she came in, but Nyx waited a full minute, while Angus kept working.

She said, "Thanks for that gun."

No response.

"I said, thanks for the gun."

Without looking up, Angus said, "What gun?"

"The pistol."

"Ach, I don't know about no pistol."

Nyx fished the pepperbox from her boot and laid it on the workbench and said, "You left it here yesterday, with a note."

Angus picked up the pistol and inspected it, turning it over in his hands and then setting it back down.

"Yah, well, I didn't."

Nyx felt the panic rising again.

"Then someone else was here. No one else can come here. No one can know we're here. That was our rule, right? Was someone else here?"

Angus raised his eyebrows.

"You mean no one else, apart from that big fella you brought over for dinner and a cuddle?"

"You're angry about that?"

"Not as such."

"This is serious."

"Yah, it is."

Nyx set her jaw. "Was someone else here?"

Angus's voice dropped lower. "Not exactly."

"But you're saying someone else was here, *inside*."

"Yah."

"Did they take it? Tell me they didn't take it."

Nyx's gaze went to the canvas bag atop the cabinet in the kitchen.

His concentration now broken, Angus wiped his hands on his shop towel, then went to the kitchen and retrieved a whiskey bottle and two shot glasses and motioned for Nyx to sit across from him at the table.

He filled the glasses, slid one to Nyx and said, "*Zum wohl!*"

Angus tossed back the shot and let out a sigh.

"Okay, girl, here goes. People come here all the time. They come to drop off guns, and then they come back once they're fixed."

"Yes, I know, so who—"

"And you know that I don't know who them people are. And I don't want to know."

"Yes, but—"

"They know I'm here. But they don't know you're here. Not that we know." Angus stopped talking, stared at Nyx and then at the glass. A moment passed and then she downed the shot. "So, it don't bother me that folks bring me guns to work on, since we can use the money. And, no, it don't bother me that you brung your friend."

"Then what's the problem?"

"Well, a couple things, I suppose." He refilled his glass and drank it. "I didn't put that pistol there, and I didn't write no note."

"So someone broke in and left it there?"

"Yah. Seems like. Now, it could be that this person wanted me to have it and wrote 'For you,' meaning for me. And they didn't feel safe leaving it on the porch."

"Doesn't seem likely."

"No, especially on account of I recognize this gun." Angus held up the pistol. "Construction, design, and Damascus steel. Uncommon for here."

"So whose is it?"

He turned the handle to Nyx so that she could read the initials inscribed on it.

"J.B."

"Yah, Jonas Bauer. This here is a pistol your father owned."

In her mind's eye Nyx saw the cigar box on the windowsill of her parents' bedroom. She remembered opening the box, seeing the pistol and wondering why it was there.

"How do you know?"

Angus leaned back in his chair and said, "Well, he had me fix it once on account of it didn't have no spark. That, and also my cousin told me he found it after what happened to your parents."

"Kamp?"

"Yah, he told me he got it off of Danny Knecht when he caught him."

"So, Kamp brought it here."

"No. He told me they took it off him when they strung up Danny Knecht."

"Who's they?"

"I don't recall that he said."

"Kamp can tell us, and that would lead us to whoever put it here."

Angus shrugged. "*Mebbe*. There's something else."

He unfolded a piece of paper and smoothed it out on the table. A wanted poster.

"Oh, I saw that already. It doesn't look like me."

"Yah, well, did you see this?"

Angus unfolded another wanted poster. It read:

$1500 REWARD

Will be paid in gold coin for the apprehension

DEAD OR ALIVE

of

the **MURDERER NICKEL GLOCK**

Beneath the writing was a hand drawn portrait of a man's face.

Nyx stared at the poster for a few moments, then said, "Fifteen hundred?"

"Yah."

"Fifteen hundred for him and only a thousand for me? That's not fair."

Angus laughed. "No, it ain't."

"And who is Nickel Glock?"

"I don't know, but he looks one hell of a lot like Kamp, don't he?"

16

The Unlimited rolled to a stop a half mile before the station at Mauch Chunk. At first Kamp thought he was just hearing the typical sound of train wheels grinding the tracks, combined with the rumble of anthracite shifting in a hopper.

But now he discerned individual sounds, men shouting as well as a banging noise, persistent and loud. He climbed down from his box car and walked alongside the idled train. When he reached the front, he turned his head up to look at the engineer, who stared straight ahead, stone-faced.

Kamp called up to him, "*Was ist?*"

Without looking down the engineer said, "Troublemakers."

Kamp looked down the tracks to the station. On the platform beside a passenger train, a crowd pulsed and surged. Rocks pelted the side of the train parked beside the platform. He heard breaking glass and a woman screaming.

"What's it about?"

The engineer took off his hat, scratched his head and said, "God damned Irish louses want money, but they don't want to do nothing for it."

"Which?"

"Why, the miners. They'd rather throw a rock than work an honest day." The engineer craned his neck to look down, and he studied Kamp's face. "Say, don't I know you?"

EMMA WYLES PEERED out the front window onto Third Street. Or, rather, she looked at the window itself, without a single scratch or pock. She might have admired the plate glass longer had it not been the fourth one she'd bought in the past year.

"Irish confetti" is what people called it when bricks sailed through the window. She didn't know who was doing the damage, nor could she fathom why any Irish person would be involved. Blaming outsiders is always convenient, she knew, and much easier than holding the real culprit, Black Feather, accountable.

Wyles had grown accustomed to this and other forms of harassment, but she knew that her role in the community had thus far given her a large measure of protection. She'd cared for hundreds of families in the area, including those of Black Feather executives.

Still, they wanted her gone, as she represented part of the living memory of their misdeeds. Eventually, she assumed, they'd step up their efforts. In the meantime, there were babies to deliver and prescriptions to fill.

She filled the mortar with ingredients in the correct proportions, picked up the pestle and started grinding. At first she didn't notice the two women in long dresses and bonnets who came through the front door. Wyles didn't pay attention until they stood facing her, and she smelled whiskey. The women pulled back their bonnets to reveal that they were men.

As the first man went to the front door and locked it, the second one said, "I was wondering whether you got anything for a headache."

KAMP KNEW HE SHOULD AVOID the train station at Mauch Chunk, skirt the commotion and continue on his way. But he wanted to understand what was going on, and in order to do that, he needed to get close.

He walked alongside the passenger train and toward the platform, noticing right away that the mob wasn't entirely made up of Irish miners.

Kamp heard German swearing combined with imprecations in an Irish brogue. All of it was directed at the people on the train. By the time he reached the platform, members of the mob had begun smashing locks on the train doors and trying to get on. He walked up to a porter in a black wool uniform, who was leaning against a pillar and taking in the scene.

The porter said to Kamp, "You won't be getting anywhere today, not on a train. That's sure."

"Why the ruckus?"

The porter pulled in a long breath, sighed, and began, "Yah, well, these hoofties here don't want them hoofites on the train, they don't want them to get off."

"Why not?"

The porter turned to him in mocking disbelief and said, "Why not? Because them on the train are here for jobs in the mines. There ain't enough work for them that's already here. When we was heading into the station, I told them on the train, just wait a couple of months. All those angry fellas throwing rocks will be dead from hard labor. Then yous can take their jobs, and they won't complain so much."

Kamp's gaze drifted above the porter's head to a poster that had been affixed there. It began, "Wanted, the Murderer Nickel Glock," and beneath the text was a drawing that most certainly looked like him.

E. WYLES FELT her heart thudding in her chest, though her expression remained flat. She scrutinized the men's faces and decided she hadn't seen either of them before.

The first man cleared his throat loudly and spat on the floor.

He said, "Lady, my headache is getting worse, an' you're a druggist. I bet you can make a whole lot of things feel better."

The man produced a knife with a shiny blade and held it up before her. The second man pulled a length of lead pipe from his sleeve and swung it, taking out a row off large bottles on a shelf along the wall.

Wyles said, "That's enough."

"Oh, that's nothing," the man said.

THE MOB ON THE PLATFORM SWELLED, and unable to break into the train, men tried to crawl through windows or jump in through the vent in the roof of each passenger car.

As the tumult neared its crescendo, a fine four-in-hand carriage with a driver and one passenger, and two paddy wagons drawn by teams of horses pulled up to the station. Men in wool uniforms, some black, some blue, leapt out, truncheons at the ready.

Kamp scanned the scene and saw a girl, perhaps eight years old standing at the edge of the platform and holding the hem of her mother's plain dress. Instead of watching the uniformed men wailing on the miners, she was staring at him.

She looked at Kamp, then at the wanted poster on a pillar above her head, then back at him. Her eyebrows shot up, and then she started tugging at her mother's dress and pointing.

He couldn't hear her above the din, but Kamp could see what she was saying.

"It's him! It's him!"

"THE POLICE WILL BE HERE SOON. You need to leave now."

The man with the knife said, "That's a good one, lady. You need to learn how to stop giving orders and start taking them."

As he said it, he lunged across the counter and reached for a handful of her white blouse.

Wyles pulled a pistol, raised it, pressed it to the man's forehead and fired. The slug exited at the back of his head, taking clumps of brain and skull with it.

As the second man bolted for the door, she trained the gun on him and squeezed the trigger. The bullet went through his left cheek and out his right. She fired three more times into his back and head, then waited for him to breathe his last.

She put the pistol back in its place beneath the counter and walked to the front door. When she put up the sign that read "Closed for the Day," E. Wyles noticed one of her bullets had gone through the glass.

So much for the new window.

THE UNIFORMED MEN quickly gained the upper hand on the miners, who, truth be told, were already starting to fade when the paddy wagons appeared. The police and Black Feather security men bludgeoned some, handcuffed others, and the rest they chased off.

The girl's screaming grew louder. "He's there. That man in the picture. He's right there!"

Kamp looked for an easy way to get off the platform without being mistaken for a miner and without being recognized by anyone else. A solid wall of uniforms blocked his exit.

At the moment the girl finally convinced her mother to turn and see what her daughter was pointing at, Kamp felt a rough hand on the back of his neck as a burlap sack was jammed over his face.

"You're coming with me."

17

Joachim S. Thaler stood atop his carriage, pulled a small tin of Turtle Island Tobacco Bits from his vest pocket and put a pinch in his mouth. He watched the riot drawing to its conclusion with some miners being led from the station in shackles and others left bleeding on the ground.

Reducing their pay had made them angry, but it was the arrival of potential replacements that turned them murderous. Wherever he looked, Thaler saw productivity lost. If the miners were here, they weren't down the hole shoveling. He'd need to fix that.

As he savored the hit of nicotine, Thaler saw a police officer leading another man with a burlap sack on his head.

He climbed down from the carriage and called out, "You there. Halt."

The hand on Kamp's elbow took a firmer grip and pulled him to a stop. He could tell that whoever had called out was standing directly in front of them now.

"Where are you taking this man?"

"He's not supposed to be here."

Kamp thought he recognized the voice of his captor when he first heard it. Now he was certain of who it was.

Thaler spoke without hurry. "Well, if he's a miner, he needs to be in the mine."

"He's not a miner. He's one of them that rouses the rabble and gets them to misbehave."

"An agitator."

"Agitator."

"Take off that bag. Let me see him."

When the sack came off, Kamp squinted against the sunlight, and before his eyes could adjust, Thaler slapped him hard across his face. The pain in Kamp's jaw made his eyes water and nearly buckled his knees.

When Thaler finally came into clear focus, Kamp saw wavy, flaxen hair, oiled and combed straight back to reveal an unlined face with a straight nose and eyes the color of a glacial pond.

Thaler said, "Do you know the trouble you're causing?"

The man holding Kamp put the sack over his head again and said, "Time to go."

"You're taking him to the police station, then?"

"No, we have a different place for this kind."

NYX WANTED TO TELL HIM. In fact, the longer she worked beside Aodh, the more she yearned to confess everything about the past two years. She wanted to describe her parents and how, whenever her mother made a pie, she always ended up with a smudge of flour on her right cheek. She wanted to tell him what it felt like to be gathered up into her father's arms and to be loved.

Nyx wanted to be close to Aodh and to feel him. But she wouldn't allow it. That was a risk. If anyone ever recognized her, they'd assume Aodh knew all along. And if she never told him who she really was, he could honestly say he never knew.

And maybe she also didn't want to risk him telling someone else. Beneath that, most importantly, she didn't want anyone to know her.

Still, she needed information, and Aodh was her only source.

As they hewed lying side by side in their tiny crevice, she said, "Where was everyone today?"

"How's that?"

When I went for my *Gezähe,* it seemed like half the men weren't there."

"They musta been somewhere else."

Nyx picked up irritation in his voice, but she tried to sound nonchalant. "Oh, well, do you know where they might've been?"

He stopped hewing for a moment, sighed, and said, "I heard maybe there was gonna be an action."

"What kind of action?"

Aodh slammed down his pick. "Christ, Nef Bahr. Let me work."

He crawled backwards out of their space, and Nyx followed him. As he stood facing her with his hands on his hips, she felt a surge of lust that started at the base of her spine and radiated. It was so powerful she almost lost the ability to speak.

"What kind of action?" she said, forgetting her fear but still stifling the urge to devour him.

He wiped the sweat from his brow with the back of his hand. "A protest at the train station, all right?"

"A protest for what?" She couldn't help picturing him taking her then and there.

He winced. "Jaysus."

"What kind of protest?"

"If I tell ya, will ya shut up?"

"Yes."

"Scab train, full of men the company wants to take our jobs. Some of us was going down there to stop it."

"Some of us, as in Irish?"

"Irish, German, any miner who wants to keep working." He turned and crawled back into his crease.

She called after him, "Then how come you're not there?"

"You keep your secrets, Nef Bahr, an' I'll keep mine. Now leave me be."

E. WYLES ASSUMED that the police would arrest her for murder. Even if she explained the circumstances first, they wouldn't care, given her adversarial relationship with the Judge.

They'd never liked each other, to put it mildly. She didn't hide her disdain for a man she considered to be a manipulative, mendacious, power hungry bastard. Over the years, they'd managed not to clash directly until Wyles came to the defense of Nyx Bauer and upstaged the Judge in his own courtroom.

Nevertheless, Wyles hurried now to the police station to make the case that she acted in self-defense. When she burst through the door of the police station, she saw the low-brow High Constable, Samuel Druckenmiller, with his feet up on his desk, face hidden by the broadsheet newspaper he held in front of him.

"Constable, I need your help."

"Good morning to you, too, Emma," he said, without lowering the paper.

"My shop was invaded. I was forced to defend myself."

Druckenmiller rustled the newspaper. "Says here that Native Plants and Medicines is having a sale. You know Native Plants and Medicines, the outfit across the street from your place."

"Don't goad me, Constable."

"Says they're having a sale on liver and kidney tonic. Sasparilla, too."

Wyles slapped the newspaper out of his hands. "Goddamnit, you fool, people are dead."

Druckenmiller stared at her with brow furrowed and mouth agape.

He said, "Easy, easy now. Just give me a minute once, and we'll perform a full investigation."

He glanced across the room at a uniformed officer, Falko Stier, and then at the gun cabinet. Stier unlocked it and pulled out an 8-gauge shotgun.

THE THREE OF THEM WALKED back across the South Side with Falko Stier leading the way, shotgun held across his chest. While they walked, E. Wyles told them the details. As they approached the door to the pharmacy, Stier went into a crouch and slowed his walk.

He said to Wyles, "Is it locked?"

She nodded and gave him the key. He crept toward the door and gently turned the key in the lock. Stier braced himself for the sight of the dead men and for the possibility that he might be attacked by their associates.

"Wait here, ma'am," he said.

Falko Stier raised the shotgun, kicked the door and went in. She heard his boot heels clicking on the floor, first at the front of the store and then at the back.

Druckenmiller called to him, "*Was ist?*"

"*Nix.* Nothing."

E. Wyles went in and surveyed the room. The bodies were gone, and all of the gore, even the blood-stains, had been cleaned. The floorboards were already dry.

Certain there was no danger, Druckenmiller walked into the shop. He saw Wyles staring at the spot on the floor. He took off his hat and cocked his head to the side.

"If you'll allow me to say it, ma'am, I don't see no victims lying there. Do you?"

She was too dumbfounded to put him in his place. Wyles stared at the spot where the first man had stood when she shot him, then at the place where she'd stood. Every trace of what had happened was gone.

Druckenmiller produced a silver flask from his jacket and unscrewed the cap.

He raised the flask and said, "To the dearly departed, wherever they may be."

Then he took a long pull and then offered the flask to Wyles, who declined.

Falko Stier returned to the front room, shotgun at his side and said, "I've found no evidence of a crime. You said it was two men, wearing dresses."

"That's right."

Druckenmiller took another long pull and smiled, eyes shining from the drink.

He said, "Ach, *mebbe* they was angels."

Wyles tried to regain her bearings.

She said, "I shot them. I shot them both with this gun."

As she said it, Wyles went behind the counter to retrieve the pistol. But when she reached under the counter, she found that it was gone, too.

"It was right here."

Druckenmiller said, "So, help me understand on account of you being much smarter than me. You're saying that two imaginary fellas, wearing imaginary dresses, come in here. And you shot them with your imaginary gun."

"Oh, for the sake of—"

"Pardon me for asking, Emma, but have you been tasting some of the more powerful medicines you got here?"

"Stop being an ass. For once."

Druckenmiller put his hat back on and walked out the door. Falko Stier tipped his hat to her, said, "Ma'am" and then left as well.

As soon as they were gone, E. Wyles resumed mixing the compound she'd started before it happened. But she couldn't stifle the fear she'd felt only once before, the fear that she was alone and exposed, no ground beneath her feet. And this time, she feared, there'd be no branches to break her fall.

KAMP TRIPPED and tore a hole in the knee of his pants before the man hauled him up by the arm and forced him to start walking again. His jaw ached, and he still wore the burlap sack on his head, but the commotion was fading and with it, the danger.

The man stopped him and took the sack off his head. Kamp felt a lump rising in his throat when he saw Shaw's father, Joe, staring back at him.

Joe put his hands on Kamp's shoulders and studied his face. Kamp had a couple scratches and a small cut on his chin, where the butt of Falko Stier's gun had hit him.

He took a step back and looked at Joe, who wore an old, ill-fitting police uniform.

Kamp said, "You mean no one noticed?"

"Noticed what?"

"No one noticed you weren't an actual policeman?"

Joe said, "I've told you this before. *Òpinkòk* never notice anything."

WHILE HE RODE THE TRAIN, the district attorney B. H. Grigg penned a letter to the Honorable Tate Cain, notifying him of an indefinite leave of absence.

He didn't mention the appearance of the silver coin, the calling card of the Fraternal Order of the Raven. According to local legend, the recipient of the coin faced certain death.

He explained none of this in his letter and listed his rationale for the leave as "special circumstances."

He'd heard the rumors regarding the demise of his disgraced predecessor, Philander Crow. The official story was that at the end of a booze-soaked evening, Crow had committed suicide by gun but not before shooting the prostitute with whom he'd been consorting. This story struck anyone who knew the man as patently ridiculous.

Another rumor was that Philander Crow was executed for attempting to expose the members of the Fraternal Order of the Raven and bring them to justice. Grigg had also heard that on the morning of the day Crow died, he'd found a silver coin on his desk at work.

B.H. Grigg couldn't prove any of it, and proving it wasn't his intention. As the train rolled into the station, he scanned the platform, looking for anyone who might be lying in wait.

Aside from a man and woman and their small child, the platform was empty and quiet. He hopped off the train and searched the station until he found a U.S. Mail letter box.

He dropped the letter to the Judge in it, then hurried out. Grigg buttoned his wool coat against a cold wind and started his march across the city, unaware of the cloaked figure who'd followed him off the train.

18

The two men didn't speak until they were at least a mile out of Mauch Chunk. The clatter of the town gave way to warblers and wind in the trees. Kamp focused on the feeling of his feet on the gravel to distract himself from the throbbing in his jaw.

He hadn't called for Joe and wouldn't have known how to find the man even if he'd wanted to. But in the same way he knew that Joe would find Shaw and Autumn and bring them to safety when the need arose, he knew Joe would do the same for him.

Joe understood what it meant to be an outsider and a fugitive. He knew he could never move freely in daylight without putting himself at great risk.

Kamp glanced sideways at Joe and took in his profile, the bump along the ridge of his nose, the granite jaw. He looked at the man's scarred knuckles and at the shabby uniform he wore.

"Where'd you get that outfit?"

Joe looked at his clothing as if it weren't on his own body, shook his head and made a wry face. To explain how he'd peeled the jacket and trousers from the corpse of a man he'd had to kill would be to place the burden of knowing on Kamp. It wouldn't add to Kamp's understanding and would only further contaminate his dreams. Some stories weren't meant to be told.

So Joe shrugged and focused on the sun that warmed his face.

NO ONE DARED TO ENTER the room at the bottom of the mine unless summoned by Dis Padgett, who sat at a small wooden table.

He lit a candle, warmed his hands and let waves of satisfaction wash over him. He'd heard the action had been a rousing success. The scabs had been terrorized, and even though dozens of miners had been beaten and arrested, they'd made their point.

More important was that he'd incited and then ordered the men to riot. He'd taken their rage and frustration and used it for his purposes.

Dis Padgett opened the beer bottle he'd brought for the occasion. The smell of it took him back to the first sip he'd ever taken as a small boy. In a field of waving barley under a magnificent sun, his grandfather had uncorked a bottle and handed it straight to him. He'd held it with both of his small hands, then pressed the bottle to his lips and tilted his head back, letting the beer trickle onto his tongue and down his throat.

His grandfather had said, "Tha's a good lad," taken the bottle back and downed the rest in one swig.

Padgett lost himself for a moment in the memory as feelings of pride mixed with a sense of loss. He pulled himself out of it by reminding himself there was a great deal still to be done, more moves to make and obstacles to overcome. For now, though, he wanted to savor his victory.

Dis Padgett took a gulp and called out, "Connor."

A stout miner with a wide face and no shirt came hustling into the room. "Yes, Pater."

"Connor, you know the trapper boy called Short Pinky."

"I do."

"Bring me that dear boy. I want to celebrate."

AS NYX AND AODH TRUDGED out behind their seventh car, a man went rushing past them. Moments later the man came back with the trapper kid, Short Pinky, in front of him. The man held the boy by his collar.

"What's going on?"

Aodh lowered his head. "Never mind."

"What are they going to do with that boy?"

"Patience, Nef Bahr. Patience."

On their way out of the mine mouth, they heard excited chatter about the riot and rumors of what would happen next. Imprisonment? Execution? The mountaintop hummed with the news. Even the wraiths who worked the slag heap spoke of it.

Nyx and Aodh walked away and down the mountain, waiting until they were out of earshot. For once, Aodh spoke without prompting.

"All right, now listen, Nef Bahr. And I donna want you to speak until I'm finished."

Nyx nodded.

"You remember that son of a bitch, Butcher, the one who got the free ride down the mountain? Yes, well, in one way he was the last man who stood between Padgett an' what he wanted."

"Which is what?"

"Rule everything down below by driving out the Germans. Butcher was the last one that mattered, last one with pull. Padgett can do whatever he wants now. That young German boy we seen back there, Short Pinky, belongs to him now."

"*Belongs* to him?"

"Every Irish will follow Padgett. No reason to do otherwise. And no choice."

"I'm German."

Aodh turned his head and raised an eyebrow. "I'm aware of that."

"So what will they do when—"

"You're with me. You wonna have any problem, long as tha's so."

"I heard people saying Padgett's trying to make things better for the miners."

"Yah."

"And that he's just doing what he has to."

"Well, tha's what he wants miners to think."

"But—"

"He wants to make things better for Padgett. Me an' some of the other men intend to set things right. It's what you call a work in progress. The only thing standing in our way is—"

Aodh stopped talking when he saw two men approaching them. One wore a shabby blue uniform and the other wore a slouch hat. He had pale skin and had a hitch in his gait. Nyx recognized them immediately and broke into a run.

KAMP WATCHED THE FIGURE, covered head to toe in coal dust, running at him. If it were a demonic phantasm, he'd question anew his mental state. But since it appeared to be a real person, Kamp wished he'd brought a gun. He didn't have the strength for a round of fisticuffs, and his jaw hurt.

But as the figure got closer, he saw a smiling face and outstretched arms, and even though Kamp still didn't know who it was, he smiled and opened his arms, too.

NOW THAT HE'D ESCAPED BETHLEHEM and the reach of the Fraternal Order of the Raven, B. H. Grigg could investigate the plot against Wendell W. Kamp. For starters, he wanted a closer look at the file on Kamp at the Pennsylvania Hospital for the Insane.

Grigg didn't believe in the idea of insanity, as such. If a man committed a crime, that was his nature, and he deserved punishment. He recalled the matter of a man named Elijah Sample, a villain who'd cut down his family in cold blood. A jury had found Sample not guilty by reason of insanity. Grigg also knew that a mob made up of peaceful, law-abiding neighbors had hanged the fiend Daniel Knecht so that he couldn't escape justice via the same route.

Even though Grigg wasn't one to ponder the whys and wherefores of men's motives, he now found thoughts of this type turning in his mind as his boots crunched the gravel path to the hospital.

He'd gotten past the guard by displaying credentials that showed him to be a sworn servant of the County of Northampton. And while he couldn't claim to have an appointment with Dr. Alistair MacBride, Grigg sounded convincing when he said he was there on "official business."

He stepped smartly up the impressive marble steps leading to the portico and underneath it, the front door. Grigg felt excited that he'd kept the element of surprise.

Before he reached the top step, though, Dr. Alistair MacBride burst out the door, extended his hand, and said, "Mr. Grigg, so good to see you again. We've been expecting you."

NYX THREW HER ARMS AROUND KAMP'S NECK and gave him a bear hug.

"It's me, it's me."

"I see that," Kamp said. "But who is that?"

Nyx surprised herself with a laugh she hadn't heard in years. She licked her fingers and wiped away the coal dust from her cheeks and forehead, then lowered her voice to a whisper and said, "Me."

Then Nyx gave Joe a hug as well and said, "I didn't expect to see *you* out here. What's with the ridiculous get-up?"

She turned to Aodh to make the introductions. It occurred to her in that moment that she didn't know whether Aodh could be trusted with the truth about Kamp and Joe.

"Aodh, this is my, um, cousin, Wendell and his friend, Joe."

He extended his hand. "My name is Aodh Blackall. And you three better get your story straight about how you know each other, else I'm liable t' think you're lying."

Joe, Kamp and Nyx looked at each other for a long moment, then all broke into laughter.

MACBRIDE USHERED GRIGG into his office and offered him a seat on the red velvet divan. Grigg noticed the fine wood paneling, burnished to a shine and a fern in an ornate porcelain vase.

Two attendants entered the room, the first carrying a sterling silver tea service and the second a tray of crumpets with a variety of jams.

MacBride handed Grigg a cup of tea before dismissing the attendants, who closed the door when they left.

Grigg took a sip, steadied himself, and said, "What do you mean you were expecting me? I didn't have an appointment."

MacBride pursed his lips and then sighed. "So they haven't told you?"

"Who hasn't told me what?"

"Oh, dear."

Grigg had assumed that MacBride was associated with Black Feather and probably with the Order of the Raven. He may even have been a member. As such, he didn't expect MacBride's cooperation. But now, Grigg felt his throat constrict and felt his hands and feet go cold.

"Dr. MacBride, I'm just here to see the file you presented, the one with the photographs of W.W. Kamp, if I may."

Two large men in white uniforms entered the office.

MacBride looked at the men, then back at Grigg and said, "I'm afraid that won't be possible."

ONCE THE WARMTH OF THE REUNION began to dissipate, the four of them realized they were standing together in broad daylight and that each of them was in grave danger. Nyx knew she had to explain to Aodh the truth of her relationship to Kamp and Joe, at least part of it.

She turned to him and said, "Kamp helped me one time and for that I'm grateful. And Joe is Kamp's—"

Aodh said, "You donna hafta explain, Nef Bahr. That history's in the past."

While Nyx and Aodh talked, Kamp studied Nyx and marveled at the transformation. She'd changed her name, her clothing, hair, voice and skin color. No wonder the wanted poster looked nothing like her. She'd utterly adopted the persona of the working man, except for the moment when she'd seen him and dropped her disguise.

He wondered what her Irish friend may have noticed there.

Nyx said to Kamp, "Where are you on your way to?"

"Oh, just going piece way up—"

Joe raised his hand. The four of them listened to the wind in the branches.

Aodh said, "I donna hear—"

The crack of the rifle made them scatter and take cover in the woods. They crouched low, listening. The second shot told them where the shooter was.

Nyx pointed in the direction from which the sound had come.

"Angus."

19

The foursome ran for the cabin, weaving their way through the trees with Nyx in the lead. They heard one more shot and then silence as they drew closer.

When they reached the edge of the clearing, Nyx signaled for Kamp, Joe and Aodh to slow down and get low. The cabin came into view, and they saw Angus standing on the front porch, a rifle across his chest.

When Angus saw them, he smiled and said, "Remember, normally I shoot on sight, but in your case I'll make an exception. Hurry up once."

He held the door open as they filed into the cabin. Angus locked the door behind him, then put water on the stove to boil and ground some coffee beans.

Kamp said, "We heard the shooting."

"Oh, yah," Angus said, "I was just testing a gun." He motioned to a rifle resting in the rack.

Kamp said, "You weren't testing it by shooting at someone, were you?"

Angus forced a laugh. "Ach, cousin, you know me." He poured four cups of coffee. "Yah, well, I seen a couple fellas at the tree line. Maybe two. Don't know."

Nyx said, "More people have been coming around. Someone even broke into the cabin."

While she spoke, she dipped a washcloth in the hot water and wiped the coal dust off her face. Now Kamp could see the way Nyx's face had changed. It was thinner, more angular.

"It's not safe here," he said.

"Tell me about it."

Joe said, "You can come with us."

"Where?"

Joe took a sip of coffee, paused, then said, "Up the line."

Aodh, who'd been standing at the window and looking out turned around and said, "If you want to speak freely, I can step outside."

Nyx looked at Aodh and then Angus.

"I'm not leaving. I'm not finished yet," she said.

Kamp said, "Finished with what?"

Nyx pulled the pepperbox pistol from her boot, held it up and said, "Besides, not everyone wants to hurt us. Someone left this for me."

Angus turned to Kamp. "It wasn't you, was it?"

He shook his head.

Nyx set the pistol on the table in front of him. Kamp recognized it immediately, recalling the moment Daniel Knecht pressed it to his own temple and yanked the trigger.

Angus said, "When was the last time you seen this gun?"

Kamp closed his eyes and pictured the scene in the front yard of the Bauer's house, the grim carnival that led to the hanging of Knecht. He remembered firing the pistol into the air in the hopes of jolting the mob from its collective nightmare. When that failed, men in the crowd dragged him away. The pistol had been lost in the melee.

He opened his eyes and said, "Three years ago."

"Any idea who mighta brung it?"

"No."

Angus went to the gun rack. "Yah, well, in any case I want yous to take this rifle."

He retrieved the Henry and handed it to Joe. Aodh looked at the pistol, then the Henry and at the assortment of weapons on Angus's workbench.

"Jaysus but you've got an arsenal."

The room fell silent and then the attention turned back to the Henry.

Joe said, "What kind is this?"

"A repeater," Kamp said. "You can fire sixteen times without having to reload." He turned to Angus and said, "Thanks, cousin, but we don't need it."

"It's mine anyway," Nyx said.

E. WYLES NEVER GAVE much thought to personal safety, and she'd only put the pistol under the counter at Kamp's insistence. Her daily existence revolved around caring for others, and she'd assisted hundreds of individuals and families in their time of greatest need.

People knew she worked tirelessly in the pharmacy and that, barring an emergency, she'd be there during business hours, and usually later than that. For these reasons, Wyles believed the community tolerated her as an outspoken and uncompromising woman.

They were willing to overlook the fact that she hadn't married, and even though they gossiped behind her back, the people of Bethlehem showed her the utmost respect in person.

But starting the day the two men in drag invaded her store, that changed. She saw it in cold stares and stiff postures. She heard it in strained tones and clipped words. And she heard the whispers.

Someone had apparently labeled her with a term. She'd never heard the word before, but now she heard it in whispers and low murmurs.

Passing a tavern on Fourth Street, she'd heard a man say, "Here I thought she was just odd. Truth is, she's what's called a 'tribade.' "

No matter how many lives she saved or babies she delivered, and no matter how much pain she alleviated, E. Wyles was being reduced to a term, a word that signaled her expulsion and empowered others to harm her.

Her role and standing in the community would have been safe if she were the only person who could provide what she provided. But now there was competition.

The day after she shot the two men, she'd seen a drop in business, and for the first time, Wyles noticed customers going to the pharmacy across the street. The second day, she had four customers, and on the third day, she had none. A continuous stream of people began to flow in and out of Native Plants and Medicines.

By lunch time of the fourth day, Wyles had worked through her entire backlog of prescriptions, and she'd received no new ones. She contemplated leaving early, something she'd never done before.

As she placed the "Closed" sign in the window, she saw a man emerge from Native Plants and Medicines and walk straight across the street toward her.

"Miss Wyles, Miss Wyles, may I have a word with you?"

"I'm sorry, we're closed for the day."

"Miss Wyles, if I may, I'm in need of your assistance."

He was a small and sturdy man with close-cropped hair and a clean shave. He wore a starched white shirt with stainless steel sleeve garters, no necktie, wool pants and shiny, black brogans.

"Please come back tomorrow. I open at eight."

She saw the color rising in his cheeks.

"I'm so sorry," he said.

"I'LL JUST BE GOING. Thank you for your time." Grigg tried to sound confident when he said it.

Alistair MacBride leaned against the edge of his wide mahogany desk and filled his Meerschaum with cherry smoking tobacco.

"Oh, not at all. Please, stay." MacBride struck a match on the desk, dipped it into the bowl of the pipe and sucked down the flame. "May I know your first name, Mr. Grigg?"

"There's really no need—"

"Your given name. What is it?"

"Bartholomew. But that's not what people call—"

MacBride breathed out the smoke. "Bartholomew, I can see I must be frank. Your condition demands it."

Grigg looked at the men guarding the door and felt his pulse hammering in his temples.

MacBride continued, "We know about what's happening to you."

"What's happening is that I came to ask if I may see your file on Wendell Kamp. And now I'll be on my way."

MacBride said in a pitying tone, "Oh, Bartholomew, it's so hard to admit we need help, isn't it?"

"Not really."

"It's sad when everyone can see it but you."

"See what?"

"Your recent behavior. Strange actions, deception. Fear, delusions of persecution. Depravity of various sorts."

"Who told you *that*?"

"Oh, a number of people."

"Like who?"

"That's not germane to the—"

"Who?"

MacBride sat up straighter on his desk and gave Grigg the look of a disappointed father.

"Well, your minister, Ebbenstick, for one. He said—"

"Eberstark," Grigg said.

"Yes, him. He said you've lost your footing."

"He's a fool."

"And several of your neighbors. And your superiors, of course." MacBride picked up a ledger from his desk and read from it. "Multiple instances of prevarication, perseveration and grandiose pontification. Paranoia."

"Garbage."

"And fraternizing with a known criminal." MacBride looked up from the ledger.

"What criminal?"

"The murderer Nickel Glock."

"Oh, for heaven's sake. You know there's no such person as—"

"I suspect the cause may be what we call fragility. Soft brain."

"Cause of what?"

"Madness. I'm afraid, Bartholomew, you're insane."

"They're lying."

MacBride took a thoughtful pull on the pipe and raised one eyebrow. "They're lying? They're *all* lying? And you're the sole possessor of the truth? Is that it?"

"Drop this farce at once."

MacBride let out a long sigh, pursed his lips and shook his head.

"It's not your fault, Bartholomew. There's no shame in your illness. And you must know that you're in the right place. We have the finest moral treatments."

There was a gentle knock at the door, and a tall, skinny bald man entered the room. He had thick eyebrows and a white coat with blood spatters on the lapels.

"I'd like you to meet Dr. Schultheis."

20

The little pharmacist standing in front of E. Wyles wrung his hands and stared at the ground.

She said, "What's the problem?"

"The problem?"

"Yes, what do you need?"

"We're running out of medicines, ingredients, supplies, everything."

"Like what?"

"Oh, right." He fished a folded paper from his pocket and read from it. "*Infusi Taraxaci*, *rhei*, *potassae tartratis*, *hyoscyami*, willow bark, jimson weed..."

As he continued on down the list, E. Wyles realized he'd caught her off guard. She'd assumed her competitor would be antagonistic and hostile. Instead, here was this bashful, well-scrubbed little cherub.

"...*Podophyllum, Theae folium,* ephedra, mandrake, and laudanum." He looked up at her and smiled. "Long list, I guess."

She said, "What's your name?"

"My full name?"

"Sure."

"Uwe Wedekind Eugen Schiffhorn the Third."

"Oh, boy."

"Yes, but no one calls me that."

"What do they call you?"

He blushed again. "Pickler. Everyone calls me Pickler."

Wyles unlocked the door and said, "Come on in, Pickler."

KAMP NEVER ASKED Joe where he lived, and he always thought it was better that way. Joe had a well-earned reputation for vigorous self-defense of person and property or for cold-blooded murder, depending on one's perspective.

Kamp had the utmost respect for Joe, based on the way he treated Shaw as well as for accepting him into their family. He also knew that Joe's people had been driven into hiding in successive waves of violence and persecution and that Joe had borne up under it.

It was dangerous enough for Joe to have taken Shaw and Autumn to his home. If anyone other than Lenape recognized them as Kamp's family, they'd be punished. And if anyone saw Kamp there, the entire community would be subject to harsh repercussions.

Joe took off his blue wool jacket and turned from the road onto a narrow trail that led through thick undergrowth. Kamp followed, and they walked in silence between tall trees and over a large deadfall.

They'd hiked at least five miles back already, well beyond the sounds of society and far enough for Kamp to forget his fear they'd be discovered. He was hungry, though, and Kamp hated marching on an empty stomach. The sun had begun its slide behind the mountains, and soon they'd be walking in total darkness.

"Not far now," Joe said.

PICKLER FLICKED THE SWEAT from his brow with his first two fingers and said, "Thank you. Thank you ever so much."

"You're welcome."

In the failing light of late afternoon, Wyles surveyed the gaps in the rows of bottles, canisters, boxes and vials on her shelves.

By the time she finished filling Pickler's order, the little pharmacist had made seven trips back to Native Plants and Medicines.

He turned to go, then paused, turned around and said, "It's most kind of you to help me."

"Why wouldn't I?"

He looked at the floor. "Considering the circumstances."

"You mean that I'm losing my customers, and you're taking them?"

He nodded without looking up.

Wyles said, "People need medicine. What's happening to me isn't the customers' fault, and from what I can tell, it isn't yours, either."

He looked directly at her for the first time and said, "They're wrong about you."

Then he turned on his heel and closed the door behind him. Wyles watched the little pharmacist cross the street and disappear into Native Plants and Medicines.

It occurred to her that since Black Feather's first attempt to ruin her had failed, they'd changed their tactics. Pickler was going to kill her with kindness.

KAMP CAUGHT THE SMELL of stew on the night air well before he saw the light in the window. It carried him back in his mind to the first meal Shaw ever made for him, and it carried him forward to find them.

He hadn't pictured the home where Joe might live, but the waft of supper called forth images of a wigwam, a longhouse or a collection of both, only a remnant of the Lenape's rich tradition but a community still.

Instead, he saw a single wooden cabin, a small A-frame whose contours he discerned by moonlight. In the window a candle burned, and by the light he caught a glimpse of Shaw. He leapt up the steps and grabbed the brass door handle. Locked. Kamp pounded on the door but had to wait for Joe to unlock it.

When he did, the door swung open and Autumn ran and hugged him hard around the legs. Shaw followed her and put her arms around them. The pain, all of it, vanished in that moment. When he stepped back to look at them, he saw tears streaming down their faces. He gathered up Autumn in his arms. He looked into her eyes, one brown and one blue.

"I missed you, Daddy," she said. "I missed you so much." Then her eyes went wide and she said, "But I *loved* riding the train."

ANGUS POURED ANOTHER CUP OF COFFEE, took his seat at the workbench and hunched over an assemblage of metal parts.

Nyx tried to engage him. "How's your work going?"

"Say what?"

"Your work, your gun." She pointed to the workbench. "How's it going?"

"Good."

"Who's it for?"

"Don't know."

Taciturn, even for Angus.

Nyx pulled up a chair and looked directly across the table, and cradled her chin in her hands. Angus didn't respond, and Nyx kept staring until he finally looked up.

She expected him to smile, but he didn't.

"What's wrong?"

"I done a terrible thing," Angus said.

SHAW FURROWED HER BROW. "You're saying they found someone who looks like me?"

"Sort of like you," Kamp said.

"And they stuck her in our house?"

"Don't worry. She's got someone who looks like me to keep her company. I'm sure they'll keep the place nice until we get back."

"I can't joke about it."

Shaw put her face in her hands, then stood up from the kitchen table and went to the window. "Did they find a kid who looks like her?" She motioned to Autumn, who'd fallen asleep in a cot by the fire place.

"They said they had a child who died when their house burned down."

Shaw spun around to face him. "We're going back there. Tomorrow."

Kamp put his arms around her, but she shook him off.

Joe said, "*Nichan*, don't wake the girl."

Shaw put her head down and balled her fists. "We can't let them shove us out again. I won't let them."

Joe put his arm around her shoulder. He gently rubbed his thumb across the crescent-shaped scar above her right eye.

"You're here now. We're all together, and we're safe."

ANGUS LIT A LANTERN and then pulled on a heavy coat.

"Follow me."

Nyx put on her coat as well, and the pair went out the back door. They marched through the woods for a few minutes with only the sound of their boots on the forest floor and the squeaking of the lantern as it swung by its handle.

Nyx said, "Aren't you going to tell me what happened?"

"I was out hunting for rabbit."

He said nothing more after that and kept walking until they reached a low hill with no trees. Angus slowed at the top and then stopped, crouched down and held the lantern at arm's length.

Nyx saw the bodies of two men on the ground. One had a long beard and the other wore a straw hat with a black ribbon around it.

Angus held the lantern over the corpses. "I come upon these two. They didn't hear me."

"And you mistook them for rabbits? What in the—"

"I heard them talking."

"Jesus, it's not a crime to have a conver—"

"Goddamn it, girl, they was talking about *you*. What they was going to do to you. How they was going to bring you back once they was finished. They had these."

Angus reached under the body of the man with the beard and pulled out wanted posters of Nyx and Kamp.

"You didn't have to shoot them, though, right? They wouldn't have found us."

Angus hardened his gaze.

"They was all the way up here, say not? Forty miles from Bethlehem and not a half a mile from our cabin. They knew where to look."

"Who are they?"

Angus shined the light on their faces.

"I don't know."

Nyx fished through the pockets of the man with the straw hat and found a folded piece of paper. She unfolded the note, held it next to the lantern, and read it aloud.

"Be careful, Abner. I love you."

Nyx looked at Angus. "Know anyone named Abner?"

"Yah, plenty. But not this Abner." Angus looked up at the moon and then back down at the bodies. "I suppose there's only one thing to do now."

"What's that?"

Angus stared down at the corpses. "Get some spades and start digging."

21

Joachim S. Thaler hooked his thumbs into the belt loops of his bespoke wool trousers, pulled in a deep breath, leaned back and surveyed the town of Mauch Chunk. His new home wasn't perched high enough for him to escape the din, but that didn't matter. In fact, he liked to hear the clatter of commerce, and to be above it.

The veranda on which he stood was nearly complete. The workmen, a gang of burly Swedes freshly arrived to the new world, hunched and squatted at the edges, laying the final slabs of sandstone and filling the spaces between them. After that, they'd build a majestic stairway that led down to the valley.

If it hadn't been a beautiful day for taking the air, Thaler might have joined the Swedes in their labor. He marveled at how hard they toiled for a paltry

196 | KURT B. DOWDLE

wage, how they sweated and groaned. But then again, he remembered, hard work is its own reward.

Normally he wouldn't have needed them on Sunday, but the work had to be finished on time. He considered shouting an encouragement but didn't want to break their concentration.

Thaler turned and went in the mansion, also under construction and also nearly finished. Soon, the Gujarat teak bookshelves would be lined with all of his beloved tomes, and soon the stone fireplace would glow. It helped, he thought, to step back on occasion from the ugliness of the affairs of men and to take perspective, to reflect on what the good lord had bestowed upon him. A magnificent home, a warm hearth, an exquisite view.

Still, there was business. The gathering was only a month away. In addition to overseeing the completion of his mansion and grounds, Thaler had work to do, starting with the appointment set to commence directly.

He looked out the back window and saw a figure emerge from the trees. Thaler pulled the watch from his vest pocket. Noon. On the dot.

AFTER JUST A DAY INSIDE the Pennsylvania Hospital for the Insane, B.H. Grigg began to lose his sense of time. At first, he'd been shackled to a bed in a small room in the cellar with no light. There was no way to discern the passage of time, so when he was eventually brought back upstairs, he didn't know what time it was, or even what day.

They'd taken his clothes, in which he'd shat and pissed, hosed him down with cold water and given him the drab uniform all the patients wore.

They shaved his head but let his beard grow, and they strapped him on his back to a bed without a mattress in a room without heat.

Grigg still didn't feel insane or even believe in the concept. He assumed that MacBride's plan was to drive him mad by removing the components of his identity one at a time.

He'd stopped straining against the binds at his wrists and ankles, because they'd begun to cut into his skin and because they didn't give. He became motionless and to quell the panic, Grigg forced himself to conjure memories that calmed him—picking apples with his father, walking to church alongside his sister, skipping a stone across the surface of a pond.

At the moment the blood stopped pounding at his temples, the door of his room swung open, and the two large attendants entered.

"Someone wants to talk to you," the first one said.

"YOU WANTED TO SEE ME."

Joachim S. Thaler extended his hand, but his visitor didn't shake it. They stood on the stone patio behind the mansion.

"Truth be told," Dis Padgett said, "I didn't want to see you before, and I don't now."

Thaler's mouth turned up at one corner. "And yet, here we are."

"Your man come to me three days ago, said you wanted a parley."

"Might I offer you a drink?"

"You might."

Thaler turned and went in the back door. "Follow me." Once inside, he retrieved a whiskey bottle and two tumblers. He poured three fingers in each and handed one to Padgett.

Thaler held up his glass. "*Zum Wohl.*"

"Yeah, and your mother, too."

THEY TOOK THE SHACKLES OFF Grigg's ankles so that they could lead him to a room with a concrete floor and a sturdy, rectangular table in the center. The attendants strapped him to it and left him there for what may have been hours.

When the door creaked open, he couldn't see who came in until the oval-shaped face of Dr. Schultheis hovered above his own.

Shultheis grabbed him hard by the chin and leaned in closer to inspect his face and head.

"Yah, you are suitable."

"Suitable for what?"

"For being cured of madness."

Schultheis left the room. The attendants covered his eyes with a blindfold and then left as well.

Now Grigg began to go insane.

PADGETT DRAINED HIS DRINK then motioned for Thaler to pour him another.

Padgett said, "I'll gladly finish the bottle for ya, but I donna think tha's why I'm here."

"Why do you think you're here?" Thaler took a sip of his own drink.

"No, lad, this ain't hide and seek."

Thaler studied Padgett's face. He noticed the black whiskers and blue eyes but most of all his skin. It was clean, porcelain white, devoid of color. Not even a freckle.

"I can give you what you want," Thaler said.

Padgett stared into his glass and shook his head and said, "You canna give me no devil's bargains. And you canna give me what's already mine."

Thaler's expression didn't change. "You wouldn't be here if you didn't want something."

"Why don't I tell you what you want and we'll go from there?"

"Fine."

Padgett motioned out the window and said, "You want them workhorses out there to finish your porch, so you can enjoy the view. You want them moles in the mines to keep filling seven cars a day, so your own coffers fill with gold. You want the good lord to keep blessing you in such a fine and fancy way. You want that black river to keep flowing out the hole. But if the miners ainna doing their seven cars a day, the coal, the money, the lord's blessings, they donna flow."

"Go on."

"An' you want me to get them to shut up and get back in line and work. Full bore. You know all they need is my say so."

Thaler pulled a tin of Turtle Island Tobacco Bits from his vest, unscrewed the cap and put a pinch inside his lower lip, then said, "And for you to get what you want—which is absolute power in the mine—"

"I already have that."

"If you had it," Thaler, said, "you wouldn't be here. In order for you to get it, you need it to be all Irish."

"In time."

"No Germans."

"I can make it so, certain as I can drink your whiskey."

Thaler shook his head.

"Alas, you can't. The panic is still on. So many men, so much desperation. Masses of men willing to kill just for the chance to die in the mine."

"An' you bastards intend t' keep it that way."

"You can't stop it. You can't keep going to the train station and throwing rocks."

Padgett poured himself another glass and downed it. "Foxes have holes and birds have nests, but the son of man—"

"I can make certain your men will keep working."

"Tha's good. But truth be told, I donna care if they're Irish."

"How's that?"

Padgett said, "Maybe them Hungarians come cheaper than Irish. You'll get yourself a bargain."

"And you won't have to compete with any Irish for control."

"Maybe."

"It's going to cost you."

Padgett looked at Thaler and noticed the faint lines across his forehead.

"Yah, boss, it's gonna cost you, too."

AFTER SCHULTHEIS LEFT, GRIGG SWEATED through his clothes, and when his body temperature eventually fell, he began shivering.

The door creaked open, and he heard boot heels on the concrete floor.

Grigg caught the scent of jasmine and musk, and he felt a hand removing the blindfold. He blinked against the sunlight in the room, and a face came into focus.

She had high cheekbones, blue eyes, a fine nose, a square jaw and blonde hair. The woman pulled up a chair, and when she removed her coat, Grigg saw that her right hand and forearm were missing.

He recalled a story Kamp had told him about a bear, and his heart began pounding anew.

She said, "Your efforts to expose the Fraternal Order of the Raven haven't gone unnoticed. You know that, right? *Not* gone unnoticed."

Grigg didn't answer, and Adams slapped him hard across the face.

She traced the red mark she made on his cheek with the nail of her index finger. "You were a lawyer. And a stylish one, they tell me. Handsome, clean-smelling." She scanned him from head to toe. "And now, this."

Grigg met her gaze. "Get me out."

"Tell me where Kamp is."

"I don't know."

"Tell me where Nadine Bauer is."

"I don't—"

Adams slapped his face again.

"No one knows you're here, Bartholomew, and no one cares." She stood above him and gently stroked his forehead with the back of her hand. "I'm the only person who can help you now."

"I can't answer any of your questions."

"But you do know what they intend to do to you."

"No."

"Tomorrow morning at eight o'clock the doctor will take an instrument somewhat like a screwdriver. He'll ease the instrument all the way in at the corner of your left eye and then exercise it vigorously. The bad news is that you'll never be the person you once were. The good news is you'll be blissfully uninterested."

22

"Jaysus, Nef Bahr, but you're quiet today."

In fact, she was simply exhausted. She and Angus had spent the night digging a deep grave and rolling in the bodies. When Nyx left for the mine just before first light, Angus was throwing the last shovelfuls of dirt into the hole.

Now, lying side by side in their tiny space, Nyx fought sleep. She focused on the sound of the pick hitting the coal and on Aodh's breathing.

A memory began to play on the back of her eyelids. In it, she looked out her bedroom window at the mob kicking and spitting on the fiend Daniel Knecht. She saw a man she only vaguely recognized as her neighbor, Kamp, place himself between the mob and the accused murderer.

206 | KURT B. DOWDLE

She watched him struggle in vain to keep them from finishing their grim business. Nyx saw the rope go tight and the noose bite into Knecht's neck.

Then the memory became a dream. Nyx felt the rough fibers of a hanging rope around her own neck. She imagined trying to throw it off and running, going past the point where anyone could look for her. Even in her dream, there was no such place, or no way to find it. Her body dissolved, and she became the color and texture of the mine itself.

When she emerged from the dream, she looked at Aodh, lying on his side, twisted up and sideways, hacking into a crease. He was working without a shirt, and the sweat poured from his head and over his powerful shoulders. Purple scars from the explosion covered his back.

He knew some of her secrets. He'd met Angus, Kamp and Joe, and he must have discerned that their shared history was secret, and significant. If he went digging, he would surely determine who she was.

He paused his axe. "I can hear you thinking, Nef Bahr."

"Really."

"You're trying to figure out how much I know about you, and whether I'll figure out more."

"That's not at all—"

"Well, it donna matter t0 me. Donna matter who you are up there, or were."

"But I want you to—"

"Fill your cars, an' leave it at that."

Then he put his coal axe back in motion. Nyx crawled to where he was working and put her hand on his shoulder to stop him.

"HOW LONG CAN WE STAY, JOE?"

They'd been chopping wood for the better part of two hours before Kamp asked his question. Joe rested the head of his eight-pound splitting maul on the ground and leaned on the handle. He took a couple deep breaths, blowing great clouds of steam when he exhaled. Joe tilted his head back and saw ravens twirling and tumbling in the sky.

"How did they do it?"

"Who?"

"*Òpinkòk.* How'd they get rid of you? You own your place. That's what they care about, isn't it? If you own it, they can't make you leave."

"Right."

"So how'd they kick you out?"

"They made up a story about me. They used imposters, people who looked like us. Replaced us with them. Made us disappear without anyone knowing."

Joe wiped the sweat from his brow and said, "*Òpinkòk* pretend their laws apply to everyone but only apply them to protect each other."

"What's your point?"

Joe stared past Kamp. "What they're doing to you violates their way."

"Are you asking me if I'm telling you the truth? Are you saying you don't trust me?"

Joe raised the maul and swung it down hard, splitting the wood block into chunks.

ALONE AND LASHED TO THE BED, B. H. Grigg tried to force himself not to remember. Memories from his boyhood flooded his consciousness anyway, his mother's fingertips on his forehead and her smell of jasmine, his father's laugh in the next room, the first girl he kissed.

The memories wanted to play on his mind's stage to exhort him to live or maybe as a summation of moments. To allow himself to indulge them would be to plunge headlong into madness. If so, his last memory of himself would be dark and lonely indeed. He needed rational thought now as well as to be in the present. Grigg slowed his breathing, focusing on each inhalation as the onrush of pictures and sensations gained intensity.

NYX FELT HER SENSES heightened beyond what she thought she could bear. She laid her fingertips on Aodh's shoulder and began to caress it.

He stopped working, and she felt him shudder.

"I have to tell you right now," she said.

"Tell me what?"

"The truth. All of it. I don't want you to wonder. I'll show you."

KAMP STOOD UP A LOG and an instant later, Joe's block buster came down, gliding past Kamp's ear and splitting the log cleanly in two. He stood up another one, and again Joe's maul hit it square. They continued without stopping until Joe, out of breath, sweat soaked, stood up and paused.

Joe turned to face him and said, "You can stay here as long as you want to." Then he turned away again.

"But."

"*Òpinkòk* will find you one day, maybe today, maybe tomorrow."

"Not necessarily. I won't bother anyone."

"They'll put my home to the torch. My daughter and my granddaughter will die because of you."

He respected this man and the sorrows he'd endured. Joe's words tapped into the well of shame Kamp thought he'd taught himself to ignore.

"We'll have nowhere to go."

"You're beginning to understand, *nkwis*."

WHEN THE TORRENT OF MEMORIES subsided, Grigg found himself exactly where he'd been before it started, strapped to the wooden bedframe with leather belts and iron buckles. As his mind cleared, his thoughts turned to escape.

He reckoned he had at least twelve hours until his appointment with the surgeon. Grigg wiggled his hands and feet, testing them against his binds. Large movements were impossible, but there was some give, a fraction of an inch, in the bind on his left ankle. By moving his left foot back and forth, it loosened ever so slightly.

NYX FELT AODH starting to relax as she massaged his shoulders. She wanted to free herself of the rough wool shirt she wore and beneath that, the bandage that flattened her breasts. Aodh reached back and ran his hand along her hip.

"Nef Bahr, I don' know what you have in mind, but I think it's time for you to get back to work."

"I want you to know who I am," she said.

Aodh turned to look at her, their faces inches apart.

"I already do," he said and unbuttoned the first two buttons on her shirt.

The moment was broken by a deep rumble in the mine and then shouting. Nyx and Aodh listened to the sound of approaching feet and men's excited voices.

"I know he's in here," one said.

Another said, "This way."

Nyx and Aodh scrambled backward out of their tiny space. Men in black wool uniforms, led by a miner, rushed into the room.

The miner pointed a finger and said, "There he is. That's him!"

GRIGG WAS DRENCHED IN SWEAT from the work of freeing himself. He could turn his left ankle in the bind now, and he moved his foot back and forth until it came free.

For a moment he savored the ability to bend his knee and lift his leg off the bed. Then he remembered he had to free the other foot and both hands. He slowed his breathing and focused his attention on his right hand which was still bound fast to the frame.

He found that he could turn his wrist a fraction of an inch. After a few turns, the strap loosened. It was a matter of time until he slipped all the cuffs, but he didn't know how long he had.

When Grigg heard the bolt slide and the door open, he slipped his foot back in the bind. He couldn't tell who'd entered the room until the face of Alistair MacBride appeared above him.

The doctor surveyed him head to toe, and in a soothing voice said, "My goodness, Bat, you look an awful mess."

"Bat?"

"That's your nickname, isn't it?"

"No."

"That's not what your mother said."

Grigg breathed a long sigh and closed his eyes.

"Indeed. They talked to her."

"Who did?"

"Representatives of the hospital went to her home to deliver the news and to console her. In the course of their visit, she told them stories of your youth, reminiscences of childhood pastimes, frivolities, hypocorisms, and so forth. They said it was evident that she loved you so very much and that she wept and wailed."

"I don't understand why you need to—"

"Son, no one wants to be the bearer of bad news, but they did what they had to do. They explained that her son, Bat, had suffered a devastating break with reality and that, in spite of the hospital's best efforts to save him from himself, he took his own life."

"This gets you nothing."

"Don't you think it was better that she heard it from them?"

"What makes you think—"

"Don't you realize that's better than your mother having to learn of it by reading the newspaper?"

MacBride let the question hang and surveyed Grigg's body. His gaze fell on Grigg's left ankle. With his first two fingers, he inspected the cuff and discovered how loose it was.

He gave a pitying look and said, "Oh, Bat, we had such high hopes for you. You had so much potential."

"WHAT AM I BEGINNING TO UNDERSTAND?"

Joe didn't answer Kamp's question and instead went back to chopping wood.

Kamp persisted. In a loud voice he said, "What don't I understand?"

Joe paused with the maul resting on a split log. "You all think everything is about you," he said.

"Who?"

Joe rarely showed anger, but his eyes flared now.

"You. *Òpinkòk.* White men. You drag your problems with each other wherever you go, and then you make all of creation suffer."

"I don't."

Joe stared a long moment at him. "You brought shame on them."

"How?"

"I don't know, *nkwis.* That's between you and them."

"But I let it go."

"Yes, well, they didn't."

NYX BRACED HERSELF. She'd been running for more than a year, and now she was caught.

Instead of grabbing her, though, they knocked down Aodh and kicked him until they were certain he wouldn't overpower them in spite of their numbers.

When they hauled him to his feet, blood trickled from his nostrils and left eye socket.

He slurred when he said, "Jaysus, boys, all ya had to do was ask."

The Black Feather sergeant, a stout man with a salt-and-pepper moustache said, "Don't give us no trouble."

Nyx said, "What's this for?"

Aodh said, "Peace, Nef Bahr."

"What's this for?"

As the black wool uniforms dragged Aodh out of the room, the sergeant looked straight at Nyx and said, "Shut up and get back to work."

23

Officer Falko Stier had never been much of a reader. He liked to speak with his hands, to communicate with action and not to confuse things with words. And to this point in his life, without realizing it, he'd strongly resisted the notion that words could change his perception of how things are and how they ought to be.

He was rummaging through a cabinet in the police station, searching for shotgun shells when he found a sheet of paper at the bottom of the drawer.

It was an old police report, bearing the official crest of the city and the signature of a hero, the fallen Deputy Chief of Police, Markus Lenz. But what led Stier to read the report wasn't Lenz's name but another name, Wendell W. Kamp.

Kamp. That wrong-headed, stiff-necked son of a bitch who didn't understand the meaning of law and order. The fact that the man had once been a sworn officer of the law infuriated Stier. The thought of him made Stier wish he'd gotten rid of him when he had the chance.

He recalled, of course, that he'd been under strict orders not to kill him. And those orders were all that had prevented him from dropping the lit match and setting that rotten asshole ablaze.

Alone now in the station, by the light of his lantern, Stier read the report, written in pencil:

At midnight, the prisoner began speaking incoherently in his cell. He appeared desperate and then withdrawn. At one thirty-five a.m. the prisoner complained of hunger and thirst. I went to the kitchen, and when I returned, the prisoner was hanging by the neck in his cell. He had affixed his own belt to the rafter. I freed the prisoner from the makeshift noose and laid him on the floor. Efforts to revive the prisoner were unsuccessful. Wendell W. Kamp perished at one forty-three a.m. Signed, Markus Lenz, Deputy Chief of Police, Bethlehem.

Stier felt a pronounced shift in his thinking, though at first he didn't know why, and he tried to deny the realization. It must have been a mistake.

Kamp obviously hadn't killed himself, so why did Lenz say he had? Maybe he'd confused Kamp with someone else, or maybe there was another person with the same name. Perhaps the report was a forgery.

As minutes turned to hours and the dark of the night shift gave way to dawn, Falko Stier arrived at a series of conclusions. He felt certain that someone, probably Lenz himself, had lied. And if the report were a lie, it was possible that Lenz concocted a story to cover up what he'd intended to do. That raised the possibility that Kamp had acted in self-defense.

Falko Stier wasn't a man given to creating chains of assumptions based on speculation, but if Kamp had acted in self-defense, it stood to reason that the police meant to do him wrong. They could still be doing him wrong now.

As the first rays of morning slanted through the blinds, Stier tasted bile on his tongue. He couldn't tell if the bad taste came from not eating or from the gut feeling that his reality had just crumbled on the basis of mere words.

WHEN MACBRIDE LEFT THE ROOM, the attendants filed back in, and after scolding Grigg and slapping his face a few times, they cinched all his binds even tighter than before.

As the attendants left the room, the first one said, "Don't go nowhere," and the second one laughed.

Grigg immediately set about loosening the binds once more. He knew he could slip them, although it would take hours. He began twisting his wrists and ankles simultaneously, as if each were the tumbler of a safe, and he the safe cracker. He kept shifting and turning, working without thought or reason, letting his limbs communicate directly with each cuff.

Losing sense of time and even of himself, his body writhed in a rhythm that loosened the binds, imperceptibly at first and then with discernible progress. Sweat flowed from his pores, soaking the iron buckles and leather straps, a mad baptism.

He didn't notice the perspiration or the way layer upon layer of skin burned off from friction. By the time he arrived at the silence of pre-dawn, all physical sensation had fallen away, and there was only motion, the working of flesh and bone against the binds.

NOTHING PREPARED FALKO STIER for a world in which basic reality had come into question. He set down the police report and gazed out the window at the grey-purple dawn.

For the past year, he'd overheard enough drunken ramblings of men in the holding cell to know that the citizenry believed wholeheartedly in the existence of a secret society called the Fraternal Order of the Raven.

They believed in it and feared it, so much so that they didn't speak of it in public, at least not when sober. Stier didn't believe the rumors, but from the story Lenz concocted in the police report, Stier felt he had glimpsed a malicious plan. Had Markus Lenz answered to the Order?

Stier knew he couldn't tell anyone. It would be best to put the page back at the bottom of the drawer, precisely where he'd found it.

But the flicker of bewilderment and anger he'd felt upon first reading the report now burst into a small flame in his chest. Something wasn't right. He folded the form into thirds and slipped it into his pocket.

B. H. GRIGG THRASHED IN HIS BED. His left hand slid from its cuff, then his right foot. In a single motion he ripped off the right cuff and then finally his left foot came free.

He stood, balling his fists at his sides and arching his back. The sun was nearly up, and soon the attendants would return to take him to the surgical theater. He was still locked in his room and still trapped behind the doors and walls of the hospital. But Grigg felt no fear.

He knew there was a way out. He would escape the building or shuffle off the mortal coil, it mattered not which. His eyes went to the metal lattice on the window. He gripped it with both hands and pulled. It didn't give. He turned and scanned the room for anything he could use, some kind of implement he could use to escape, or to fight.

The room was bare, except for the bed itself. One of its legs could do some damage. If he flipped the bed over, maybe he could wrench one of the legs free.

Grigg heard voices in the hallway. They were coming for him. He turned over the bed as quietly as he could and tried working one of the legs. No luck.

He braced himself for the entrance of the attendants, determined to go down swinging. A bit of iron the underside of the bedframe caught Grigg's eye. It was an implement, a metalworker's file, affixed to the center rail.

Around the file was wrapped a piece of paper, which he unwrapped and read the handwritten scrawl:

"If you're reading this, you're probably an unlucky son of a bitch like I was. Use this here as a means to effect a dramatic escape. Your Friend, A.T."

Grigg grabbed the file, went to the window and started sawing through the lattice. The soft metal yielded to the tool, and though the process made a loud noise, he made very good progress.

Within minutes, he'd cut through a few of the thin bars along the right-hand side. He gripped the lattice again with both hands, and this time it gave. Grigg bent it back far enough so that he could get his hands on the sash.

He pulled up but found that it had been painted to the window frame. He heard the door to his room open behind him.

The first attendant shouted, "Unlawful patient exit in progress!"

The attendant lunged at Grigg, who whirled on the man and sank the file in the man's neck as far as it would go.

The attendant dropped to the floor, as Grigg punched the window pane, shattering it. He forced himself through the broken window, slicing his forearm on the jagged glass and then falling fifteen feet to the ground.

He stood up and scrambled for the wall, clutching the vines that clung to it and hauling himself over. The guard at the front gate was only able to get off one errant shot before Grigg sprinted down a busy street and then disappeared.

24

Kamp pulled on his thin work jacket and cinched his bag. Until and unless he brought his tormenters to account, he and his family could never find peace.

Shaw found him in the bedroom. She balled her fists and blocked his way out of the room.

"It doesn't matter what you did or what they made you do," she said, "or why they still care. You left it behind, you let it go. It's dead."

"Your father made a point."

"Which is what?"

"If I stay, they'll come and kill me, and you and Autumn. And your father. But if I—"

"But if you go, they won't? Think about it. If you go and do whatever it is you're planning to do, they'll still punish us."

He moved close to her and kissed the crescent-shaped scar above her eye.

"As long as they're looking for me, I can't stay here. I have to make them stop."

"No."

"Your father will protect you until then."

He took her face gently in both hands, and they kissed.

WHEN E. WYLES FIRST PLANNED her pharmacy, she'd decided to call it "Pure Drugs & Chemicals." She wanted the name to be straightforward, in keeping with her manner. She knew she'd face pressure and scorn from the community at first, merely for being a woman and in spite of her sterling reputation as an apothecary and midwife.

And at first that had been the case. Roustabouts and neighborhood toughs routinely harassed and pestered her. That was the overt kind of friction. Less obvious but more pernicious were sideways shoulders and turned backs, the language of bodies that whispered their disapproval.

But people couldn't deny they needed her help as a midwife, though at first they tried. One woman, then another and another allowed her to assist in difficult childbirths, and her reputation grew.

Soon, men with panicked expressions sought her out in the dead of night, leading her to a small farm, a tumbledown shack, or a mansion. They summoned her to assist their wives or their lovers, and to save their not quite born babies.

The tide had turned more slowly in the pharmacy, though the change followed the same pattern. The most desperate came first, heads down, hands in pockets, all damaged in the ironworks, the mines or the war.

They'd been told by the doctor and by their families to bear up under it, but they knew she had much better remedies for pain than a stoic grimace.

With so many men mangled and in permanent agony, the trickle of patients became a torrent. Over time, E. Wyles was accepted, grudgingly. In public people still called her "unladylike" and "disagreeable." But they prayed she'd always be there.

And now her business was gone. No one came through her door. Everyone went to Native Plants & Medicines, which had undercut her prices.

To assuage their guilt for abandoning her, Wyles' former customers convinced themselves she hadn't been much help after all and that they'd been wrong to have overlooked what they considered her moral failings.

As they passed her on the sidewalk or from across the street, they all called her the same name. *Tribade.* She didn't know who'd first called her that but assumed it must've been the Big Judge.

E. Wyles wasn't given to reflection or introspection, but surveying the shelves of the store with nothing on them except dust and empty bottles, she had to wonder how life had brought her to such an unfamiliar station. At least, she thought, she was still a midwife. There would always be women in need of her services.

Wyles was deep in this thought when the bell over the door jingled and a small man entered the store and removed his felt hat.

He wore a grey ditto suit and scuffed black brogans. The man carried a business envelope and without introducing himself, he walked to the counter and handed the envelope to her.

She opened it, unfolded the typewritten form inside and began reading, "By order of the Health Inspector, City of Bethlehem, Emma G. Wyles is hereby ordered to cease and desist in the practice of midwifery, including any and all activities related to the gestation, birthing and subsequent existence of infants. Signed, Dotter, M.L., Health Inspector."

E. Wyles looked up at the man and said, "Who are you?"

"Health Inspector."

"Inspector?"

"Dotter, M.L."

"Who told you to do this?"

"County." The man sniffed and looked past her.

Wyles felt rage welling up in her belly. "Yes, but who, Mr. Dotter? What person?"

"You're unlicensed to practice, ma'am."

"Since when is there a license?"

"County requires a license."

"How do I get one?"

"You can't."

"What?"

M.L. Dotter straightened. "You can't get a license."

"Ridiculous."

"Madam, restrain yourself."

"Go to hell."

"Firstly, ladies are forbidden to become or to be midwives. Secondly, no unlicensed person may render medical services."

"No unlicensed person."

"That's correct. And currently there is no licensure process for midwives."

"So, no one is allowed to help a woman give birth."

"A licensed medical doctor may do so. Which you are not."

M.L. Dotter surveyed the rows of shelves that ringed the store, then looked down at the empty mortar on the counter.

"You also need a license to become a pharmacist."

"I *am* a pharmacist."

"Native Plants and Medicines has a pharmacist, Mr. Uwe Wedekind Eugen—"

"Pickler?"

"Mr. Schiffhorn is a pharmacist. Perhaps he can help you better understand the requirements for licensure."

M.L. Dotter put on his hat, tipped it, and left.

Wyles scrutinized the letter which bore the seal of the city. It was signed, "By order of the Honorable Tate Cain."

She choked down tears and felt the sting of grief at the back of her throat before she looked down, pulled in a long breath and regained her composure.

When she looked back up, the girl with the wide-set pale blue eyes and long, straight hair with the color and texture of corn silk was standing before her. Now tears filled Wyles' eyes.

"Let's go home."

AFTER KAMP SAID HIS GOODBYES, he walked back into the woods, skirting the town of Mauch Chunk. Along the way, he heard and saw groups of men, hunters with shotguns draped across their arms or held at the ready. Some were hunting pheasant, deer or bear. All of them, given a chance, would hunt him.

He thought about retracing his steps back to the cabin where Nyx and Angus were. Then he realized he'd just be creating same situation for them that he'd caused for his own family. If anyone discovered him there, his cousin and Nyx would suffer.

When night fell, Kamp walked to the railroad tracks and followed them south. Soon, he settled into a rhythm that let him tick off the miles without having to think about having left his family.

25

Only when she went back to the mountain the day after they took Aodh away did Nyx realize how much his presence and protection had meant.

As soon as she set foot in the company store to retrieve her *Gezähe*, Nyx knew she'd suffered a dramatic drop in stature. The clerk, an Irishman who'd replaced the German before him, handed her the ring to which her tools were affixed.

But they weren't the ones she'd used the day before, the tools she'd carefully maintained, gleaming and sharp. The ones he gave her were blunt and rusted.

"This is bullshit," she'd said, as the clerk looked past her to the next man up.

Nyx had been expelled, too, from the work crew to which she and Aodh had previously belonged. They should have given her another hewing partner, but now she was alone. And as long as she was by herself, she'd never be able to fill seven cars.

For two days, Nyx worked alone, filling four cars each day. On the third day, she thought she'd collapse from exhaustion. Her taut muscles and iron will weren't enough to carry her through.

She let her coal axe fall to her side, and she slumped against the wall. A light bobbed toward her, and she heard footsteps crunching on the floor.

"Sir?"

It was a boy's voice. Nyx looked up and saw the trapper kid, Short Pinky. He held a blunt coal axe.

"Yah."

"I'm ready to work with you, if you'll let me."

Nyx looked him up and down. "Go back to your stool."

"Sir?"

"You're better off sitting and reading books."

"I need real work. Trapping don't pay nothing. And if I don't have no money, I can't pay for no candle to read by."

"You're shit out of luck, kid."

"I can do it. I'll show you."

Nyx considered her prospects. By herself, she'd never get paid. And no one else would work with her.

"Seven cars," she said. "That's what we're after."

KAMP FELT THE LIVING HUM in the rails and knew the train was coming. He hustled down an embankment, ducked into the underbrush and waited for the engine to pass.

He'd walked all night, probably twenty-five miles with a good fifteen to go. By the time he made it to Bethlehem, the dawn chorus had begun, murmurs and chirps and then well before first light, bird songs in full throat. He had to pick up the pace.

He passed by his small farm and crept to his house. No sparks issued from the chimney, but when he pressed his hand to the glass of a downstairs window, it was warm. And when he peered into the main room, he could see red embers winking in the fireplace.

He forced down his rage. Breaking in would accomplish nothing, so Kamp turned and headed for town. He crossed the New Street Bridge in time to see the first golden rays of dawn pouring into the river. His waking thoughts began to flow together with a dream, and it was all he could do to will himself across the bridge and to the back door of E. Wyles' store.

Kamp fished the skeleton key from his pocket and turned it in the lock. He barely noticed the eviction notice posted on the door and made straight for the cellar and the wooden cot Wyles used whenever she had to sleep there. By the time he hit the thin mattress and pulled the wool blanket over himself, Kamp was already asleep and dreaming of a scene he'd witnessed as a boy, a hawk driven to the ground by large black birds.

AODH AWOKE ON THE HARD BENCH, squinting against the sunlight streaming through the window in his cell. He shielded his left eye, the one that wasn't swollen shut. Caked blood filled both nostrils, and he struggled to breathe. With great difficulty, Aodh sat up.

When the jailer walked past, Aodh said, "Friend, how about some water?"

He got no reply.

FOURTEEN HOURS AFTER THEY STARTED, Nyx poured the last bucket of coal into the seventh car and started pushing the car along the tracks.

Short Pinky, who'd been silent all day said, "Didn't think I'd make it, did you?"

"Make what?"

"You didn't think I'd hew my share."

"I wasn't thinking about you, no."

"But I did it."

"Uh-huh."

"And I can do it again tomorrow. Faster."

Nyx pressed her shoulder hard into the back of the car, burning the last of her strength.

"Yah, well, right now we need to finish for today."

Everyone else had gone home, except for the new trapper kid. He sat in the dark beside the stack of books Short Pinky had left behind.

As Nyx and Short Pinky pushed the full car toward the massive door, the kid swung it open and let them pass. Nyx grabbed all the penny dreadfuls as they went by. When they reached the surface, she handed the books to Short Pinky, and they parted ways without a word.

WELL AFTER SUNDOWN the jailer turned the key in lock of Aodh's cell and entered it. He was followed by three uniformed policemen, one of whom carried a bucket of water, a scrub brush and a bar of soap. Another carried a prisoner's uniform.

"What's the occasion?"

The man with the bucket set it down and lathered the brush.

The jailer said, "We can't have you looking like dog shit."

"Mind telling me what I done wrong?"

"You gotta go before the judge t'morra."

One of the officers held him by the shoulders and another scrubbed the coal dirt from his face. When

Aodh turned away, the third officer gripped him by the throat.

The jailer said, "It ain't for me to say what you done wrong, and it don't matter. Hearing is tomorrow morning. And make sure you're wearing the uniform."

"Yah, well, can I have a drink?"

"Why, sure."

The jailer tilted his head toward the bucket of soapy water, then turned and left with the policemen following.

B.H. GRIGG WRAPPED HIMSELF IN NEWSPAPERS and sat down in an alley. He couldn't control the shivering and feared he wouldn't last the night. He reasoned that he must have reached the other side of Philadelphia, given how far he'd fled. But asking for help was still too dangerous.

He had no shoes, no food, no money. And the wounds to his wrists and ankles had to be cleaned or else he'd die from gangrene.

Grigg stood up, sloughed off the papers and shuffled to the street, passing a few drunken walkers and a solitary carriage pulled by a bony draft horse. He pulled himself along the side of the street until he found a low-slung brick building with a candle in the window and sparks spewing from the chimney. A sign over the door read, "Philadelphia Home for the Needy."

He knocked twice, and the door opened. A woman wearing a blue dress and a white muslin cap looked out at him.

He opened his mouth, but before he could speak, she said, "Oh, you poor dear" and put her arm around him. The smell of baking bread filled his nostrils as soon as he stepped inside. Relief mixed with extreme fatigue overpowered Grigg, as a nurse led him to a room upstairs, where she washed and bandaged each of his wounds before he collapsed.

KAMP THOUGHT THE SOUNDS of Wyles working upstairs would wake him, but they didn't. Neither did he know what time it was when he woke up, but it was dark outside.

He swung his legs over the side of the cot, planted his feet on the floor and tested the strength in his legs before standing and letting all of the soreness surge through his body, radiating from his right hip up through his chest and down through the soles of his feet.

When he made his way up the stairs and into the back room of the pharmacy, his footfalls echoed louder than he thought they should.

He felt along the counter until he found a lantern and a box of matches. He lit the lantern, held it up and saw bare shelves. When he moved to the main room of the store, Kamp saw that it, too, was nearly empty, and judging by the layer of dust on the floor, no one had been there for days.

He went to the front window and saw a sign there, written in Wyles' neat hand.

"Closed until further notice."

A powerful growl rippled through his belly, and he realized there was no chance of finding food unless he left the store. He laced up his boots, pulled on his work jacket and slouch hat and went out the back door to steal some dinner.

26

Short Pinky didn't show up at the crossroads where they'd agreed to meet the next morning. Nyx waited for a minute or two, then set off for the company store to retrieve her *Gezähe*. But the front door was locked, and no lanterns burned inside. She saw that a note had been affixed to a post.

In pencil scrawl it read, "Courthouse."

Since Nyx functioned outside the patterns and rhythms of day-to-day society, she couldn't know what story might have caught the interest of the general public, what constituted "news." But as she headed for the Carbon County courthouse in the town of Mauch Chunk, it became clear that the entire region was caught in the thrall of an unfolding drama.

The carriages streaming into town reminded Nyx of sleighs she'd seen pulling up in front of her home on the morning her parents had been found hacked to death in their bed. On the faces of people passing her on the road, Nyx saw that same heightened sense, fear mixed with arousal.

By the time she reached the front steps of the courthouse, a crowd of hundreds already swarmed there, shoving and jostling to get in the door, miners mostly. But there were plenty of visitors from farther away, judging by the quality of the carriages and clothes. Nyx spotted Short Pinky at the bottom of the jailhouse steps.

When he saw her headed in his direction, he looked at the ground and said, "I'm sorry, sir."

"*Was ist?*"

"*Shtore* was closed. They told me to come here. I know I should've—"

"What's going on?"

"Your man Blackall is going in front of the judge."

"That so."

"Yah, and there's a rumor a bloodthirsty fugitive is prowling the local environs."

"What?"

He looked up at her. "Nyx Bauer. They say she's around her somewhere. Boy, I'd like a crack at that bounty myself. Thousand bucks. Just imagine."

He stared into the sky and pictured fortune and glory. By the time he looked back down, Nyx had already disappeared into the mob.

She elbowed her way forward, making a direct line up the courthouse steps until she reached the doors and a bailiff put his large palm square in her solar plexus.

"No admittance."

"I need to get in."

Nyx leaned harder into his hand, the crowd pressing in behind her. She had a fleeting worry that he'd feel her breasts, but she dismissed it and pushed even harder.

"I demand you let me in."

"Yah, well, who are you?"

She pulled her hat off and looked him in the eye.

"Family of the accused."

The bailiff didn't allow her to pass, as such, but he bent his arm just enough to let her slip by. As soon as she was in the door, the bailiff locked the doors to a shower of curses.

Nyx took a seat at the back of the courtroom and surveyed the spectators. A few of the miners she recognized. Most, she didn't. There were also men in bespoke wool suits and women in fine silk dresses and furs.

One wealthy-looking man sat apart from the rest. He had hair the color of flax, lightly oiled and combed straight back. As soon as her gaze lit on him, he turned to face her. In spite of having been caught, she held his gaze.

Nyx recognized him as the man in charge of the mine, the man who'd openly challenged Dis Padgett. Her heart started thudding in her chest, but she didn't turn away.

Thaler looked at her for a long moment, as one might regard a bird wheeling across the sky. Then he shifted his attention to door at the side of the court-room.

Two men in blue wool uniforms entered first and took up positions on either side of the bench. Two more bailiffs entered, leading Aodh, who wore the drab uniform of a prisoner.

As soon as he appeared, loud cheering erupted from the gallery, accompanied by just as many boos. Another prisoner was led in behind him, and then another. The three of them sat in wooden chairs be-hind a table.

The prosecutor, a tall, dour sort, entered next and took his seat. With each arrival, the raucous crowd voiced its opinion. Finally, the judge entered.

The bailiff said, "All rise. The Honorable J. Blasius Grimp presiding."

Nyx noticed that this judge had none of the style or bearing of the Big Judge Tate Cain. He was short and hunched over with a few strands of greasy hair dragged over a bald head. His walk was a kind of slow, teetering shuffle, and he ascended to his platform with the grace of a porcupine climbing a tree.

But then he settled into his high-backed wooden chair, raised an oversized gavel and slammed it hard enough to rattle the windows.

In a deep baritone he said, "Order."

The room fell silent as the judge looked over three sheets of paper in front of him.

"Defendants, rise." All three stood up. "In the matter of Carbon County versus misters Reginald Bream and Maurice O'Shea, the charges are criminal mischief, mayhem and disturbing the peace."

Loud booing erupted from the gallery, and each bailiff's hand went to the pistol on his hip.

The Honorable J. Blasius Grimp waited for the clamor to die down, then said, "There will be silence in the gallery, or you will leave. Gentlemen, you may be seated."

Bream and O'Shea sat down.

"In the matter of the people of Carbon County versus Aodh Blackall, the charges are the creation of a subversive and illegal society, inciting a riot, and murder of a sworn officer in the first degree."

Aodh said, "Sworn officer?"

"A certain Robert Mettis was a detective in the employ of Black Feather Extraction."

"Who?"

"Robert Mettis."

"Butcher?"

Irritation flashed across the judge's face. "Indeed."

"I never touched Butcher. Not once. You boys should really—"

The prosecutor, who'd been silent until now, cleared his throat.

"Your honor, as part of his investigation into illegal activities in the mine, Mr. Mettis played the role of fire boss and then company clerk. In the course of performing those duties, he completed his investigation."

Nyx's heart slapped against her ribs. What did they know about her, and what would they be willing to fabricate?

The judge said, "We honor and esteem the efforts of Mr. Mettis, who made the ultimate sacrifice on behalf of the people of Carbon County. I've read the investigation in its entirety, and it's a sad tale. We live in a fallen world. That is certain."

PERSISTENT KNOCKING ROUSED B.H. GRIGG from a dreamless sleep. His wrists and ankles ached, as did the hip on which he'd landed when he launched himself through the broken window and onto the hospital grounds. He didn't feel sick or hungry or crazy, though. A vast improvement.

Grigg remembered he'd been taken to a private room on the second floor of the almshouse. Again, he caught the waft of baking bread, and he allowed himself a moment to savor the smell and feel the comfort of a warm bed.

But the knocking downstairs continued, and he felt compelled to find its source. He forced himself out of bed, then limped to the window overlooking the street. On the sidewalk a man in a police uniform stood beside a woman wearing a hooded cape.

Adams.

He scrambled out of his room, down the stairs and into the kitchen, where a woman was preparing the morning meal.

She noticed his appearance and his distress and said, "Is everything all right?"

Grigg heard the sound of the front door opening, followed by loud footfalls going up the stairs.

He paused long enough at the back door of the almshouse to notice a loaf of sourdough on the counter. He also saw a small office just off the kitchen.

Grigg ducked into the office and found a metal box, locked, on the shelf. When he shook it, he heard coins clinking.

The woman in the kitchen said, "What in the name of Jesus!"

But he'd already hit the back door running with the bread under one arm and the cash box under the other.

THE HONORABLE J. BLASIUS GRIMP sat in silence in his high-backed wooden chair and peered down at the three men before him.

"Mr. Bream, Mr. O'Shea."

The men pushed back their chairs and stood.

"I've considered the facts of your case, and I've reached my conclusion. You are foul, dim-witted men, hardly more than common beasts of the field, incapable of charting your own moral course. Yours is a low and petty existence. You know that."

Bream scratched his left ear, and O'Shea stared at the floor.

"Regardless, I believe the lord in his grace, and the commonwealth in its mercy can put you back on the right path. For that reason, I sentence you to a period of imprisonment of no fewer than two and no more than three years in the Eastern State Penitentiary, where, under the ever-watchful eye of god, you will be corrected."

A miner at the back of the courtroom blurted, "Jaysus, what bullshite," before an officer clubbed him with a baton and dragged him out the back.

At the same time, bailiffs guided Bream and O'Shea through the side door. While J. Blasius Grimp waited for calm to settle, he packed the bowl of his pipe with blended tobacco and lit up.

When silence returned, he set down the pipe, sniffed once, and cast a baleful eye on Aodh.

"Rise."

ANYONE WHO SAW GRIGG SPRINTING down the street would have pegged him for a fugitive from justice. He heard gasps and shouts, as many stepped aside to let him whoosh by. He heard police whistles, too.

The cashbox dug into his ribs, and his legs burned, but Grigg put his head down and picked up speed. He ducked down an alley, crossed a main street, then ran into the next alley, and so on, until he'd traveled a mile to another part of the city.

The commotion gradually diminished, and the houses grew. He peeked around a corner and saw no one on the street, save a man or woman here and there, outfitted in servants' clothes. He searched for a house with no smoke from the chimney and no one visible inside.

Grigg knew as soon as one of the neighbors spotted him, the police would come running, so he went for the stone patio of a stately brick home built in the Georgian style.

He peered through the windows of the French doors and saw no one inside. He looked back over his shoulder and then tried the brass handle. It turned, and he crept in and set his bread and cash box on the mahogany dining table.

He tiptoed for the main staircase and listened. There was no sound except the steps of the family cat, who padded toward him on the gleaming wood floor, brushed his leg with its whiskers, then turned and sashayed away.

Grigg ascended the main staircase in silence, intending to move past the second floor and up to the third, where he knew he'd find the master bedroom and in it, the wardrobe. As he crossed the second floor landing, though, Grigg heard soft moans floating from the powder room.

He took three small steps and peered in the door to see someone who must have been the man of the house in a tender embrace with the maid.

When he stepped back toward the staircase, Grigg stepped on a floorboard that creaked.

The maid said, "*Qu'est-ce que c'est?*"

Grigg froze where he stood. He let a moment pass, then another, and soon the moaning started afresh. He moved to the next landing, slipped into the bedroom and found a rack of stylish wool suits. He dressed quickly and found that the shirt, the vest, and the pants all fit. He selected a pair of polished ankle boots in fine black leather.

Grigg put on the hat, carried the boots and tiptoed back down the way he'd come. The passion had intensified below, and he heard louder moaning and a steady rhythmic slapping.

He tried not to step on the same plaintive floorboard but hit it anyway, and it gave another loud crack.

The man of the house said, "Oh, that goddamned cat," and he emerged from the powder room, cheeks flushed, sans pants.

He came face to face with Grigg and said, "By god, who are you?"

Grigg tipped his hat and strode down the stairs. When he reached the dining room table, he took all the money from the almshouse cashbox and stuffed it in his pockets. He left by the back door, closing it behind him.

AODH STOOD STRAIGHT, SHOULDERS BACK. Nyx had never seen his skin clean before, and when he turned to scan the gallery, she glimpsed his white face with red in his cheeks. His eye was still swollen shut, and his bottom lip had been split.

The judge said, "I've considered the facts of your case as well, Mr. Blackall, but before I render the verdict, I must make a further comment." He set his pipe down and surveyed the gallery. "The work of a man's hands is sacred in the eyes of god. Labor is verily a great blessing, and the coal mine is a divine engine that powers the coming of his kingdom."

The judge let his gaze settle on Aodh. "But all have sinned and fallen short of the glory of god. And the machine needs a driver. It can't function on its own. It can't drive itself. When men disobey their masters, anarchy ensues, which is what we have here."

Nyx turned in her seat to look at the exit and saw a dozen men in blue uniforms filing in and lining the back of the room. She craned her neck to see the balcony. Another dozen officers peered down from there.

The judge continued, "The court is equal parts justice and mercy. Judgment must be rendered and every effort made to correct and even to save the evildoer. I have considered the facts of this matter, and I find that god alone, in his infinite mercy, is fit to extend mercy to this scoundrel, this foul fiend."

A wave of anger rippled through the gallery. Nyx scanned the crowd for Dis Padgett, thinking that perhaps he'd speak on Aodh's behalf. He wasn't there. But she did notice the boss, Thaler, leaving by the side door with an escort of three men in black uniforms.

The Honorable J. Blasius Grimp said, "In the matter of the people of Carbon County versus Aodh Blackall, I find the defendant guilty on all counts."

Bailiffs stood on either side of Aodh, taking him roughly by each arm.

"I sentence the defendant to death by hanging."

Before the gavel landed, the courtroom erupted. Miners set upon the bailiffs holding Aodh, knocking them down and kicking them in their faces.

A moment later shots rang out from the back of the courtroom, as a trio of miners hustled Aodh out the side door.

The melee spilled onto the street in front of the courthouse, where fifty blue and black uniforms waited. Nyx charged out, searching for Aodh and spotting him a block away. His would-be deliverers had thrown a cloak around his shoulders. She raced toward him, arriving moments before his pursuers.

When she caught up to him, Nyx grabbed him by the front of his shirt. He looked at her, and when recognition flashed across his face, she knew that he could see her for the first time.

He said, "Jaysus, Nef Bahr, I love you."

Tears streamed down Nyx's face. She gave Aodh a long kiss on the lips, then said, "I'll figure out a way. I'll get you out."

"It must be so," he said, a moment before a baton slammed the side of his head. Nyx caught the butt of a shotgun in her jaw, and she spun to the ground. By the time she raised herself to her knees, Aodh had already been hauled back to the jail.

27

When he was in the war, Kamp learned about stillness. He learned by observation, and then he taught himself. In the silence before the bullets flew and then in the shrieking of the first hot clash, when the cannonballs whizzed and bounced past him, he remained in the same place, silent until the shot presented itself.

He sat now in the woods fifty yards up the mountain behind his house under a clear, black sky dotted with stars but no moon. He settled under a wool blanket covered with leaves and branches. Men, even trained soldiers, could pass within inches of him and never know he was there. He sat with the Sharps across his lap and waited for sunrise.

By following the ritual of taking a position, concealing himself and focusing on the target, Kamp was able to detach from the ruminations and regrets, the torments that otherwise assailed him. At sunup, no one stirred in his house. An hour later, nothing, and he started to think perhaps the house was empty and that he could go there.

He checked his watch. Ten-thirty. He began to tense his muscles and joints gently, imperceptibly, in preparation to move.

Now the man impersonating him stepped onto the back porch and looked up the mountain in his direction. He took a long swig from Kamp's favorite coffee mug. Kamp stretched his fingers, then gripped the Sharps and raised it so that the tip of the barrel peeked from his makeshift blind.

A twig snapped behind him, and he heard the crunching of leaves. But no voices. His heart rate began to rise and with one long breath, Kamp brought it back down and listened. Two people coming toward him without talking. Hunters.

The footfalls grew louder. If he were to move now, even the slightest twitch, he'd have to come up firing. The two might be innocents, kids maybe. He remained still, and the movement behind him stopped. A minute passed, and Kamp's left hand curled around the forestock. He let his index finger rest on the trigger.

The man on the back porch scanned the mountain behind the house and poured out the last of his coffee, a signal to the men in the woods, the all clear.

The hunters started walking, and when the two tromped past him, Kamp saw that each carried a shotgun.

The first man said to the second, "That goddamned guy's not around here. I'm starting to think he ain't nowhere."

NYX STOOD IN THE STREET and watched the ebbing melee. Miners vanished, some running, some shambling in the direction of the mountain. They still had to earn their pay. Once the miners dispersed, the police followed. Half went back into the courthouse and the other half to the tavern. The mere spectators went to their carriages and rode away. They'd all gotten their money's worth.

Nyx watched in a stupor, brought on in part by being hit in the face but mostly because her world had crumbled again.

A sob rose in her throat, and she stifled it. To stand there and cry would be call attention to herself and to admit defeat. As she pondered whether and how she could proceed, she saw the boss, Thaler, climb in his fine carriage. And then she felt a tug at her sleeve.

She turned and saw it was Short Pinky.

He said, "Ready?"

"For what?"

Nyx stared at the fine carriage which had started to roll.

"Ach, to go back to work."

"Not today," Nyx said, and she followed Thaler's carriage.

THE HUNTERS REMAINED on Kamp's property, walking the perimeter, scanning the tree line, hiding in the forest. Kamp stayed put, silent and invisible. He kept his gaze trained on the house, watching, waiting.

After four hours, he heard one of the hunters say, "This is goddamned bullshit. Let's go."

The other said, "They ain't gonna like that."

"Next shift starts soon anyhow."

Kamp waited until they were gone, then stood up, stretched his legs, scattered his blind and walked back over the mountain.

OFFICER FALKO STIER WATCHED two of his fellow officers drag themselves through the door. They wore heavy wool shirts, trousers and work boots. Hunting clothes. Under normal circumstances, their attire wouldn't have caught his notice. Everyone hunted.

But his world had shifted, and he no longer trusted it.

To the first man through the door he said, "Where ya been?"

The man bristled. "Not how ya been? Not *wie gehts*?"

"Where," Stier said, surprised at the tension in his own voice.

"Yah, well, I don't answer to you, no how."

Stier felt as if he might lunge for the man's throat, but he couldn't locate the source of his hostility. He'd worked alongside this man for six months and never had an issue with him. He turned his attention to the second man and said, "What were you hunting?"

"Huh?"

Falko Stier looked directly at the man. "I said, what was it you was hunting for?"

"Rock dove."

The High Constable Sam Druckenmiller, sat at his desk, boots off and feet up.

He said, "Christ, Falko, what got up your ass?"

Stier looked from Druckenmiller to the first officer and then the second, trying to discern whether they shared a secret.

Stier said, "Where's Clutch and Fenstermacher?"

Druckenmiller said, "Who?"

"They're supposed to be here now, according to the schedule."

"They're on special assignment."

"Special assignment?"

"Yah."

"What's special assignment?"

Druckenmiller cocked his head to the side and scratched his ear. "I don't know that these are the type of questions you need be asking."

NYX WONDERED where Thaler's carriage was going, and that was partly the reason she followed it. More than that, she realized she wanted to say something to this man. She needed him to know what Aodh meant to people, what he meant to her.

Nyx walked along the side of the road, keeping the carriage in view. The horses picked up the pace as they approached the bridge over the river, and Nyx thought she'd lose sight of the carriage.

But it turned before it reached the bridge and began to wind its way up a mountain road. She saw that it was headed for a brick mansion that overlooked the town.

The closer she got to the mansion, the more aware she became of her dirty clothes and face. If asked, she couldn't pretend she just happened to be strolling through the neighborhood. Anyone who saw her approaching the mansion would know she didn't belong there, so Nyx left the road and slipped through the tree line.

KAMP KNEW. In the moment between the Minié ball making contact with his skull and the chunks of his brain blowing out, he knew he would never be himself in the way he was before.

BARTHOLOMEW H. GRIGG walked into the train station. The bandages on his wrists and ankles felt good, and the suit, the hat, even the socks and ankle boots fit just right. He went to the ticket window.

The woman behind the counter let her gaze linger on him a moment, then said, "How may I help you?"

Grigg felt for the wad of cash in his pocket and said, "Virginia, please."

By the time Adams figured out where Grigg was going, he'd already boarded the train, and by the time she ran across the platform, hand curled around ivory handle of the pistol in her muff, finger on the trigger, the train had left the station.

NYX SKIRTED THE FRONT of the mansion when she saw a gang of well-muscled men laboring on a sandstone patio and insulting each other in a language she didn't know was Swedish.

She swung around the side, picking her way through the brush and staring up at the impressive, brick edifice. Apart from the workmen, she didn't hear anyone until she reached the back, where Thaler's carriage sat parked. Another carriage, a lorry with a padlock on its door, pulled alongside it.

The driver climbed down from his seat, produced a skeleton key on a chain affixed to a chain on his belt, and unlocked the carriage doors.

Immediately, the Swedes appeared and started unloading the carriage on the orders of their squat foreman, a bald fellow with thick arms and a heroic beard.

He said, "*Skynda på!*"

The men hauled crate after crate, carrying each one through the service doors at the back of the kitchen. Nyx drew as close as she dared, but she couldn't see what was stamped on the crates. One of the men unloaded a box, set it on the ground next to the carriage, then grabbed another one and took it into the mansion.

As soon as they'd emptied the carriage, the men hustled back around the front. The driver snapped the reins, and the carriage disappeared down the hill.

All that remained was the box the workmen forgot. Nyx stepped from cover to get a closer look.

The box was stamped, "U.S. Army."

Nyx wanted to go in and find Thaler, because she knew he was in there and because she wanted to make him know her mind.

But first she wanted to look in that box.

A shotgun blast thundered close by, and Nyx looked up to see the squat foreman glaring at her.

In his thick Swedish accent, he said, "The second shell won't be no warning."

FOR A FLEETING MOMENT when he stepped off the train, Grigg considered assuming a new identity, starting a new life. He'd outrun the Order, and he had enough money to get started. He could simply become someone else and be done with the past.

Then he remembered the silver coin they'd put in his desk. They'd driven him from his home and his profession. They'd had him tortured and driven mad at the hospital, and they'd kept pursuing him once he'd escaped. He'd never outrun them, because they'd never stop.

And Grigg thought about Kamp, a man he himself had pursued. Now, he thought, he could see the world through Kamp's eyes.

KAMP WALKED on the tracks back to Bethlehem. He'd learned nothing from spying on the impostors living in his house, nothing except that armed men prowled the woods, waiting for him.

He focused on the railroad ties at his feet, letting himself fall into a trance while he walked. Memories ticked past his mind's eye with the click-clack rhythm of train wheels. A thin, bare branch of a maple tree, the freckles across the bridge of Shaw's nose, Autumn's fingers reaching for him. His father's cold knuckles across his cheek, a hard march across frozen fields.

Night had fallen by the time Kamp reached the edge of town. He pulled the brim of his slouch hat low and looked at the ground as he walked. When he turned into the alley behind E. Wyles' store, his belly let out a plaintive growl. He dreaded the thought of having to go back out and pilfer.

But when he reached the back door of the pharmacy, he breathed a sigh. A light burned inside.

28

Kamp couldn't see who was in there, and it could have been someone who meant him harm. After all, this was the same back door he'd stumbled out of a year before, kerosene-soaked and vomiting after Officer Falko Stier threatened to set him on fire.

But the exhaustion, the frustration, the scars and the years it took to accumulate them—all of it had whittled Kamp's will to a sharp point. He rapped knuckles on the door.

Locks turned, the door opened, and Wyles' face, beleaguered as his own, stared back at him. She didn't smile but simply stepped aside and let Kamp enter before shutting the door and locking it again.

"This light should be out," she said and turned the flame on the lamp all the way down. "Are you all right? Are you hurt?"

"*Wie gehts*, Emma?"

"It goes. What do you need?"

He noticed her sleeves were rolled to the elbows, her blouse spattered with blood.

When Wyles took off her blouse and washed her hands, face and neck, Kamp turned away. When he turned back, she was dressed again.

He said, "*Vass geht au*? The blood."

"What?"

"What's going on, Emma?"

Kamp stood facing her and waited.

She said, "I'll fix you something."

He took a step closer. "Why is the store empty?"

"Not now, Kamp. Come home with me. I'll fix you supper and explain everything."

She put on her heavy coat and picked up her riding gloves. Kamp took her by the shoulders.

"I can't. No one can see me."

FALKO STIER HAD NEVER HEARD the words "special assignment" before, not in his training and not in his two years as a sworn officer of the law. Perhaps it was because he'd already become suspicious, but to him, those words rang false. They were meant to hide something.

And when he'd pressed Druckenmiller for an explanation, the man wouldn't answer and instead responded with a veiled threat.

Just before his shift ended, Stier stuffed the police log books from the past three months in his rucksack and took them home.

THE HALL OF RECORDS BURNED long before B.H. Grigg went looking for it, and the locals in Fredericksburg regarded him with suspicion and bemusement when he asked them where it was.

But eventually he found a kid with threadbare pants, no shirt and a straw hat who pointed him toward the Spotsylvania Courthouse, which had somehow outlived the war.

"It's thataway, sir," he'd said.

He'd tossed the kid a sliver dollar, compliments of the Philadelphia Home for the Needy.

Grigg talked his way past the clerk at the front desk of the courthouse by claiming to be an insurance man from a neighboring county. He'd even affected the correct regional accent. Finding the exact information he wanted proved harder than finding the courthouse, though. All of the war records were stacked in loose piles in an unlit cellar.

KAMP HAD ALWAYS DEPENDED ON WYLES and her lifelong, staunch refusal to be shaken. Looking at her now, he realized something had changed.

In all the time he'd known her, she'd always addressed people directly, chin out and shoulders back. It wasn't a provocation, merely a statement. And she looked everyone in the eye.

Now, her eyes were downcast.

"They're taking it," she said and kneaded her forehead with her fingers.

"Taking what?"

"My practice, the store, my reputation, all of it. Piece by piece."

As Kamp fixed two cups of coffee, Wyles told him the tale, from the men she gunned down to losing her customers to the visit from the health inspector.

When Wyles finished, she paused, took a sip of coffee, then said, "Where's your family?"

FALKO STIER FOUND NOTHING about special assignments in the log books he read. He scoured every page, searching for those two words. Hunched over his kitchen table and reading by candle flame, Stier hunted for something he'd never wanted before. He wanted to find truth in words.

The muscles in his neck ached, and his eyes grew tired. Special assignments didn't exist, as least not in the official police record. His suspicion grew alongside his anger.

B.H. GRIGG DIDN'T FEEL ANGER. Irritation perhaps, and frustration. He wasn't surprised that the records in the cellar of the Spotsylvania Courthouse weren't organized in any fashion. Relegating something like a war to neat sheaves and orderly columns takes time.

But what Grigg needed—a name and the person who went with it—he needed now. He couldn't spend days riffling through thousands of pages. For all he knew, the Order might descend on the courthouse at any moment. He picked up the lantern and walked out of the cellar.

When he reached the front desk, the clerk said, "Son, you been down there so long we was about to send a search party."

"Very kind of you."

"Hope you found what you was lookin' for." The man screwed up his face. "Say, what was it you *was* lookin' for?"

"A name, a man's name." Grigg tried to hide his irritation.

"So you found it then?"

"What?"

"The name."

"I didn't."

Grigg put his top hat on, tipped it, and turned to go.

"Mercy me, son, you look like you got the fantods. You said you was a insurance man?"

"That's right." Grigg tried to remember exactly the story he'd used to talk his way in. "I'm an insurance man."

The clerk's tone went flat.

"What kinda insurance?"

AND THEN IT WAS KAMP'S TURN. He told Wyles about how, upon being driven from their home, he'd found Shaw and Autumn at Joe's house and about how he had to leave. He told her about the armed men prowling the woods behind his house, waiting for him to show himself.

He finished by saying, "And now I'm back where I started."

Wyles sat across from Kamp with her elbows propped on the table and fingers interlaced under her chin.

She paused for a long moment and then said, "They can't win."

Kamp looked at her across the table at his old friend who, in an instant, had recovered her resolve.

"Yah, well, you might want to tell them that."

"I know you. I know why they're coming after you."

"You do."

"The same reason they're after me."

Kamp rubbed his forehead with his left hand. "But I'm not a threat."

"Of course you are," Wyles said. "What you are, who you are."

"I'm not anyone."

Wyles studied him, his blue eyes and the marks of time on his face. She reached across the table and took his hands in hers.

"Do you know what people always ask me about you?"

"No."

"They always lean close and whisper, why'd he do it? Why'd Kamp try to keep the mob from killing Daniel Knecht? And I always tell them the same thing."

"What's that?"

"I tell them—"

A pounding came at the back door and then a pleading voice.

"We require assistance. Please open the door."

WHEN SLEEP BEGAN TO OVERTAKE Falko Stier, dreams mixed with reality. His mind drifted back to the moment he'd doused Kamp in kerosene, struck the match and held it above the fallen man's face.

In that instant before he gave himself over to sleep, Stier felt weightless and free from the burden of judging and in that instant Falko Stier saw that he'd been manipulated and deceived.

As he put his head down on the table, he knew that words could never set things right, but actions could.

GRIGG WANTED TO RUN from the courthouse. To answer the clerk's question would require him to tarry, but not answering would provoke the man's suspicion.

The clerk leaned forward. "I said, what kinda insurance did you say you was in?"

"Life."

"Life insurance?"

"That's right. Why?"

"Shoot, ain't none of us got insurance, not in this life, no. But that ain't the point, is it?"

"Point of what?"

The clerk leaned back. "Life insurance ain't for the dead man. It's for them that's left behind."

Grigg felt sweat beads popping out on his forehead. "That's right."

KAMP CRACKED THE DOOR and a man stared back at him, hat in hand, deep furrows across his forehead.

Kamp said, "*Was ist?*"

"What?"

"What's the problem?"

"My wife needs a doctor. Please help us."

"No doctor here."

Kamp closed the door and locked it. Wyles tried to push him out of the way.

"Move."

"Bad idea, Emma."

"This man needs help."

"You're not a doctor. And you don't know what this man needs. He's probably lying anyway."

Wyles drew back her fist and punched Kamp in the shoulder where he'd been shot two years before. When he pulled back in pain, she swung the door open and pulled the man inside.

IT ANGERED ADAMS that Grigg escaped from the Pennsylvania Hospital for the Insane and from the Home for the Needy. Then again, she loved things that were hard to kill.

Even the bear, especially the bear that fixed its jaw on her wrist, taking her hand and wedding band along with it. And the girl, too. Nyx. She'd escaped along with Kamp's cousin, the freak Angus.

Adams loved to return in her mind to the moments she ambushed her quarry, each a consummation of desire and malice. She slowed each memory at the instant of recognition and relived the twitch and tingle it gave her.

But they didn't pay her to enjoy it. They paid by the kill, and they didn't appreciate her recent string of misses. And so she had to focus on the task at hand and her anger at Grigg. Her train had pulled into Fredericksburg six hours after his, and she wasn't certain she'd find him.

But by posing as his jilted wife and enlisting the help of the citizenry, Adams found people who pointed her in the right direction. They put her onto the road to the Spotsylvania. One family with a husband, wife and three daughters even gave her a ride in their humble wagon.

By the time the sun began to set, the courthouse came into view, and a light still burned in the window.

THE CLERK RUBBED THE WHISKERS on his chin and studied Grigg.

"Do you love the lord?"

"Do I what?"

Grigg reached behind his back for the brass door-knob, while still looking at the clerk.

"I said, do you love the lord?"

"Of course."

"And have you squared your account with him?"

"Say again?"

Grigg dared not turn his back on the clerk, but he couldn't find the knob with his hand.

The clerk's tone turned stern.

"You have a troubled heart, friend. I can tell."

ADAMS BID ADIEU to the family who'd given her a ride to the courthouse.

The youngest daughter said, "We can wait here if you need a ride somewhere else."

"That's very kind of you, but I'll be on my way."

The little girl said, "Well, then, good night."

Adams felt for the ivory handle of the .45 and headed toward the courthouse.

A BEAD OF SWEAT ROLLED down Grigg's cheek.

"I'll be going now."

Grigg was dimly aware he'd dropped the regional accent and was speaking in his own voice.

The clerk said, "You stay right there," and he reached under the counter.

Grigg spun, reached for the doorknob and twisted it. Locked. His heart slapped against his ribs as he waited for the blast.

THE MAN STOOD DOUBLED OVER, head down and panting.

Between breaths, he said, "My wife needs your help. She's having a baby. Something's wrong."

Kamp studied the man, whom he didn't recognize. He wore a frock coat with a velour collar in the Victorian style and black leather brogans.

"Take her to the hospital. Lots of doctors there."

"Christ, Kamp."

The man stood up and looked at Kamp. "We don't have any money."

Kamp said, "Don't do it, Emma."

Wyles put on her coat, turned to the man and said, "Where is she?"

Kamp hustled after Wyles, who chased the man down the dark alley, before turning onto Third Street and running toward the stacks of Native Iron.

When they ducked down another side street, Kamp wished he'd brought a pistol. He rounded the corner and saw a wooden carriage, a caravan with the back doors open, and a figure lying inside. A candle illuminated the scene.

The man crawled into the caravan and threw his arms around the figure there.

He wailed, "No!"

Wyles knelt beside the body and then turned to Kamp and shook her head. When Kamp got close enough, he saw a woman's body naked from the waist down and covered in blood.

The man rose up and said to Wyles, "If you'd gotten here sooner, she'd have been saved. They both would have." Then he fixed his gaze on Kamp and said, "This is your fault. Yours." The man jabbed the air in front of him as he said it, then threw himself across the bodies of his wife and dead child.

Wyles climbed down from the caravan, closed the doors and started down the street. Kamp waited a moment longer and looked at the gold lettering painted on the black doors.

It read, "Royal Traveling Show. Performances Nightly."

He caught up to Wyles three blocks later, grabbing her by the elbow and forcing her to stop running. She pulled away hard, but he kept his grip.

"Where are you going?"

"The coroner needs to be informed."

"We didn't see anything, Emma. We weren't there. You tell Oehler, and he'll know you tried to help them. You'll be arrested. And by the time he gets there, the bodies, the carriage. It'll all be gone."

"Stop it, Kamp. Once and for all, stop it."

"Some guy shows up at your back door and you just want to help—"

"People show up at my door all the time. You did."

"It's not what it looks like, Emma."

"That woman was dead. That baby was dead. That was real."

"But you don't know why they put them there."

"They?"

"Black Feather. And the Order. They're controlling—"

"Jesus Christ. You're out of your mind."

She shook his hand off her arm.

"That man saw me, Emma. And he saw you with me. You realize—"

Her eyes blazed.

"Don't you dare hurt him."

"My point is that since he saw us together, you're not safe. No one who cares about you is safe."

Wyles turned on her heel, put her head down and started walking toward the pharmacy.

"Emma, think about it."

"I'm not listening. I need to stop at the store and then I'll—"

Wyles stopped talking as she turned onto Third Street and saw the flames spewing from the door of her pharmacy.

She ran to the front window and was repulsed when the heat blew it out.

Kamp grabbed her hard by the elbow.

"It's finished," he said.

They turned and ran to the alley, where Wyles' horse was tied. Wyles climbed into the saddle and reached for his hand.

"I can't. Just go."

"Get on."

In the distance they heard the bells of the fire brigade and the clatter of hooves.

Kamp took her hand and hauled himself onto the horse. His head began to spin immediately, so he shut his eyes hard and pressed his cheek against her back. Wyles shouted, "Ya," snapped the reins, and took off down the alley.

"THAT'S RIGHT, DOOR'S LOCKED. That's so you can't leave."

Grigg turned to look at the clerk, expecting to see the barrel of a gun. Instead, there was a bible opened on the counter.

"Please unlock this door. I need to go."

The clerk shook his head gently. "Brother, you said you's from Wildcat Corner, ain't that right?"

Grigg couldn't remember where he'd said he was from.

"Yes, Wildcat Corner."

"So you know Pastor."

"Who?"

"Pastor Fosdick? Eustachius Fosdick over at Mount Hor Baptist Meeting House. You go up there, don'tcha?"

"Of course."

"So you know him."

"He's a good man. Now, if you'll permit me to leave."

Grigg scanned the counter for a set of keys and didn't see them. The clerk rubbed the whiskers on his chin.

"Yes, sir, a good, good man. Courageous, too. 'Specially for what he done."

"Yep. Would you be so kind as to—"

"You know he was a surgeon."

"Who?"

"Pastor."

"No, I didn't know that."

"Well, that's because he don't like to bring it up no more. Never did, actually. But pastor was a sawbones in the war. Tried to fix 'em all, too. Rebel, Yankee, didn't make no distinctions. Some folks didn't like that. But I respect it immeasurable. To pastor, it was just the lord's work. Blood an' guts t'ain't neither blue nor grey."

"No, they're not."

"They're all red." The clerk chuckled and shook his head.

"True enough."

Then the clerk stopped laughing, turned sober and said, "That man has the divine hands, you know that."

Grigg thought he caught the sound of boot heels outside the front door. He looked at the door knob and saw it jiggling.

In a quiet voice, he said, "I think we might want to—"

"Say, let's us share a word from the good book, an' then you can be on your way."

Grigg stepped to the side of the room. "Really, I think we should—"

The clerk cleared his throat, looked down at the bible and started to read.

"From Paul's letter to the good people at Philippi. 'Be careful for nothing, but in everything by prayer and supplication with thanksgiving let your requests be made known unto God. And the peace of God, which passeth all understanding shall keep—' "

The first bullet split the lock, and the second blew it clean away. Adams kicked the door open and shot the clerk in the chest. He clutched the wound with both hands and gasped for breath as blood poured onto the bible.

Adams crossed the floor and put the gun to the clerk's forehead.

She said, "Where is he?"

The clerk let out a gurgle and motioned to the front door.

Adams spun on her heel and saw nothing but Grigg's coattails disappearing into the darkness. She turned back and put the fourth bullet in the clerk's head.

29

Nyx went back to the room at the bottom of the mine, the one she'd shared with him for six months, where they'd lain side by side, hacking away, dreaming of each other. The room had been their only sanctuary. Now it was contaminated and bereft of all but darkness and dust.

She fought the urge to shut down, to lie there in surrender. Nyx willed herself to pick up the coal axe and start hewing. Soon, she'd drifted out of her consciousness so that all that remained was muscle and bone.

Short Pinky took his place alongside Nyx. There was none of the fire she'd felt with Aodh, of course, but she made room for him all the same.

Nyx filled five cars by herself, and she felt no fatigue. Sweat spilled from her chin as she hacked and shoveled. Only when Short Pinky took her by the elbow did Nyx snap from her trance.

"What?"

He waited until she came back to consciousness, then said, "That's it."

"What is?"

"We hit the seven. Let's go." He cupped his hands around his mouth and yelled, "Done!"

Soon, the hurrier and the thruster, Irish girls, appeared. The hurrier wore a leather belt with a heavy chain she attached to the front of the car. The thruster took her place behind the car and pushed. When the car began to roll, Nyx and Short Pinky fell in behind it.

Short Pinky gave Nyx a gentle elbow to the ribs and said in a low voice, "Never seen these two before. They're replacing us, ya know."

"Who is?"

"Germans out, Irish in. One by one. Now that your man is gone, someone'll take his place soon enough. And mine. And yours."

Nyx grabbed Short Pinky's jacket and stopped him in the dark tunnel. "Who's replacing us?"

"Ach, you know who it is. That guy with the blond hair, the boss."

"Thaler."

"Yah, that guy. And Padgett. Padgett says he wants what's best for the miners, but who knows what he really wants? He's in bed with that Thaler."

GRIGG DIDN'T KNOW ADAMS, but he'd heard a few things, murmurs and veiled side comments about who she was and the role she played. They never used her name.

He wasn't privy to full explanations of their sordid dealings, because they never trusted him and didn't want him to interfere.

Nevertheless, Grigg had discerned that they trusted Adams and her ability to make their problems vanish. And considering that she'd followed him this far, he had no doubt she was relentless. But she'd also made a mistake. She'd shot the clerk before questioning him.

It was possible that the clerk had given her the surgeon's name before he died, but Grigg doubted it. She'd find him again, that was certain. But for now, he'd performed another death-defying escape, and he set his sights on the humble village of Wildcat Corner and the steeple that rose from its center.

He brushed the dirt and dust from his jacket, tucked in his shirt and straightened his back as he headed for the front steps of the church. He paused to look up at the wooden sign above the door.

It read, "Mount Hor Baptist Church. Souls saved."

He went around the back and knocked at the door. When no one answered, he let himself in. Grigg stepped lightly into the hallway and paused to listen. Somewhere in the building, a floorboard creaked, but that was all. He waited another long moment, heard nothing and then started down the hallway. He dared not call out for fear of meeting another hostile pursuer, another antagonist, another gun.

But when he reached the office at the end of the hallway and peered in, he saw a man in shirtsleeves hunched over an open bible on the desk before him. When Grigg knocked at the door, the man didn't startle. Instead, he remained motionless for another full minute, then said "amen" softly and turned to greet his visitor.

The man stood up, extended his hand and said, "Brother, I don't believe we've met. Eustachius Fosdick, servant of the lord."

Grigg removed his hat with his left hand, shook the pastor's hand with his right and said, "B.H. Grigg, District Attorney, Northampton County, Pennsylvania."

OFFICER FALKO STIER STARED down at the sign at his feet. He knew it used to read, "Pure Drugs & Chemicals." Now all that was left was the charred remnant and the wrought iron bracket that had held it up.

Stier saw city firemen inside, hosing down the embers. The shelves had burned along with the wooden counter where the pharmacist had plied her trade. Shattered glass covered the floor. He didn't see the remains of any inventory.

He walked to the back of the pharmacy, a storage area that the fire hadn't consumed. He found a kitchen table and on it, two ceramic coffee mugs. Wyles been there recently, and someone was with her.

Stier called out, "Anyone seen her?"

The fireman closest to him mumbled, "I'm working here" and tossed a shovelful of ashes toward the door.

Stier talked a little louder. "Did anyone see her?"

The man stopped shoveling. "Her who?"

"The pharmacist. Wyles."

The fireman stood up and tilted his helmet back on his head.

"Not that I know."

"She didn't die in the fire?"

Irritation flashed across the fireman's face. "Unfortunately, no."

"You're certain?"

He turned to look at Stier. "Ach, I don't see no bones. Do you?"

Stier felt the first flame of rage tickling the base of his skull. He stood up straight, spine stiffening.

"You don't hafta be so ugly," he said.

The weary, soot-smudged fireman leaned on the handle of his spade. "Yah, well you don't hafta ask so many goddamned questions."

Stier felt the anger spread through his chest, as he stepped to within an inch of the fireman.

"How'd it start?" The fireman looked past him and said nothing. Stier took a handful of the fireman's coat. "How did the fire start?"

The fireman muttered something under his breath.

"What did you say?"

The fireman met Stier's gaze. "I said you can go fu—"

Stier slammed his elbow into the fireman's jaw. The man doubled over, and Stier stepped past him to the back door.

His mind flashed to the scene of Kamp lying in that very spot, soaked in kerosene. Stier saw the lit match in his own hand, hovering inches above Kamp's face.

Why did I think I was right then? What if I'm wrong now?

GRIGG KNEW he'd found his man. He pulled the photograph, creased and nearly falling to pieces, from his pocket and laid it on the table.

"Pastor, if you'll allow me to get straight to the point."

"By all means."

Grigg pointed to the man standing next to the table in the picture.

"I believe that's you."

Fosdick slid the photograph closer to inspect it.

"I believe you're right."

"What about the man on the table? Do you remember him?"

"Where was this?"

"Fredericksburg."

Fosdick looked again, then stared up at the ceiling. "Son, I can't say I remember. There were so many."

Grigg gently turned the photograph over and pointed to the scrawl on the back. "Is the writing yours?"

"Appears to be."

"You wrote, 'Captain W.W. Kamp, deceased.' "

Fosdick leaned in and scrutinized the handwriting, then looked back up at Grigg.

"Why'd you say you need to know?"

"He needs my help."

"Not if he's dead, he don't."

"Pastor, Kamp is alive. I know he's alive. You wrote 'deceased.' Why?"

Fosdick sighed and then reached under his desk and produced a bottle and two shot glasses.

"Son, this is between you, me an' the lord. Understand?"

He poured two shots, slid one across the desk and raised the other.

"To Jesus."

Fosdick savored the whiskey for a moment, then said, "Fredericksburg. Last day. This fella come in shot up, like you see there. I removed the bullet, fixed him up best I could but knew he wouldn't make it. That man went cold dead right at the end."

"And then?"

"Well, I said the prayer I always say at the moment I give one of his children back to him. And right when I finished praying, his eyes opened. He come back."

"But you said he was deceased."

"I lied."

"Why?"

"While I was working on him, they come over with a camera, big camera on long legs. They set it up and took photographs. Appears they took it right before he come back to life. Then they left. A week later they come see me with that very photograph. They insisted that I put my name to it an' verify the death."

"Who were they?"

"By that point, he'd been shipped back. Philadelphia, I b'lieve."

"Who took the photograph? What were their names?"

"They didn't say, and I didn't ask. They told me they was reporters out of Richmond. Didn't believe that, though."

"Why not?"

"There was a darkness on both of them. It's not my habit to dissemble, of course, but I didn't trust them, not at all."

"What did they look like?"

"Don't recall that, either. Except he wore fine clothes, clean and tailored. And she wore a velvet cape with a hood."

"She?"

"That's right. Petite l'il woman. Blond hair under that hood she wore. A fine face, but hard. I lied to 'em an' wrote that there. Never heard from 'em again and was glad of it."

"Thank you, pastor."

"Both of 'em had blond hair, come to think of it. His was blond an' wavy, combed back."

"Very helpful. Thank you."

"Now let's have a word from the good book. How about a verse from Paul's letter to the Philippians?"

"I'd rather not."

KAMP DIDN'T KNOW where Emma Wyles lived, he now realized. When they were kids, yes, he went to her family's house every day in the summer. Her parents referred to him as "a fixture" at their supper table. But when he'd returned from the war, Wyles was gone, her family's house sold, her parents departed.

And by the time they met again, a necessary distance had grown between them and, as such, Kamp didn't visit her at home. Nor did he wonder where she lived.

He had to go to her house now, though. They both did. Kamp couldn't open his eyes, lest the vertigo overwhelm him, but he knew they were traveling up the road over South Mountain. Somewhere near the top, Wyles turned off, and he could feel the horse picking its way along a narrow trail. He vomited once but was otherwise steady as he clung to Wyles. A few minutes later, the horse came to a stop.

He leaned over and let himself slide off the horse's back. Once he'd steadied himself on the ground, he opened his eyes and saw a sturdy cabin built into the mountainside and surrounded by trees. Kamp heard a crow in the distance but nothing else. No hooves, no voices, no creaking wheels. He smelled the breeze and caught a whiff of sulfur from Native Iron.

Wyles unlocked the padlock with a skeleton key, and the girl with porcelain blue eyes and hair the color and texture of corn silk opened the door.

Wyles went straight to a bedroom, while Kamp surveyed the cabin. It was clean and spare, exactly what he would have expected. On a table by the back door, he saw an empty basin, and under the table, a large black medical bag.

The girl walked past him to the bedroom door, knocked softly and entered. He heard them talking but couldn't make out the words. The door swung open, and Wyles walked out. When Kamp looked in, he saw tears streaming down the girl's face. Wyles put the medical bag in the basin and then carried it all out the back door.

When she came back in, she said to Kamp, "Let's go."

The girl launched herself across the room and threw her arms around Wyles' neck.

"No."

Wyles kissed her forehead and said, "Go to your brother's house."

When he went back outside, he saw that Wyles had harnessed the horse to a cart. She emerged from the cabin alone.

"Get in."

Kamp climbed in the cart and lay down on his back. She covered the cart with a canvas tarp and cinched it tight at the corners. Soon the cart began to roll.

Wyles called back to him, "Where are we going?"

"Up the line," Kamp said.

30

Whe Falko Stier got back to the station, it was still dark, though he could hear the dawn chorus. He was alone in the station.

He started with the file cabinets that lined the back wall of the main room. Every drawer had a new brass lock on it, and he couldn't find a key. As the morning light came streaming in, Stier scanned the room and saw that the loose papers that typically covered every flat surface were gone. Someone had done a thorough job of cleaning up.

If there were one person Stier could count on to be careless, it was the High Constable. He went to Druckenmiller's desk and found that it, too, had been cleared of clutter. But the drawers weren't locked. The top drawer was stuffed with softcover novels and broadsheets.

Stier heard someone trying the front door. It was the next man reporting for work, a new officer named Storch.

"Open the door."

"Give me a minute."

"It's cold out here."

Stier kept digging through the drawer until he felt a paper at the bottom. He pulled it out, glanced at it and shoved it in his pants pocket. He went to the door, unlocked it and swung it open.

Storch scowled at him and said, "We're locking the door now? Jesus Christ."

AODH HEARD THE SKELETON KEY turn and looked up to see the jailer approaching him in his cell with breakfast. He expected a hard biscuit and thin coffee.

Instead, the man carried a feast of eggs, sausage and warm bread on a tray. Aodh's heart sank.

The jailer set the tray on the bench next to Aodh.

"You got a visitor," the jailer said.

FALKO STIER DIDN'T KNOW that Aodh Blackall's day of wrath was approaching. He just wanted to get home, build a fire and warm his feet by it before dropping off to sleep. As he walked the mile from the police station to his home, he unfolded the paper he'd taken from Druckenmiller's desk.

It was a handbill for something called the Royal Traveling Company, and it read,

"An Authentic Presentation of a Medieval Master-piece. *THE HARROWING of HELL.*"

On the front was a picture of a man cradling a skull. Inside the cover, there were hand drawings of several cast members. The portrait of the lead actor bore a striking resemblance to someone he knew. Before, he'd only seen the broad outlines of the conspiracy. Now he began to comprehend it in full.

But Falko Stier didn't feel like thinking. He wanted to let his body rest, to let the pain and anxiety drain from his limbs.

He let himself in the back door of his small house at the edge of town. He unlaced his boots, went to the fireplace and arranged the kindling and logs. When he stood up to retrieve a match from the mantle, he saw it, and his heart began slapping against his ribs.

Next to the box of matches was a newly-minted silver coin with a locomotive on the front and on the back, a smiling face beneath a cap in the Phrygian style.

DIS PADGETT WAITED for the guard to leave before he said anything to Aodh, who'd begun wolfing down his breakfast.

"Rest easy, lad. This meal wonna be your last."

Aodh took a mouthful of scrambled eggs and washed it down with coffee.

"Easy for you to say."

"There's plenty of trouble to go around, believe me."

"That so?"

Aodh stared down at his plate while he finished his meal.

"Yes, and more."

Padgett rolled two cigarettes on the bench, lit both and handed one to Aodh.

Aodh took a drag and said, "I know what they get. What do you get?"

Padgett stood up and looked out the small window at the top of the wall.

"You think it was me who put you in here."

"I know it was."

"Why?"

"Because they couldn't do it without your permission."

"Jaysus, Blackall, you're the one that was schemin' to hit back against Black Feather. Now you're payin' the price. And besides, they donna care a squirt o' piss about what I think."

"Tha's not true. Yer dancin' with them. Tha's why I'm here. Tell the truth."

Padgett took another drag and watched the smoke twist toward the window.

He said, "You know, when they came for him, when they intended to do all manner of evil—"

"Jaysus, don't start."

"When they came to do all manner of evil to your poor brother, who was it put a stop to it?"

"I'm not talkin' about then. I'm—"

"When I found your brother, Butcher had his cock stuffed down his throat. I didn't hear nothin' from your brother but a whimper 'til he seen me. Was me who clouted Butcher in his skull with my shovel."

"I told you—"

"That you can believe. Just lucky I'm not sittin' here beside you for it."

"I doubt it's luck."

"Well, you owe me."

"You do what you do for your reasons, not mine, not my brother's."

Padgett took the last pull on the cigarette, then dropped it on the floor.

"You know, there was a line o' fellas, pants open, waitin' for Butcher to finish. Tha's no lie. And you know I paid for savin' your brother from that. Bosses didn't like that I kept them miners from gettin' their pleasure. Said I hurt morale."

Aodh felt the rage well up from his gut and spread through his chest and across his shoulders.

"Casey is gone, Dennis. There's no call for you to insult his memory. If you'll just tell for what reason you came—"

"You always was an ungrateful bastard."

Aodh balled his fists.

"Leave," he said.

"Yah, Casey is dead an' buried, but that little German friend o' yours, he's alive and well."

"Dennis, stop it."

"What's his name, Naf Bear? Donna worry, now that you're gone, he can keep me warm."

Aodh launched himself at Padgett and gripped him hard by his throat. He didn't see the blade drop from Padgett's sleeve and didn't feel it go in his back, just above the kidney.

Aodh's legs went weak, and his grip loosened. Padgett wiped off the blade on Aodh's prison shirt before letting him fall to the floor.

He stepped over him on the way out of the cell, saying, "You know, back when we was home, your mother liked to have a taste herself."

Padgett waited until Aodh's body became still, then shouted, "Guard! There's a man down."

The jailer came running. He looked at the carnage and said, "Christ, this isn't good, isn't good at all."

"He came at me half out of his mind," Padgett said, "It was all I could do to defend myself."

KAMP LAY HIDDEN under the canvas tarp and felt the to and fro motion of the cart. Neither of them spoke for the first hour or so, and they only stopped once at Shawnee Creek so that Wyles' horse could have a drink.

When they cleared the outskirts of the town, and farm and field gave way to forest and meadow, Wyles broke the silence.

"Are you there? Are you awake?"

"Say, Emma, who was that girl at your house?"

"I'll take that as a yes."

Wyles eased back on the reins and brought the horse to a stop. "We're safe."

He pulled off the tarp, sat up and squinted against the morning sun.

Wyles said, "I assume we're going to see your family."

"Not necessarily."

"Why not?"

Kamp rubbed his left temple. "I'm never getting to somewhere they're not chasing me, am I?"

She turned in her saddle to look at him.

"You're exhausted, and hungry."

"Tell me the truth, Emma. This is just like when we were kids, sort of. That was a good time."

"This is real," she said, "and not as much fun."

In the distance they heard the clatter of hooves and the creak of wagon wheels. Kamp lowered himself back down and covered himself with the tarp.

On the road behind them, a carriage came into view, and another one behind it. Wyles waited for the first to pass and then the second. A well-dressed family rode in each one.

The man driving the second carriage tipped his hat to Wyles and said, "Ma'am."

She heard more voices on the road and soon saw two men, hunters, walking side by side, each cradling a shotgun.

They stopped to leer at her.

She said, "Where's everyone going?"

One of the hunters said, "Where are *you* going?"

Wyles shook her head and without emotion said, "Answer the question, please."

The second hunter said, "You hafta answer now, Horace. She said please."

"What're you doing out here all cold and alone?"

Wyles sat taller in her saddle.

"I have a question, too," the first hunter said. "We're lookin' for a fella, fella with a bounty on his head." The hunter produced the wanted poster of Kamp from his pocket, unfolded it and held it up. "You seen this son of a bitch, *mebbe*?"

Under the tarp Kamp tensed his muscles. He didn't have a weapon, but he could surprise them.

"No," Wyles said.

"Sure about that?"

She held the saddle horn, shifted her weight and looked up the road.

Wyles said, "Where is everyone going?"

"Mauch Chunk."

"For what?"

The first hunter said, "What do we get if we answer?" He closed the action of the shotgun and held it at his side. "You hear me? What do we get?"

Wyles pulled the .45 and pointed it at the man's crotch.

"You get to keep your balls. Horace."

The second hunter said, "Hanging. Everyone's going to see that troublemaking son of a bitch hang."

Wyles shifted her gaze to the first hunter. "Are you two going to Mauch Chunk?"

Before the first hunter could answer, the second said, "No."

"Good."

LIKE EVERYONE ELSE, Officer Falko Stier knew what the silver coin meant. He'd heard the stories. Some of them sounded like pure bullshit, some not. The coin signaled the ultimate fall from grace. Police officer or no, he'd become a marked man.

He couldn't report for work, couldn't follow any normal routines for that matter. They'd find him soon enough, but he wouldn't make it easy for them.

While he gathered up a few days' worth of food and a change of clothes, he tried to imagine who could help him, but no one came to mind. He no longer trusted his fellow officers.

But he remembered there was that guy, the lawyer. Stier hated the sound of his voice, all smooth edges and slippery words, all the bullshit that guy said. What was his name? It was on the tip of his tongue. Gig? Greg? Grigg. That was it.

Why did this *klootzak's* face appear just now, he wondered. As he stood with his hand on the brass doorknob, ready to run, Stier remembered that Grigg defended Kamp. They told him Kamp was nothing but a troublemaker and a louse. But Stier remembered that when he was a kid, they told him Kamp was a war hero. What changed? Who was telling the truth?

Of course, it didn't matter, as such. Stier stared at the coin in his hand and knew it meant he had to act.

WHEN THEY'D GOTTEN CLEAR of the hunters, Kamp heard the clop of hooves and the squeak of their wagon wheels but nothing else.

"Emma?"

"Kamp."

"We need to go to Mauch Chunk."

"For what?"

"She's going to be there."

"You don't know that."

"We're going."

Wyles pulled back on the reins, and the horse stopped.

"You don't know anything about what's going on there, who'll be hanged, or why. Regardless, it isn't about Nyx."

"How do you know?" Kamp peeled back the tarp and sat up.

"You need to worry about your family. Not Nyx." He heard irritation in her voice.

"They're fine. Joe's taking care of them."

Wyles turned in the saddle to face him. "Tell me why, then. Tell me why she's so important."

He swung his leg over the side of the wagon and jumped to the ground.

She said, "Tell me."

Kamp brushed the dust from his slouch hat and put it on his head. He buttoned his thin work jacket and started walking ahead of her.

"Well, then, it's better if we split up here, anyway," he said.

Wyles started the horse, pulled alongside him and said, "We're in this together."

Kamp kept walking and without looking at her, said, "This isn't going to work."

"Get in the wagon."

"I'll see you later."

"Get. *In.*"

"I'll find you once I know she's safe."

"You want them to kill you. That's it, isn't it?"

"Go ahead. Find a place to stay."

In one motion E. Wyles swung her leg over the saddle, dismounted and stood facing Kamp with the reins in her hand.

She tilted her chin up, pulled in a sharp breath and stared at Kamp until he met her gaze.

"You're giving up," she said.

Kamp felt a stab of grief in his throat as he looked at his friend. He saw the small creases at the corners of her eyes, the lines across her forehead. And then he caught a fragment of a memory of swimming in the creek with her, surfacing through green bubbles, coming up for air and looking into that same face, unlined.

"Come back. Kamp, please." Tears welled in her eyes.

"I'll see you later, Emma. I'll find you."

"Think of your family, Kamp. Think of them."

"I am."

31

Nyx brushed her fingers along the barrels of the rifles that filled Angus's gun rack. Angus was already at work, re-boring a Pennsylvania long rifle by the light of three candles on his workbench.

Without pausing to look at Nyx, he said, "Don't touch none of them."

"I didn't."

"Don't even look at them."

"Jesus."

Angus's fingers stopped, and he said, "I know why you ain't at the mine."

He glanced at Nyx and then resumed his work. "And I know why you're wearing them clean clothes."

"We don't have to be dirty all the time."

"You're going to—"

"Stop."

Angus spoke without emotion. "You're going to town today to see your man."

"It's not your concern."

"It's wrongheaded."

"No one knows who I am."

Angus sharpened his tone and glanced at Nyx. "Bullshit. And even if they don't, someone will see you and—"

"Shut up!" Nyx balled her fists hard enough to drain the blood from her knuckles.

Angus looked back at his work and let his fingers start again.

"Be sensible, girl. He's a good man, and he don't deserve what they're giving him. But you didn't bring him to his grief. You don't know what he mighta done or not done. Just go to the mine and—"

Angus realized that the room had gone silent. Nyx was gone, and when Angus scanned the gun rack, he saw one open space.

AODH CAME TO FACE DOWN on the floor of his cell, and he felt heavy pressure on his lower back. When he tried to roll over, the pressure increased.

The jailer, said, "Lie still once. Doctor's on his way. He'll be here directly."

"For what?"

"He's got to fix you up and make sure you don't miss your last appointment."

The jailer leaned close enough for Aodh to feel the breath at his neck.

"What did you say to your friend that made him do this to you?"

"Leave me be."

The jailer slapped him across the back of his head.

"A fella doesn't come down to the jail to shank another fella in the kidneys, not just for laughs."

"Feck off."

"Not for nothing."

"Yah, well, you'd have to ask him."

"Ach, I wish I could, but Mr. Padgett's gone."

KAMP FELL into a steady walking rhythm. With his hat pulled low, no one could see his face. More important, the people in the line of carriages streaming past him wanted to see a hanging. They wouldn't be looking for him.

He brought to mind Wyles and the points she was trying to make. That he was giving up. That by walking to Mauch Chunk he'd be recognized and then killed.

He brought Shaw to mind, her face and the constellation of freckles across the bridge of her nose and the crescent-shaped scar. Then he pictured Autumn, the moment he first held her and then the moment Joe spoke her true name and lifted her toward the sky. Kamp imagined her eyes, one brown iris and one blue.

If he offered himself up to the populace alongside the man condemned to hang, would they forget about Nyx? If he surrendered himself to the Order of the Raven, would they leave his family in peace?

And then Kamp caught a fragment of another memory, a man running toward him, the fiend Daniel Knecht, sprinting up the path that ran past his home. He pictured himself hefting the spade in his hands and then swinging it into Knecht's ribs and saving him from a bullet in the back. If he hadn't swung that shovel, Knecht would have been killed and the nightmare never would have started.

He flashed to the instant he found Knecht in a barn. Knecht said something. What was it? Something Latin.

"*Quia merito haec patior.* For this I suffer deservedly."

And then Knecht pulled back the hammer and pressed the pepperbox to his temple and said, "How's that for a joke?"

Kamp tried to recall what else Knecht had said but couldn't. He tried to remember where Nickel Glock came from and failed at that, too.

He turned and saw another column of carriages coming up behind him. Maybe it was better to let it all go, to stand there and turn his face to the passersby, let them see him.

Or perhaps he could walk straight to town, surrender. Maybe they could just stand him alongside the condemned man.

ANTON "DUNY" KUNKLE WALKED ALONE on the side of the road, watching the carriages pass, ogling every woman and girl.

Fathers and brothers said nothing, owing to Duny's crazy stare and greasy locks matted to his forehead. That, and the long rifle he carried compelled them to hold their tongues.

Duny had no truck with any of them, of course. He just wanted something to distract him from the tedium of the long march to Mauch Chunk, the shithole to which he'd been sent. It had to be coming up soon.

He looked ahead of the carriages and saw another solitary figure, standing on the side of the road. Even at a hundred fifty yards, Duny recognized the build, the jacket and the slouch hat. Kamp.

Duny wasn't accustomed to good luck and put no faith in it. And yet here it was. He put Tate Cain's warning out of his mind and replaced it with the thrill of getting a reward for gunning down this son of a bitch here and now.

He widened his stance and took a steady position, then raised the rifle to his shoulder and pressed his cheek to the flame maple stock.

Kamp stood still and looked ahead at the town of Mauch Chunk spread out before him. He gazed up and saw a raven wheeling beneath a cloud, tracing its parabolic path and for a moment becoming lost in it.

Duny Kunkle pulled in a slow breath and sighted the head. He softened his grip on the rifle as his lungs filled. Kamp was giving him his shot, making it easy, like he knew it was coming. Duny waited only for the inhalation to crest so that he could fire on the way down.

But the click of the set trigger alerted the driver of a passing carriage, a respectable father of four who'd been ignoring Duny until this point. The sound drew the attention of this man, who immediately deduced the would-be assassin's intentions.

As Duny's finger lit on the trigger, the man said, "Christ almighty."

Kamp heard the shout and ducked an instant be-fore the bullet whizzed past. He hurtled into the bushes at the roadside. Duny couldn't reload fast enough to fire again or even to protect himself from the man who clambered down from his carriage and clouted Duny on the ears.

B.H. GRIGG COULDN'T RETURN to Bethlehem, couldn't practice his livelihood, couldn't resume his life. But the knowledge he'd gleaned on his journey to Vir-ginia was enough for him to initiate the escape from his predicament.

One of the individuals who'd taken the death pic-ture of Kamp was assuredly Adams, the woman hunting him. Grigg didn't know the identity of the man who'd been with her. He thought it might've been MacBride, the fiend in charge of the Pennsylva-nia Hospital for the Insane. But MacBride didn't have wavy, blond hair. Who was with Adams?

He'd solved the mystery of whether and how Kamp had died and then returned to life. But how did Kamp get to the Hospital for the Insane? And how did he get out?

Grigg hitched a ride on a U.S. Mail carriage to Washington, D.C. by convincing the driver he was a

government official who'd been ambushed by brig-
ands. From there, he spent the last of his cash on a
train ticket back to Philadelphia.

32

Joachim S. Thaler knew he needed muscle, not necessarily for actual protection but to project power, to intimidate and deter. He pulled the front door closed behind him, locked it and took in the scene below from his front porch.

He saw carriages streaming in from the south, citizen spectators. From the north, people walked in ones, twos and small groups. In spite of his order that all workers report to the mine, they were going to town for the execution of their comrade.

There would be unrest, no doubt, and almost certainly violence. But Thaler knew that in the back of every miner's mind was the realization they needed the work and the pay just to survive. Wholesale insurrection would make their lives worse.

So, Thaler surmised, whatever trouble might arise would be a token gesture, at best. Aodh Blackall was a hero to them but still a man destined to go the way of all martyrs. His death would justify their anger and satisfy their bloodlust at the same time. The miners would feel better in the end. And he'd been assured the execution would happen inside the jail and out of sight of would-be rioters.

He called to the foreman whose team was laying paving stones in the driveway.

"Go tell the Swedes."

"Sir?"

"When we go to town, you and your crew are coming with me."

FINDING ALISTAIR MACBRIDE wouldn't be the hard part. The challenge for B.H. Grigg would be getting the information he wanted without being captured. In spite of his considerable ability to escape, Grigg had no intention of going back in the Pennsylvania Hospital for the Insane.

And so when Grigg stepped off the train in Philadelphia, he walked to the hospital, assuming that MacBride wouldn't have arrived for work yet and that when he did, the doctor would enter through the front.

Grigg stood beside the road, fifty yards from the wrought iron gates at the entrance and the guard house beside it. He intended to flag down MacBride's carriage, deceive the doctor via subterfuge, then demand information, by force if necessary.

An hour passed. MacBride should have arrived by now. Maybe finding him would be the hard part after all. Grigg felt sweat beads forming beneath his mustache. Someone could recognize him as an escapee. And Adams might not be far behind.

He straightened his coat and hat, then strode to the entrance, hailing the guard with a nervous wave.

"I say, you sir."

A man emerged from the guard house and inspected Grigg, but he didn't speak.

Grigg moved closer, looking at the gates and the high brick wall surrounding the property and then at the guard.

"I'm afraid this won't be enough."

The guard gave him a flat expression. "Enough for what?"

"Oh, no, no, no, not enough at all."

"State your business."

Grigg looked past the guard. "I need to speak to the man in charge here. What's his name, McBurr? I need to talk to him."

The guard shifted his weight and straightened his spine.

"Send a letter."

"You don't understand. They're coming now. Right now. This won't be enough."

Grigg waved his arms at the hospital gates as he said it and then jammed his hands in his coat pockets.

"Who's coming?"

"Them."

"Who's them?"

Grigg lowered his tone, leaned in and said, "They deploy their foul fiends to kill the innocent."

The guard put his hand to the pistol at his right hip. Grigg's eyes went wide.

"*I'm* not the threat. The threat is there. A secret society! A murderous cabal!" He turned and jabbed his finger toward the city. "They're coming. I need to speak to the man in charge. To explain. Let me in."

The guard walked back to the guard house, closed the door behind him and locked it.

Grigg went to the door and started pounding on it. "Please, I beg of you. Just give him a message from me. Tell him—"

"He's not here," the guard shouted through the door.

Grigg kept pounding. "What did you say?"

The door swung open and the guard put his pistol to Grigg's forehead. "Doctor isn't here."

"Where is he?"

Grigg raised his eyes to look at the barrel.

"Out for the day. Now if you'll—"

"Sir, I have very important information for the doctor. It will save us all."

"Well, in that case you're doomed."

"Why's that?"

"Doctor's up the line."

"Up the what?"

"He went to Mauch Chunk, okay? If you know where that is, you can go find him." The guard slammed the door and muttered, "Goddamn lunatic."

WHEN KAMP REACHED THE CABIN, Angus was locking the door and heading down the steps.

"Morning, cousin. "

Kamp had never seen Angus startle before, but he did so now.

"Oh, Jesus, you gave me a fright. *Wie gehts*?"

"It goes, it goes. You?"

Angus buttoned his wool coat and picked up his rifle, a Sharps.

"Going hunting?"

Angus scanned the woods surrounding the cabin. "Not as such."

He tried to walk past Kamp, who took him by the elbow.

"Then where?"

Angus looked him in the eye and said, "Where I'm going, cousin, you can't come."

"She can take care of herself."

"Then what are you doing here?"

33

It was supposed to happen inside the jailhouse. The Honorable J. Blasius Grimp wanted it that way. Black Feather wanted it that way. The hanging frame was supposed to be built on the ground floor, at the front of the gallery.

The pines they intended to use were freshly felled and bucked at the base of Sleeping Bear Mountain and then hauled to Black Feather's sawmill at the edge of town. From there, a team of two draft horses pulled the lumber in a wagon to the base of the courthouse steps. The horses were flanked by officers wearing black wool uniforms and holding gleaming shotguns with fine maple stocks that blazed in the morning sun.

All who saw the passing wagon knew its purpose. Those who weren't watching the road when it passed heard the clop of hooves and caught the smell of pine. Talking ceased when the wagon went by, as if it already held the corpse of the condemned man, rather than the materials for the gallows. From the selection of the trees to the delivery of the lumber, it all went smoothly and fast.

The trouble started with the carpenter, a Mennonite named Horn. He didn't know why they'd summoned him to the courthouse. He thought they probably wanted him to build a chair or a desk.

When they told him they wanted a hanging frame, the carpenter surveyed their faces and said, "No."

The sheriff said, "Hanging is tomorrow. And this convict, Blackall, he's a scoundrel, a fiend. He deserves punishment."

Horn said, "Vengeance is mine, sayeth the lord. I won't do it."

The sheriff knew he wasn't making any headway, so he lied.

"Blackall has done things to children. Horrible things."

"I don't know that he did or he didn't," Horn said.

The Honorable J. Blasius Grimp said, "We'll pay."

"Nope."

"Best money you'll ever see."

Horn fixed his gaze on the judge, adjusted his hat and said, "You'll pay me twenty dollars for coming up here for nothing. And then I'll be on my way."

Grimp raised his hand to strike the carpenter, but the sheriff intervened before he could land the blow.

Shouting and cursing ensued, but Horn would not be moved. When the commotion died down, the sheriff instructed the town bursar to open the cash box and handed Horn his twenty dollars.

As he walked away, Horn said, "Just remember that him that guides the accused, he don't want to stand on no rickety platform. And then there's him that stands underneath and pulls the lever. The weight of the drop could bring the whole works down on him."

They watched the carpenter disappear down the road carrying his toolbox, and the sheriff said, "Yah, well, it won't happen now, not today."

"What won't?"

"The *benka*."

"The what?"

The sheriff faced the judge. "Ach, the hanging. That was the only guy who could do it right, and fast."

J. Blasius Grimp wondered what the world was coming to if a man would turn down good money for building an instrument of justice.

He fished the round tin from the pocket of his robe, took another pinch of Turtle Island Tobacco Bits, settled it between his lip and gum.

"Fucking Mennonites," he said.

GRIGG ONLY WANTED a hot bath, a shave and a clean outfit. When the train pulled into Third Street Station, he jumped from it and ran so fast that all Adams saw were the soles of his shoes.

No one could have known he was back in Bethlehem, and so great was his desire to get clean and feel safe that he sprinted in the direction of his house. While he ran, he considered the possibility that the Order had ransacked his home or even burned it to the ground.

When his house came into view, however, nothing seemed amiss. He retrieved the skeleton key he kept in the downspout and turned it in the lock. But before he turned the knob and pushed the door open, Grigg hesitated.

He recalled a story about an incident involving a businessman, a Black Feather executive named Ownby, who'd put his hand to a warm knob and twisted it an instant before his house exploded. At least that's what Kamp had told him.

Kamp swore the Order had set a trap for the doomed Ownby, and Grigg saw no reason they wouldn't do the same to him. He went around to the back of the house, dismantled the window frame next to the backdoor, removed the pane, and set it on the porch.

As soon as he was inside, Grigg saw that a wire had been strung across the back door. He stepped closer to inspect it and saw that the wire was attached to an apparatus affixed to a bundle of dynamite. He saw the same setup inside the front door, too.

Grigg moved as quickly as he dared, careful not to take a step or open any drawer without first checking for a trap. He guessed he'd have an hour or more before whoever they'd assigned to keep watch took notice and alerted them to his presence. He took in a long breath, sighed and realized he needed a hot bath to put himself right, no matter the risk.

He started a fire in the stove, heated the water and filled the tub. Grigg stepped into the bath and gently lowered himself, letting the pain, distress and grime wash off. He gave himself a clean shave and then tilted his head back and allowed himself to luxuriate in the hot water.

HE'D ALMOST GIVEN UP on checking for signs of life inside the lawyer's house. Each day for the past week, he'd walked slowly by the house and scanned for an open window or a new milk bottle on the stoop. Checking had become a habit, a fruitless compulsion. But today, from a distance he saw a thin spiral of smoke issuing from the chimney. Grigg was there.

Grigg had just drifted off in the hot water when he heard boot heels on his front steps and then a loud rap on the door. He leapt from the tub, pulled on a pair of pants and tiptoed down the stairs.

He peeked through the wooden blinds of the bay window and saw shiny black boots and wool pants. The man wore a holster on his belt, and across his chest, he held an eight-gauge shotgun. If the man tried to break through the door, he'd hit the trip wire, and that would be that. But if Grigg warned the man, he'd diminish the chances for his own escape.

Grigg turned and retreated back upstairs. The knocking on the door resumed, and then the man called out.

"I know you're in there. Answer the door."

Grigg didn't recognize the voice. *Just give me a minute to get out of here and then you can blow yourself to kingdom come.*

He hustled to put on his best suit and retrieve the wad of cash he always kept stashed for an emergency.

"Mr. Grigg, I just need to talk to you. Open the door."

Grigg carried his shoes to the bottom of the stairs and laced them up. The banging on the door intensified, and he saw the doorknob wiggling. If the man outside put his shoulder into it, it just might give.

"I know you're there."

He finished tying his shoes, grabbed his coat and made for the back of the house.

"I'll break down the door if I have to."

Yeah, do that, asshole. Grigg hoisted one leg over the windowsill.

The man shouted, "Listen, I know what they're doing. I seen it in their records. I know they're after you. The police and Black Feather. The Order of the Raven. I know all about it."

Grigg recognized the voice now. He pulled his leg back in the window, raced to the front of the house and opened the blinds to see the brash, violent Officer Falko Stier readying himself to break down the door.

"Stop!"

STIER NEEDED NEXT TO NO CONVINCING that he should accompany Grigg on the next train to Mauch Chunk. He told Stier to keep an eye out for a slight woman with blond hair.

They boarded without incident, although the packed train thrummed with a nervous energy. All the talk they heard centered on a single topic: the execution of an Irish fiend named Aodh Blackall.

THE HONORABLE J. BLASIUS GRIMP SPAT tobacco juice on the muddy ground and said to the sheriff, "Who else can we get to build this goddamned thing?"

The sheriff removed his wool hat and scratched his scalp. "Ach, I don't know."

"How hard can it be?"

"Harder than you think."

Grimp said, "Well, get whoever you can, and get 'em to work fast."

The sheriff then recruited the one group of men he knew was available, the poor bastards in his jail. When asked if they could do it, all of them professed to have the skill to build the gallows.

The sheriff quizzed them all, selected the four who seemed least likely to fail, and promised them an early release if, in twenty-four hours, they could build a suitable gallows. All agreed.

The four convicts immediately dispensed with the notion that the structure would be built inside the jail. Hauling the planks up the steep stairs and then cutting them all to fit the dimensions of the room would cost them too much time. Much easier to do it outside, they said.

Twenty-four hours later the hanging frame stood ready enough, though if one looked closely, there was a discernible tilt to it. And just prior to finishing, the four convicts who'd been promised early release upon completion of the structure, abandoned the job and vanished down the street.

To J. Blasius Grimp's surprise, one convict returned, hanging his head.

Grimp said, "Who's this responsible fellow?"

The sheriff said, "I believe that's Smitty." He struck the man with backhanded knuckles to his ear and said, "That's for the them who didn't come back."

Grimp said, "What in god's name *did* you come back for?"

Without looking up, the man mumbled, "Tired. Nowhere to go."

THE SIGHT OF THE GALLOWS caused the town of Mauch Chunk to pulse with dread, anticipation and arousal. Delaying the execution for a day allowed the pressure to build, as those who'd been forced to wait another day grew impatient and as the late arrivals added to their ranks.

The local taverns were packed, and boarding houses bulged with the curious who'd come to see and even participate in the grisly show, if the opportunity arose.

And still more carriages rolled into town, though some veered off the main road and up the drive to the mansion on the mountainside.

THE HONORABLE J. BLASIUS GRIMP gazed up at the gallows and then back down at the square in front of the jail. Men had begun swarming on street corners. Grimp felt the mood of the street, combustible and murderous.

And then the jeering started.

"Hey, Judge, I don't think that gallows is gonna work."

"You can't kill no one with that rig, 'specially not a big son of a bitch like Blackall."

"Yah, *mebbe* we oughtta try it out with a little son of a bitch first."

"Yah, why don't we try it out with you, Judge, see if it holds!"

Sardonic laughter ensued. Alone, none of them would dare challenge him, but together, now that each man's identity had begun to melt into the mob, they'd give no thought to harming him.

No telling what they'll do once they see Blackall swing at the end of the rope, Grimp thought.

He wasn't one for backing down, though, not for anyone who might break his laws and certainly not for the stained rabble in the street.

NYX KNEW MORE than Angus thought she did. She'd watched him so many times that she could make her own rimfire cartridges and load all sixteen with one in the chamber. And Angus didn't think she knew how to handle the Henry, but she did.

Nyx wore brown trousers, a white cotton shirt and work boots. She added a grey wool cap and a dark green wool jacket with black buttons, instead of brass. She'd found the jacket in Kamp's slaughter-house two years before and kept it without telling him, tailoring it to fit her frame and waiting for an opportune occasion such as this.

She carried the Henry in a canvas duffel that also held enough food to last as long as she'd have to wait.

34

The ruse would work, not because his disguise was particularly convincing but because they wouldn't suspect anyone, least of all a fugitive, to sneak into jail.

From a street corner, hiding in the mass of men, Kamp had watched the scruffy convicts erect the structure and then steal away as soon as the opportunity arose. When it did, he saw his chance. He focused on the convict who looked most similar to him and chased the man down an alley. Kamp had cornered him, then offered to exchange clothes.

The convict realized that he stood a far better chance of escaping if he weren't wearing a prisoner's stripes and took the deal.

All Kamp had to do then was to trudge back to the jail, mumble a few words, absorb the requisite blow to the head, and he'd be safely inside. He assumed they wouldn't put him in the cell with Aodh Blackall, but maybe they'd put him close.

On his way to his cell, a bailiff slapped him hard on the back of the neck and said, "Welcome back, idiot."

The bailiff shoved him to the concrete floor, slammed the door and left. Kamp took a moment to orient himself. The cell to his right was empty, and in the one to his left, a man slumped in the corner.

"Aodh, Aodh."

The man stirred, but Kamp couldn't see his face.

Kamp raised his voice. "Hey, Blackall, it's me—"

"Yes, dear?"

The man rolled over and grinned. He had greasy hair plastered to the side of his face, and he was missing all his teeth. Definitely not Aodh.

ANGUS WAS UNACCUSTOMED TO ANXIETY, let alone panic, but now his heart slapped against his ribs. In the years since he'd left Bethlehem and moved to the woods, he'd taught himself to narrow down his world to his own activities, to need only himself.

But then Kamp had appeared, followed by Nyx. The two of them worked their way into his life, his routines. Especially Nyx. Angus hadn't known the depth of his need for them until now. And now they were both gone, both about to put themselves in harm's way.

Angus put a pistol in his belt and locked the door behind him when he left.

EMMA WYLES NEVER ASKED KAMP what happened to him while he was at war. She wasn't curious about the battles he fought or the horrors in which he participated or simply endured. By the time he returned from the war, she'd traveled far and wide herself and withstood hardships of her own.

It wasn't that she didn't care. She loved Kamp as a person with whom one's life has been intertwined since before conscious memory. She felt affection for him now but along with it a deep ache for the boy he'd been and the lost man he'd become.

And much as she detested the realization, Wyles felt sorrow for herself, for the way her livelihood and her life had been torn down.

She caught a fragment of memory, the moment her father collapsed in the front yard, how she pressed herself to his chest, taking handfuls of his wool coat, willing her breath into his lungs, and failing, pressing her head to his chest and listening to his heart beat its last.

Wyles blinked away the tears and sat straighter in the saddle as Bethlehem came into view. She'd never caved in to despair before and wouldn't now.

She realized how the enemies that plagued Kamp plagued her as well. The same forces that destroyed the upright Jonas and Rachel Bauer were those that ensnared the fiend Daniel Knecht and condemned Aodh Blackall to hang.

The men who'd driven Kamp and Shaw, Nyx and Angus onto the margins and into the shadows were all the same. They created one nightmarish scene after the other in order to distract and deflect, obfuscate and confuse. They did it for personal gain and personal enjoyment. They did it for the sake of evil but said it was for the common good.

Wyles' desperation and anger coalesced into purpose, as she pointed her horse in the direction of Bethlehem's South Side.

PICKLER DIDN'T HAVE TIME to ponder the mysteries of emotion or the machinations of men. A stack of new prescriptions lay on the counter beside his pharmacist's tools, and a line of customers stood before him, peppering him with questions and demands.

"Where's that liver tonic?"

"When's the talcum coming in?"

"Get more of that black licorice. My girl loves it."

Pickler wiped a bead of sweat from his brow with the back of his hand. If he'd had time to admit anything to himself, Pickler would have conceded that the runaway success of Native Plants and Medicines was running him ragged. He hadn't entered the ranks of his profession in order to accumulate wealth, but if that were the reward for his labors, so be it. And whether his success was engineered by the men who destroyed his competitor, well, that wasn't his business.

Pickler pushed away these thoughts as he stared into the swirls of the maple wood mortar, the last item he'd bought from Emma Wyles. He felt a fire in his elbow from so much grinding and pushed that away as well.

Of necessity he narrowed his world down to the task at hand, the ingredients in correct proportion, the scrape of the pestle in the bowl.

Pickler didn't hear her come in, didn't notice her shooing all of the customers out and then locking the door. He didn't become aware of her presence until the moment there was silence.

When he looked up, Emma Wyles was standing before him with a determination and ferocity he knew he had no chance of resisting. She didn't need to press a gun to his head.

Before he even knew what was happening, she'd packed his case with an assortment of medicines and bandages and guided him outside to her wagon.

Pickler managed only a feeble "What's this about?" as he climbed in.

35

Joachim S. Thaler stood on the veranda of the mansion on the mountainside and watched the fine carriages snaking through Mauch Chunk and then turning up the drive in his direction. He counted each one, checking them off a list in his mind.

Ten had arrived already. Three more to go. The last one, he assumed, would arrive after nightfall. Thaler also heard two dray wagons and a carriage depart the drive behind the house and move down the back road, headed for the mine.

If he'd simply called off the day's work without the distraction of the execution and its attendant hysteria, the miners would have been most suspicious. But most of them would skip work anyway, and ordering those that did report to vacate the

341

mine would allow the operatives to do their work without raising eyebrows.

KAMP MOVED CLOSER to the toothless man lying on the floor in the adjacent cell.

"Where is he?"

"Who?"

"Aodh Blackall."

The man furrowed his brow. "He tried to kill him."

"Who did?"

"Just imagine. They already condemned the poor bastard to hang. But the devil himself wanted him even sooner."

"Where's Blackall now?"

The man looked at Kamp with disgust.

"He put a blade straight to the kidneys. There. Right there."

Kamp noticed the bloodstain on the floor.

The man continued, "Didn't kill him, though. *Mebbe* he didn't want to."

"How's that?"

The man rubbed the scraggly whiskers on his chin.

"*Mebbe* Padgett just wanted Blackall to suffer all the more."

He turned his head to the side and studied Kamp's face.

The man said, "Heeeey."

"What?"

"You and me been together in this cell for, what, ten days now?"

Oh, Jesus.

Kamp said, "It's been eleven days."

The man screwed up his face. "Ten, eleven, don't matter. That's not my point."

"Eleven."

"So, we been stuck in here together goin' on two weeks."

"And?"

The man sat up and leaned toward Kamp. "And you ain't never asked me one goddamn question. Not one."

"So what?"

"So today, yer just full of questions. How come?"

Kamp returned the man's stare. "Don't worry, I won't ask any more."

"Good."

"You know what? I'm tired of your bullshit."

The man's eyebrows shot up. "What did you say?"

"You heard me."

The man turned and said, "Somethin' ain't right here."

Kamp grabbed a handful of the man's shirt through the bars. "Shut your mouth."

The man pulled away and crawled to the far side of his cell.

"Fellow who was here before, in all the days we spoke, never uttered so much as one curse. Not one. You ain't him. Matter of fact, when Smit came in here, I thought, ya know, he looked like a fella who's wanted for a crime. Fella with a reward on his head. An' then Smit flew the coop when they took him out to build them gallows."

"Wrong."

"And now you's here."

"You're mistaken."

The man gritted his teeth. "Like hell I am."

"If I'm a wanted man, why would I put myself in jail?"

"Don't know and don't care. Guard!"

SHORT PINKY SHOWED UP at the mine on the morning of the execution. He knew his employer, Black Feather Extraction, had told the miners to stay home, but he couldn't bear the thought of going to town to witness the death of a hero.

He wouldn't have anything to do at the mine anyway, because no one else would be there. And that would be perfect for him. He needed the quiet, all he wanted to do was lose himself in a penny dreadful called *The Black Spider.* He settled himself on the stool where he'd passed so many days as a trapper, lit his candle and started reading.

E. WYLES MADE PICKLER sit next to her for the ride up to Mauch Chunk. She explained the history of his employer, Black Feather Consolidated. She wanted him to understand his function as one of their unwitting cogs.

Wyles didn't intend to shame the young pharmacist. Rather, she wanted him to realize for the first time that he was putting a pleasant face on their murderous machine.

She explained how a small group of men calling themselves Black Feather controlled all of the mining, manufacturing and transportation interests in the region. She also described how their power enabled them to control the court, namely the Big Judge Tate Cain, with whom they were closely connected. She finished by telling him how Black Feather's push into pharmaceuticals spelled her own demise.

Pickler kept quiet while she talked, except to let out an occasional "gosh" or, "I didn't know that."

After she finished, neither of them spoke, and the only sounds were the creak of wagon wheels, the jingle of brass fittings in the reins and a nicker from the horse.

She glanced at Pickler, who stared into the far distance, mouth open.

After another minute, he pulled in a long breath and said, "I just have one question."

"Go ahead."

"Why Black Feather?"

"What?"

"Black Feather. How come they called the whole thing Black Feather? Where does that come from? What does it mean?"

Wyles felt a wave of irritation, and she pulled the horse to a stop.

"Have you heard a word I've said?"

"Yes, I have."

"The name doesn't matter. What matters is—"

Pickler's expression hardened. He stared into the distance and said, "Of course it matters."

She felt the rage rise from her chest into her throat.

"Now listen here. Black Feather is using—"

"Excuse me, madam, if I may. You've made a number of allegations, very disturbing allegations which, if true, call into question the substance of my—"

"I haven't called your—"

Pickler raised his voice, and the color bloomed in his cheeks. "Called into question the very substance of my character. Now, if you'll please turn the wagon around. I must return to the shop. For the customers and for the patients."

"You're coming with me. You need to see it for yourself." Wyles snapped the reins, and the horse broke into a trot. "And you need to make amends."

"To whom?"

"To me."

SHORT PINKY NEVER PEEKED at the end of the story to see how it would turn out. As he reached the last chapter of *The Black Spider*, his main concern was that his candle would burn all the way down before he could finish.

He strained to keep his fingers from skipping to the last page. Short Pinky took a deep breath and calmed himself. *Take your time.*

He'd been reading for four hours straight and had entered a state of deep focus. Short Pinky didn't feel the ache in his neck or hear the noises at the mouth of the mine.

Ten more pages to go. He read another and another until he reached the second to last page. Short Pinky felt the twinge of sadness at finishing the tale and then noticed a problem. The last page was missing, ripped off.

He felt a stab of exasperation and dread that snapped him from his reverie. Now the noises in the mine came into his consciousness.

A large hand clapped him on the shoulder, and he turned to look up at a man in a black wool uniform.

Short Pinky said, "I, I just came here to read my book. Is that okay?"

THEY HADN'T CHECKED KAMP for weapons on his way into the jail, and so he'd trudged in with the pepperbox pistol tucked into his left boot.

The man in the cell next to him yelled again.

"Guard!"

Kamp said, "You have nothing to gain."

"Guard, there's a fugitive here!"

"Listen, they'll never let you collect the re—"

An iron door slammed, silencing both Kamp and the man in the next cell.

They heard footfalls and clinking shackles getting closer, as the guards led Aodh Blackall down the corridor.

36

Kamp put his hand to the pepperbox. If Aodh Blackall recognized him, perhaps the two of them could attempt an escape.

He expected to see Aodh first, but instead the familiar form of the Reverend A.R. Eberstark, outfitted in a robe and somber black stole, came into view,

Kamp's hopes of breaking out vanished when he saw Aodh. The man he remembered—upright and powerful—was gone. Aodh Blackall was now hunched over and bent sideways at the waist, head down and shuffling, manacled hands hanging limply in front of him.

And he was surrounded by three police officers in blue wool uniforms. Behind them were two more armed men, Black Feather company police, and bringing up the rear was the sheriff.

PEOPLE STARTED PACKING THE SQUARE at dawn and soon pressed shoulder to shoulder, jockeying to get and keep the best view of the gallows. Emma Wyles felt safe moving freely in the crowd without worrying she'd be spotted, that is, if she could move at all.

She didn't care to see the execution. Rather, she knew all the town dignitaries would be in attendance, and more importantly, so would the men who ran Black Feather. The public demise of an enemy represented a victory for them, a confirmation that the law was on their side. She wanted to see these men, identify them in person so that she'd know to whom to press her case when the time came.

She also knew that somewhere in the teeming mass, or just outside it, would be Kamp and Nyx. Neither would stand by and merely witness the deed. While she feared they'd be killed if discovered, Wyles realized they had to take action, as did she. She took Pickler by the wrist.

"Stay close," she said.

JOACHIM S. THALER STEPPED UP into his fine carriage, and once he was seated, the driver closed the door behind him. Soon the carriage began to roll, and the gang of Swedes, eight in all, jogged behind it.

Thaler had told the associates who'd already arrived at his home to stay there and watch the spectacle from his veranda. He'd provided them with an assortment of telescopes and Porro prism binoculars for just this purpose.

Some of the guests, of course, wished to have a closer view, although Thaler warned against them "descending into the madness."

Thaler himself had no qualms about going. He'd be surrounded by guards, but more than that, he needed to be there. The town belonged to Black Feather, and his presence would be a reminder.

KAMP STOOD NO CHANCE of overwhelming the men surrounding Aodh Blackall. He was locked in his cell, and the pepperbox only held four rounds. Blackall himself was in no position to orchestrate a jailbreak, even if he knew Kamp was there.

So, Kamp resolved to keep quiet. The man in the next cell did not.

He said, "Sheriff, I need to speak with you this instant."

The Reverend A.R. Eberstark hissed, "Not now, man."

"This man in the cell beside me has evil intentions!"

Eberstark shot a look at Kamp, and the blood drained from the reverend's face, as if he'd seen a demonic phantasm.

The man persisted. "Sheriff, you must know, there's a plot at work here, a plot to undo the hanging."

"Pipe down, Curtis," the sheriff said.

"But this fiend next to me is *proof.* He's not who you think he is. In fact, he's none other than—"

A loud boom echoed down the hallway, followed by the sound of shattering glass.

"For the sake of Christ," the sheriff said, "what now?"

A Black Feather officer said, "Irish confetti."

The sound of bricks pelting the front of the building intensified. The sheriff pushed to the front of the group and then hurried down the hall and out of sight.

The officers closed in around Aodh, who glanced at Kamp. Kamp couldn't tell whether Aodh recognized him or not.

Soon the procession had moved down the hall and out of view. Kamp knew they'd gone out the front door by the raucous cheer that went up outside.

The man in the next cell turned to Kamp, and said, "I had to tell the sheriff. You understand, don't you?" Then he sniffed loudly and said, "If you're stuck over there in that cell, it's not as if you can do anything to me."

Kamp said, "Sure about that?"

ANGUS SAW THE FIRST BRICK SLAM into to the building's façade and saw the next one sail through a window on the ground floor.

Angus hated crowds, but now he felt compelled to descend into the mob that pulsed and pushed toward the gallows. He assumed that no one would recognize him. Given his status as an outsider and an outcast, though, if his identity were discovered, Angus knew he'd be torn to shreds.

But Kamp had to be close by, and Nyx as well. Angus didn't know when or how he'd be able to help, but he knew he had to be there when the action started.

He peeked out from under the brim of his hat and watched a half a dozen more bricks cascading onto the gallows before a man emerged from the courthouse. Angus recognized him as the sheriff.

The sheriff stood on the gallows platform and said, "By order of the Honorable J. Blasius Grimp,

Carbon County Judge, you are hereby commanded to cease and desist all seditious activities."

A man next to Angus yelled, "All *what* activities?"

The sheriff zeroed in on him and said, "Anything that would start a riot."

Another man said, "Or else what?"

The sheriff gestured to the rooftops around the square. Dozens of uniformed men had been stationed there with rifles.

A low murmur rippled through the crowd, and not another brick was thrown. The sheriff motioned to the front door, and the Reverend A.R. Eberstark appeared, followed by Aodh. When he stepped into the daylight, Aodh glanced out over the people, and when they saw him, a great cheer arose.

KAMP HEARD THE FRONT DOOR OPEN again and then footfalls coming back in his direction. Otherwise, the jailhouse was quiet.

The sheriff appeared, and before he said anything, the man in the next cell started talking.

"Sheriff, do you know who this man is?"

"Yah, it's Smitty."

"Ach, *no.*"

"Okay, tell me. Who is he?"

"He's that fugitive that's been on the loose. From Bethl'em. Just look at him. That ain't Smit."

"It ain't?"

"Jesus boom, it's that murderer, Nickel Glock."

The sheriff turned to Kamp. "What's your name?"

"Smitty."

The man went apoplectic. "It ain't him. It ain't!"

"It looks like him."

"Yah, but it *ain't*. Why, just look at that scar there on the side of his head. Smit didn't have no scar like that."

The sheriff unlocked the door to Kamp's cell, unholstered his pistol and stepped in. He grabbed Kamp hard by the chin and said, "Show me."

Kamp turned his head so that the sheriff could see the star-shaped scar on his left temple where the Minié ball had entered and where Major Eustachius Fosdick had sewn him back up.

The sheriff studied the scar for a long moment and motioned for the man in the next cell to come closer.

"See, see what I—"

The sheriff raised his pistol and fired, putting the bullet between the man's eyes. Before the sheriff could turn back to him, Kamp pressed the barrels of the pepper-box to the sheriff's throat.

The sheriff said, "You won't make it out of here, Glock, not without my help."

"It's Kamp."

37

Shaw searched the cabin, then the woods around the property, and she didn't find her father. It wasn't strange for him not to be there, but he usually told her he was leaving. Then again, she'd woken late, having had a succession of nightmares, each worse than the previous one and each involving Kamp.

At dawn, real sleep had finally overtaken her, but now her father was gone. She remembered him saying that a hanging was to take place in town, someone she didn't know, and he'd warned her to stay away. Her nightmares had involved the execution.

"Come on," she said to Autumn.

"Where are we going?"

"To town."

ANGUS ELBOWED HIS WAY as close to the gallows as he dared, a few rows back, close enough to get a clear look at the police officers who formed a wall in front of the hanging frame. Each held a shotgun across his chest.

When the Reverend A.R. Eberstark came out the front door of the jail and stepped onto the gallows, Angus looked at the ground, lest Eberstark recognize him. After that, Aodh appeared, shuffling and clinking like a worn out ghost.

From his vantage point, Angus could see a spreading blood stain on the back of Aodh's shirt. Others noticed it as well, and once the loud cheering died down, men began shouting from the crowd.

"Ain't it enough to kill him? You had to cut him first?"

"At least let him die like a man."

"And, Jaysus, what's that clown doing up there? Where's the priest?"

Angus felt the anger and unrest surging through the crowd and saw anxiety in the faces of the officers who surrounded Aodh.

One of the officers said, "Sheriff should be here."

The murmuring in the crowd grew louder and the throng began to surge toward the gallows.

The sheriff emerged, and the energy in the mob ebbed again. All eyes focused on him and not on the man who followed close behind, who wore plain clothes and a slouch hat.

Joachim S. Thaler had stepped out of his fine carriage and climbed onto its roof to get a better look and to project his authority. As soon as the sheriff emerged from the jailhouse, Thaler noticed something amiss.

The sheriff's movements were stiff and tentative, not at all his normal bearing. He noticed, too, the man behind the sheriff. In his conversation about the hanging with the judge and the sheriff, no one had mentioned an attendant. The man behind the sheriff didn't belong there.

Thaler surmised that the man was pressing the barrel of a pistol to the sheriff's kidneys.

He knew, though, that if he were to raise an alarm, the scene would explode. The conspirator would start shooting, and chaos would descend.

He decided to address the matter personally and quietly, if possible. If he could get there unnoticed, he could foil the plot, whatever it was.

FROM THE EDGE OF THE MOB, the disgraced district attorney B.H. Grigg and Bethlehem police officer Falko Stier saw a man with wavy golden hair combed straight back and wearing a bespoke suit, climbing down from the roof of a fine carriage and threading his way through the throng.

Grigg said, "That's him."

"Who?"

"The guy in charge. Thaler. That's who we want."

Falko Stier started pushing his way forward before Grigg finished the sentence. Grigg followed Stier through the hole he made. They'd have to cover a good fifty yards to intercept Thaler.

Stier led with his forearms and elbows, knocking spectators left and right. Grigg followed close behind, and they their way steadily forward.

But their progress didn't go unnoticed by several of the police officers on the roof who aimed their rifles at the pair.

THE SHERIFF STEPPED ONTO THE GALLOWS and motioned for two of the officers to bring Aodh to him. The mob erupted again.

"This ain't right."

"You'll burn in hell for this, sheriff."

"At least let him say his last!"

The sheriff said, "He had his say in life."

So preoccupied was the sheriff with affixing the noose and quieting the mob that he didn't notice the platform beneath their feet beginning to sway.

E. WYLES NOTICED and said to Pickler, "It's going to fall."

"What is?"

"The gallows. Look."

Now Pickler saw it, too. "Oh, yah, I believe you're right. They should really fix that."

She didn't hear him, because she was already pressing forward in hopes of reaching the gallows before it collapsed. Her specific concern was the kid standing under the hanging frame. His job was to pull the lever that would release the trapdoor through which Aodh Blackall would drop.

If and when the gallows gave way, the boy would be crushed. Her progress was slow, however, and she feared she wouldn't get there in time to rescue him. So E. Wyles began to shout.

"That structure is unsafe. Stop this instant!"

Her shouts were drowned out by the rising din of the mob. All the police on the rooftops noticed was a woman waving her arms and pushing frantically toward the front. Two of the officers trained their rifles on her.

THE FOREMAN OF THE SWEDES, who'd been entranced by the thrill of a criminal's imminent demise, heard a woman's voice. He couldn't discern what she was saying, but it was enough to snap him from his trance. When he did, he noticed his boss, Thaler, was no longer standing atop his carriage.

His men hadn't noticed either. The foreman scanned the mob and caught a glimpse of Thaler's wavy locks, vanishing into the mob.

He clapped the biggest Swede on the shoulder and pointed at Thaler.

"Protect that man."

The Swedes barreled into the crowd, adding considerably to the commotion.

HAVING DENIED AODH HIS LAST WORDS, the sheriff had nothing to do but finish cinching the noose and positioning the condemned man on the trapdoor.

In the rehearsal for the execution, he'd instructed the kid whose job it was to pull the lever that the signal would be two sharp heel kicks to the platform. When he heard the kicks, the kid was to pull the lever. The sheriff had neglected to mention what the lever would do.

Now the sheriff directed Aodh to the stand on the trapdoor. Or at least to make it seem so.

Back inside the jail, with the pepperbox barrels pressed to the sheriff's neck, Kamp had instructed the sheriff to make it appear as if he intended follow through on the execution. The sheriff, having no reason to believe Kamp wouldn't make good on his threat, made certain that Aodh Blackall stood beside the trapdoor and not on it.

From his vantage point on the gallows, Kamp saw two familiar faces advancing on the platform, the district attorney Grigg and the cop who'd doused him with kerosene the year before and threatened to light him on fire.

What were they doing here?

Kamp scanned the rest of the crowd and saw a gang of burly blonde-haired men also pushing closer. To the side of the platform, he caught a glimpse his old friend, Emma Wyles. She, too, was forcing her way toward the gallows. All were converging on the hanging frame, though none seemed aware of the other's presence.

The one person Kamp didn't see coming toward him was Joachim S. Thaler, who emerged from the mob, ducked behind the gallows and climbed the wooden ladder on its side.

As soon as Thaler put his full weight on the first rung, the entire structure listed.

Kamp knew his moment had arrived.

38

The first bullet slammed into the beam to which the rope was attached. The second and third bullets hit the rope, fraying it.

Kamp saw that the hanging rope was ready to snap. He grabbed it with both hands and yanked hard. The rope didn't give. Joachim S. Thaler scrambled onto the gallows and tackled Kamp, and the weight of their bodies hitting the platform caused the entire frame to shift again, timbers straining to hold it upright.

The commotion roused Aodh from his stupor. He saw Kamp and Thaler tussling at his feet, and he delivered a kick to Thaler's ribs.

The fourth bullet hit the rope, and Kamp saw that it was nearly severed. He got to his feet and pushed Aodh sideways so that he stood on the trapdoor.

Kamp kicked the floor twice, the kid pulled the lever, and Aodh dropped. When the rope went taut, it held Aodh for a second, then another, and then it snapped. Aodh landed at the feet of the kid, who now knew the lever's purpose.

NYX BAUER STARED DOWN the scope atop the Sharps. Hours before, she'd set up on a ridge a couple hundred yards up on the mountainside, digging in and getting comfortable. She'd covered her cheeks and chin with charcoal. With the combination of Kamp's sniper jacket and the dark grey wool forager's hat, she'd be invisible to anyone in town.

Through the scope she'd watched the crowd form below, watched the officers take their positions on rooftops that surrounded the square. Nyx had a clear line of sight to the hanging frame and the people gathered around it.

She saw a man in a black uniform pull his pistol and aim at Kamp. Before he fired, she pulled the trigger and saw blood mist at the side of the man's head as he fell.

Nyx fired the next four rounds at the gallows rope, fraying it but not cutting it through. If she kept shooting, she'd reveal her position, and soon someone would start shooting back.

She reloaded, looked down the scope and saw another man advancing on the gallows, which had begun to teeter in a slow, steady rhythm. Nyx curled her index finger around the trigger, preparing to shoot him. But something gave her pause. She recognized the figure. Angus.

WHEN ANGUS SAW THALER TACKLE KAMP, he knew he had to help. And when the first bullet hit the beam, most spectators ran away, but Angus kept elbowing his way to the gallows. He didn't pull his pistol yet, knowing that would invite the rifles on the rooftops to blaze.

He assumed Nyx was doing the shooting and deduced she'd situated herself on the mountainside.

At least she's safe up there.

Kamp, however, was not. The officers who hadn't run away when the shooting started now advanced on him.

The sheriff, who struggled to keep his balance on the teetering platform called to the officers.

"Take him alive."

Angus grabbed the ladder on the side of the gallows and started climbing.

Kamp didn't see Angus and didn't know he was on his way up the ladder. All he knew was that three blue uniforms on the platform were coming for him and that Nyx wouldn't be able to shoot them all.

He looked at the trapdoor. Aodh should have been able to get out from under it by now, so Kamp readied himself and then jumped through the trapdoor himself.

As he made his leap, the hanging frame finally gave way, tilting heavily sideways while breaking apart and crashing into the square with the sounds of cracking planks and the wild shouts of men.

WHEN THE GALLOWS FELL, madness descended. Every urge, barely reined in—the pressure and the pain pent up so long—all of it burst forth now, and the riot began in earnest. Bricks smashed storefront plate glass. The undertaker's office was set ablaze.

The police on rooftops, gargoyles with stiff necks, white knuckles and rigid fingers wrapped around steel triggers, kept still. The order to fire had not been given.

But one officer, a man at the corner of the building closest to the gallows, caught the fever from the scene below. His body willed him to aim at a miner with a brick in his hand and yank the trigger.

The lack of precision in his movements caused the bullet to sail high into the second floor window of the jail, where a clerk had stood transfixed by the melee below. The bullet traveled straight through her throat. She clutched her neck with both hands, blood spurting between her fingers before she fell.

The sight of it, combined with the bullets slamming into the hanging frame, convinced the rest of the officers that it was time to open fire.

THE FIRST PERSON WHO SIGHTED NYX was Joe. He'd been hiding on the mountainside himself, waiting for the trouble to start. He'd heard the first report of the rifle, and he'd located Nyx's position before she fired the second shot.

She was sitting a hundred yards or so from him and a couple hundred feet higher up. There was no trail from him to her, only trees and boulders. Joe scrambled as best he could, staying low and bear crawling in her direction. He heard her firing again and again.

They must've seen her by now.

NYX STOPPED shooting only when smoke obstructed her view of the square. She kept her rifle raised and waited for the smoke to clear. The next glimpse she caught was that of a Black Feather man with his truncheon raised over Angus's head.

Smoke covered the scene again before she could get the shot. Nyx pulled in a long breath and waited. But the smoke only thickened, so Nyx sprang to her feet, breaking cover and sprinting down the mountain with the Sharps in her left hand and the Henry rifle in her right.

Joe saw her stand up and run, though he was still a good fifty yards away.

"Nyx, Nyx."

She didn't hear him, didn't hear anything. Her consciousness had narrowed to the ground immediately before her feet. She didn't feel anything, either, not the burning in her lungs, not even the bullet that whizzed past her left ear or the one that passed through the leg of her pants, grazing her left shin.

KAMP EXPECTED A HARD LANDING, but something cushioned his fall. Kamp rolled over on the ground and saw Aodh staring back at him.

"Let's go," Kamp said.

As he said it, he heard the cracking of posts and saw the hanging frame going over, bodies spilling off the platform and hitting the ground.

He was surprised to see his cousin land ten feet from him before the hanging frame itself crashed onto its side like a felled giant.

Kamp motioned to Aodh and said to Angus, "Help me."

As soon as Angus stood up and started making his way over, a Black Feather man came up behind him with a raised truncheon and brought it down hard on the side of Angus's head. Angus fell to his knees, a trickle of blood flowing down to his chin. The man stood over Angus and prepared to land another blow.

Still lying on the ground beside Aodh, Kamp raised the pepperbox pistol and fired once. The guard caught it in the shoulder but didn't fall.

He locked his gaze on Kamp and said, "Ach, you son of a bitch."

Before he could retaliate, and before Kamp fired another shot, Angus gave the Black Feather man a sharp uppercut to the testicles and dropped him to the ground.

Angus scrambled to Kamp, and together they attempted to move Aodh. Kamp tried picking him up under the arms and Angus by the legs, but he was too heavy.

Around them the melee swirled. The rioting miners who weren't setting new fires fought hand-to-hand with the men in uniform. Some miners wore brass knuckles, which aided in their efforts.

And still the officers on rooftops fired into the square. They aimed for men making mischief, though most of their bullets missed.

WHEN NYX REACHED LEVEL GROUND at the base of the mountain, she still couldn't get a view of the square. A couple hundred yards from the fray, she stood for a moment, catching her breath, setting down the Henry and waiting for the smoke to clear.

When it did, Nyx saw Angus and Kamp struggling in vain to haul Aodh to safety. She also saw a man in uniform, the sheriff, not ten feet from Angus and Kamp, raise a pistol. As Nyx sighted the man in her scope, he fired.

An instant later she shot as well, hitting the sheriff in the chest and knocking him to the ground. Nyx dropped the Sharps, picked up the Henry and plunged into the melee.

SHAW HEARD THE DIN from a mile away. She put Autumn on her back and ran toward the plumes of smoke pushing into the sky.

By the time she reached the edge of town, the same carriages that had streamed in the day before were streaming out. Shaw had to veer off the road to avoid being trampled by wild-eyed horses. The gunfire intensified as they crossed the bridge into Mauch Chunk.

Shaw let Autumn slide from her back and turned to face her.

"You must stay here."

"Where's daddy?"

Shaw guided the little girl to a hiding place under the bridge.

"Where's daddy!"

"Don't move."

Shaw turned on her heel and ran for the center of town.

39

Kamp didn't see the sheriff standing behind him, but he heard the shot and felt the searing pain in his left shoulder blade. He heard a second shot and spun around in time to see the sheriff falling backward, blood spreading across his shirt at the center of his chest.

The foreman scanned the wreckage of the gallows and saw his employer, Joachim S. Thaler on the ground, face in the dirt. He motioned to his work gang and pointed to Thaler.

"Get him out of there."

The Swedes advanced on the square, knocking rioters out of their way as they moved.

When Thaler tried to push himself up onto hands and knees, he realized his forearm was broken at an odd angle. He saw Kamp and Angus, both bloodied and both still struggling to drag the doomed man away.

FALKO STIER CHARGED AHEAD. Grigg hesitated to ponder the likely ramifications of diving into the fray but then followed Stier in the wake the man made.

Stier became aware of the shooting behind him and noticed people scattering in front of him before he saw a figure pass by him, rifle blasting and not stopping to reload.

Nyx Bauer didn't recognize Stier or Grigg, though she'd been arrested by one and prosecuted by the other. She saw only Angus and Kamp struggling in vain to carry Aodh away.

THE FIRST OF THE SWEDES reached the spot where Joachim S. Thaler lay, cradling his broken arm. The Swede grabbed Thaler under the arms and lifted him to his feet.

Thaler motioned to Kamp and Angus and said to the rest of the Swedes, "Stop them. There's a hundred in it for each of you."

Kamp and Angus had just begun dragging Aodh away when they saw the Swedes. A moment later the first Swede fell, a bullet in his back. Then the next one clutched the side of his head and spun to the ground. Nyx was shooting them like so many tin cans on a split-rail fence.

She blasted her way across the square until she reached them, the last two Swedes fleeing before she could zero in on them with the Henry. Then a bullet hit her, and Kamp saw it happen. He recognized his jacket immediately and then the person wearing it. Until that moment, he'd hoped she'd stay hidden but knew she wouldn't.

Kamp could tell by the way she jerked sideways that the bullet entered midway up her torso. But she didn't fall and kept running straight for him and Angus. Kamp recognized the Henry, too, the weapon brought north decades before by another doomed soul. He had no idea how many shots Nyx had fired.

THE LITTLE GIRL DIDN'T LISTEN to her mother, because she couldn't bear the thought of hiding under the bridge alone and because she wanted to see her father.

Autumn trailed Shaw from a distance of a hundred feet or so, far enough so that her mother wouldn't notice but close enough not to lose sight of her. When Shaw vanished into the throng of rioters,

Autumn's heart began to pound as she sprinted forward.

Shaw focused only on finding Kamp. As she neared the jailhouse, she saw him on one knee, clearing dust from his eyes. She put her head down and barreled into the crowd, moving halfway across before she felt a heavy thud between her shoulder blades that sent the breath from her lungs and knocked her to hands and knees. Before she could turn to see who'd hit her, she felt a kick to the ribs and then hands tearing at her dress.

KAMP WAS UNAWARE of Shaw's predicament. When he wiped the dust from his eyes, all he saw was the familiar, begrimed visage of Antoine "Duny" Kunkle.

Duny slapped the hat off Angus's head and grabbed him by the hair. Angus swung for Duny's face, but Duny blocked it and punched Angus in the nose.

Blood poured from both of Angus's nostrils, and dazed as he was already from the earlier blow to the skull, Angus couldn't retaliate.

Duny said, "Look here, everyone. This here is none other than a freak, a societal deviant. This ain't a man at all. It's a lady!"

No one paid attention to him until he ripped the front of Angus's shirt, exposing the wrap Angus used to hide his breasts. Duny ripped at that, too, until Angus stood naked from the waist up, exposed to all in the square.

"See! See!" Duny yelled wildly. "Remember Agnes Kamp? Remember her? This is her. Pretending to be a man!"

Now, amidst the smoke and gunfire, a crowd formed around Duny and Angus. One man, red-eyed and drunk lurched toward Angus and grabbed his breast.

"I'll be goddamned," he said.

BY THE TIME SHE GOT WITHIN TEN YARDS of the wreckage of the gallows, Nyx understood the killing power of the Henry. She'd shot down half a dozen men.

She put the big boss, Joachim S. Thaler in her sights as he stole away, clutching his left arm.

Nyx sighted his forehead, just beneath his wavy blond hairline and put her finger to the trigger.

"I'm here. Help me."

Nyx recognized Angus's voice and turned to see him set upon by three men now. Nyx aimed and fired, hitting the first man just above his left ear and splattering gray matter on the other two, who ducked and ran along with Duny Kunkle.

Nyx took a moment to inspect Aodh, ashen and motionless in the dirt. She went to him and put her cheek to his lips to feel for breath.

Angus said, "We tried. We tried to move him. We couldn't."

"He's gone," Nyx said.

She stood up, put the Henry to Aodh's temple and pulled the trigger. The Henry didn't fire. She checked the breech, saw it was empty and tossed it to the ground.

Nyx took off Kamp's sniper jacket and put it on Angus before putting Angus's arm around her shoulder and leading him down the alley alongside the jail.

Nyx called back to Kamp. "Let's go."

40

Kamp hauled himself to his feet and began following Nyx and Angus. He scanned for threats as he moved, looking back over his shoulder one time.

When he did, Kamp saw a gang of men attacking someone. *Not my problem*, he thought. But then he caught a glimpse of Shaw's dress and then her hair. He wheeled around, raised the pepperbox pistol and fired.

One of the men grabbing Shaw put his hand to his lower back and felt the blood. He turned and found Kamp through the haze. He charged Kamp, who waited for the man to reach him, then turned the pistol sideways and brought it down hard on the man's skull, dropping him.

Kamp ran for Shaw, though once again thick black smoke swirled in the square, obscuring her and her attackers.

When he reached her, there were four men surrounding her, all with their hands on her body.

Kamp put the pepperbox to the neck of the first man and fired. Blood sprayed as he fell to the ground. The rest of the men let go of Shaw and set upon him, raining blows on his head and torso. He fired the last round of the pepperbox, hitting one of the men in the sternum.

They knocked Kamp to the ground, and more men joined in, all delivering kicks. He turned his head up to see the smoke clear enough for a sliver of blue sky to appear. And then the kicking stopped. Kamp's assailants dispersed.

Someone had driven them off, but he didn't know who until he rolled onto his back and looked up. It took a moment for him to recognize the faces of Grigg and Stier. And then he saw Shaw's face. She knelt down and cradled his face in both hands.

Kamp said, "I'm sorry, I'm sorry, I wanted to help Angus. And Nyx. I thought I could."

"Quiet, love."

She guided him to his feet as Grigg wrapped Shaw in his overcoat. Grigg and Stier guarded them as best they could.

The riot continued unabated, chaos now concealing them. The little girl still found them, running to Shaw and wrapping herself in the folds of Shaw's dress.

"I couldn't stay there, mommy. I was afraid." Tears spilled down the little girl's cheeks.

"I know, sweetheart."

Kamp looked down at his daughter and her shining eyes.

She looked up at him and said, "I love you, daddy."

Close by, a shot rang out and then a man's voice.

"And now here's the fella everyone's been looking for!"

Kamp turned, and there was Duny Kunkle again.

Falko Stier said, "Shut up, Duny."

"It's the wanted man in the flesh. Him and his Indian bitch. Glock, Kamp, don't matter what you call him. He's right goddamn there."

The remaining men in the square fell silent, and all eyes turned to Kamp.

Duny continued, "And since I'm the one what found him, and since I have this rifle and it's loaded, I'll just be taking him to collect my thousand—"

The first bullet hit Duny Kunkle between the eyes before he finished the sentence.

Kamp drew a breath and sighed. The next bullet entered Kamp's skull at the right temple, killing him instantly.

ADAMS MARVELED AT HER GOOD LUCK. She'd chased that slippery son of a bitch Grigg all the way to this godforsaken company dump. When Duny alerted her to Kamp's presence, the rest was easy.

Duny's corpse would only net her ten bucks, but Kamp's body was the real prize. A thousand for the bounty and a good deal more than that from Black Feather. And beyond that, beyond all of that, was the thrill.

She strode to where Kamp's body lay, fished through his pockets and she found what she wanted, the gold ring she'd lost a year before.

The next cold steel barrel was placed against Adams' own temple. When she stood up, her pistol was yanked from her hand by a large uniformed officer.

"What's this about?"

The Honorable J. Blasius Grimp stepped from behind the officers and said, "Disturbing the peace."

He removed the tin of Turtle Island Tobacco Bits from his vest pocket and put a large pinch inside his lip. Then he motioned to the officers to take Adams to the jail.

Autumn, who'd witnessed it all, threw herself down on Kamp's body. She pressed her ear to his chest, listened for a heartbeat and heard nothing.

"Daddy! Daddy!"

Shaw knelt beside her and cradled Kamp's face one more time.

By now Emma Wyles had reached them as well. She stood alongside Grigg and Stier, as the tears filled her eyes.

The only sound in the square was the little girl's wailing. When an officer in a black wool uniform tried to peel Autumn from her father's chest, Shaw set upon him, raining fists down on his head and back.

Grimp spat tobacco juice on the ground, shook his head and said, "Goddamned savages."

41

Joe knew about the price on his own head, of course. He'd known for the past seven years that if he were discovered in public, he'd suffer the same fate as Aodh Blackall and W.W. Kamp, or worse.

But his daughter and granddaughter remained in great danger, exposed in the center of the square. Lucky for him all of the attention was turned to Kamp's corpse, as the body had cash value.

When Joe reached them, Shaw was facing the Honorable J. Blasius Grimp.

"We will bury him," she said.

Grimp looked past her to a knot of policemen standing off to the side. He motioned to them, and one of them took Shaw hard by the shoulders. The rest lifted Kamp's body from the ground.

"No."

Shaw tried to slap Grimp across the face, but the police officer grabbed her wrist and twisted it.

Joe realized that one more aggressive move, and they would likely shoot her down. *Maybe that's what she wants*, he thought.

He approached slowly, acknowledging the officer who held his daughter. The officer gripped Shaw harder when he saw Joe.

Joe said, "It's all right. I'll take her."

Shaw turned to him.

"You can't. You can't just let them—"

Autumn tugged at the hem of Shaw's dress.

The little girl said, "We have to leave. Daddy's not here anymore anyway."

Shaw's body went slack, then she began to sob. The officer relaxed his grip, and Joe took her in his arms.

Joe departed the square, carrying Shaw, and his granddaughter walked beside him.

EMMA WYLES WATCHED the scene in the square until she felt confident that Shaw, Autumn and Joe wouldn't be harmed.

Then she turned to Pickler and said, "We're going."

Wyles knew Nyx and Angus had a head start, but both were wounded. And they may have run into trouble on the way back to their cabin, the only place they could go.

She sprinted from the square, and Pickler, who struggled to carry the medicine bag, shambled behind her. She figured she could find her way from town to Angus's cabin, but she was wrong.

Soon after departing the road, she and Pickler found what appeared to be a side trail, only to reach a cliff.

Wyles gritted her teeth and said, "Son of a bitch."

Pickler leaned against a tree, took off his hat and wiped the sweat from his forehead. Wyles put her head down and fought to stifle a scream.

A moment passed with neither of them saying anything until Pickler broke the silence.

"Ma'am?"

"Yes, Pickler."

"I think I found them."

"I doubt it."

Pickler stepped to the edge of the cliff.

"Down there."

He pointed to a spot in the forest a mile or so away, where black smoke had begun to billow.

THE SMOKE LED THEM straight to Angus's cabin. When they got within a hundred yards, Wyles slowed to a walk and listened. She heard no voices, only the crackling of burning timbers and loud popping that she took to be ignition of cartridges inside the cabin.

Wyles said, "Wait here," and she walked a wide arc around the cabin, now nearly engulfed in flames. She pushed down the memory of having been trapped with Shaw and Autumn in the cellar of their burning house years before as well as the thought that Nyx and Angus were inside.

When Wyles had nearly completed her circle, she heard shouts in the distance as well as barking dogs. Then Nyx burst from the front door of the cabin, clutching a canvas sack in one hand and a rifle in the other. Her body was bent at an odd angle as she stepped down from the porch, the back of her blouse soaked with blood.

"Nyx."

She didn't hear Wyles, or if she did, ignored her. Wyles followed her into the dense underbrush at the edge of the clearing, where she found Nyx struggling to lift Angus to his feet. The barking grew louder.

Wyles said, "Pickler," and soon the young pharmacist came running.

Nyx turned to Wyes and said, "Oh, you're here."

"Yes, and Pickler here is going to help you now." Wyles turned to Pickler and said, "Take them to Joe's."

"Where's that?"

She turned back to Nyx. "Show him. Understand? Nyx? Go to Joe's. Now."

Wyles picked up the canvas sack and the rifle and handed them to Pickler. Then she took the medicine bag by the handle and started walking in the direction of the approaching dogs.

Pickler put Angus's arm around his shoulder and said to Nyx, "Lead the way."

Wyles had only walked a hundred feet or so when the first dog, a Redbone Coonhound, reached her. It was followed by a Plott and then another Redbone. Soon, half a dozen dogs had Wyles backed up against a tall tree.

While the hounds bayed at her feet, she stood still. Thirty seconds later three men approached. Each wore an expensive-looking tweed hunting outfit with oiled boots, and they carried shotguns with fine steel barrels and maple stocks that blazed when the sun hit them.

The man in the lead tipped his cap to Wyles and gave a loud whistle. The dogs fell silent.

"A dreadful fire," the man said.

"Indeed."

"We ran here as soon as we saw the smoke."

Wyles noticed that the men were neither perspiring nor out of breath.

She said, "Yes, well, the cabin wasn't occupied."

Without emotion the man said, "Thank god. And please accept our humble apologies for the commotion." He gestured to the dogs.

Wyles inspected the men, whom she'd never seen before. They looked nothing like the locals. Perhaps they'd come up for the execution and stayed to go hunting. She doubted it. The first man spoke with an accent she couldn't place.

The lead man looked at the medicine bag and said, "Would you happen to be a doctor?"

"Not as such."

"Well, we won't trouble you further."

"Thank you."

The man tipped his cap again and whistled. The dogs bolted back in the direction they'd come, and the three men followed them.

GRIGG AND STIER SAT on a stoop across the square from the jail and watched the fire brigade hose down the embers of smoldering buildings. Then they watched as the coroner and his assistants went about the business of wrapping the corpses in winding sheets that gave the dead the appearance of outsize chrysalises.

Kamp's corpse was removed first and then the sheriff's, both placed in a police dray wagon and spirited away.

The pair noticed the Honorable J. Blasius Grimp talking to the coroner and then walking back into the jail.

Falko Stier rubbed the new whiskers on his cheeks and surveyed the scene. He motioned to the one body that hadn't been wrapped in a winding sheet, Aodh Blackall.

"Maybe they forgot about him," he said.

"Doubt it. More likely Judge wants him to rot," Grigg said. "To serve notice."

"Can't have that."

Stier stood up and crossed the square, straight to Aodh's body. He hooked his hands under Aodh's armpits and began dragging him.

"Hey. Leave him be." A uniformed officer advanced on Stier.

"Fuck you."

Stier kept dragging the body. The officer whistled to his fellow lawmen who came at once, truncheons at the ready.

Grigg sprinted across the square, waving his arms and saying, "Stop, stop at once."

The police turned their attention to him, and the first officer said, "Who are you?"

"B.H. Grigg, District Attorney, County of Northampton. May I know your name, please?"

"Well, I, it's important that you—"

Grigg continued. "And this is Captain Falko Stier, Bethlehem police."

"We don't need no help, fellas. Judge said leave this dead man be." He looked at Stier. "Now fuck off."

Stier let Aodh's body fall.

"That's it," he said.

Before he could lunge at the officer, Grigg grabbed a handful of Stier's shirt and stopped him. Then he turned back to the police officer.

Grigg said, "As I see it, you have at least two problems."

"How so?"

Grigg gestured to Aodh Blackall. "First, it's against the law to leave a dead body unburied."

"Don't matter."

"More to the point, this man isn't dead."

All eyes turned to Aodh, who'd begun to turn his head side to side.

The officer said with disgust, "Jesus boom." He unholstered his pistol and pointed it at Aodh.

Grigg said, "Pull the trigger, and you'll be arrested for murder."

The officer made a wry face. "Ach, but this god-damned guy's already supposed to be—"

Stier roared, "Get that goddamned judge out here. Now!"

JOE STOOD OUTSIDE the front door of his cabin, shot-gun propped against a post. Inside, Shaw packed everything she'd thought they'd need for their jour-ney.

It wouldn't take her more than a few minutes to prepare, but he thought that would still be too long. People had seen him in the square, and even though they might not know the exact location of his cabin, they'd find it soon enough.

He wasn't surprised when he heard footfalls ap-proaching on the trail. Joe was surprised, however, to see the familiar faces of Nyx and Angus. Both were bloody and ragged. Nyx carried a rifle and a canvas sack.

A young man Joe had never seen before trailed along behind them. Moments later, Emma Wyles appeared on the path, medicine bag in hand.

Joe jumped down off the porch, scooped Angus in his arms and carried him into the cabin ahead of Nyx, Wyles and Pickler. Once they were all inside, he locked the door. Wyles examined the gash on Angus's head, then retrieved a spool of catgut and a needle and started suturing.

Joe said, "We need to leave now."

"No," Angus said, "I ain't going nowhere."

Wyles finished the stitches and wiped the blood from Angus's face with a damp cloth.

Then she turned to Nyx and said, "Lie down on the table."

Joe said, "They saw me back there. They'll find us." Joe looked from Angus and then to Nyx, "Go back to your cabin."

"Can't. It burned."

"Who by?"

Nyx said, "I don't know. It was burning when I—"

"Me. I did it," Angus said.

Wyles peeled back Nyx's shirt to reveal the gunshot wound, a raw, ragged mess caked with clotted blood. Wyles scanned for an exit wound and found none.

"The bullet is still in there. I can go in and get it if—"

"Leave it," Nyx said.

She hauled herself to a seated position, and then she stood, though she was still bent from the pain. Nyx turned to Joe and said, "I'll stay here. I'll make sure they don't catch up with you."

Angus said, "Ach, there's no reason—"

Nyx said, "You're going with Joe. I don't know where you're going, Emma, or where—" She jerked her thumb at Pickler.

He cleared his throat and said, "Pickler."

"—or where Pickler's going. I'm not going anywhere. I'll just stay here for now and wait for him. And then Kamp and I can..."

Nyx read the facial expressions of Shaw and Joe, and she knew what they meant. Angus realized, too, that he was gone. Angus closed his eyes, pulled in a long breath, hung his head and let out a deep sigh.

The report of a rifle in the distance spurred them all to action. Joe picked up the last two boxes and went out the back door where two horses and a dray wagon awaited them.

He said to Shaw, "*Nichan, yukwe.*"

Shaw gathered Autumn in her arms and left. Angus followed them out, leaving Nyx, Wyles and Pickler.

Nyx focused on Wyles and said, "What about you?"

"We have business in town. You?"

Nyx picked up the canvas sack in her left hand and the rifle in her right. She straightened her spine and gave Wyles a flat stare.

"Best to finish all important matters once started."

42

"I ain't bringing the Judge out here, so go to hell." The police officer hardened his gaze and spoke directly to Grigg. "The judge will not be disturbed, no how. Now if yous'll just turn around and—"

Falko Stier balled his fists and started for the front door of the jailhouse.

The officer said, "Well, Je-*zus* crackers," and he raised his shotgun.

Grigg said, "Lower your weapon."

The officer aimed at the middle of Stier's back.

Grigg spoke louder. "You're preparing to shoot a fellow officer. If you do, I promise to bring the full weight of the Commonwealth down upon you."

He knew the cop could just as easily turn and fire on him, the worth of his and Stier's lives hovering near zero. But the possibility of prosecution, or maybe just tone of his voice broke the officer's concentration. He lowered the shotgun.

Stier walked a straight line, stepping through the gallows' broken bones and striding up the stairs to the jailhouse. He turned only when he put his hand to the knob and looked back at Grigg.

"Coming?"

AUTUMN WEPT until she fell asleep in her mother's arms, lulled by the to and fro rocking of the dray wagon, as Joe guided the horses down Long Run Road.

He didn't turn to look at his daughter. He knew she'd been crushed by the weight of the calamities that had befallen her, hardly different from those that had struck him so many years before. But now Kamp was gone.

Joe also knew that nearly anyone they encountered on the road could be hostile. The very sight of Lenape, especially those that wouldn't defer, was enough to provoke an attack.

Maybe that would be just as well, Joe thought. And then he looked at Shaw and then at Autumn. *Not that, not yet.*

Shaw said, "Where are we going?"

"Easy, *nichan*. Rest now."

STIER MARCHED through the ground floor of the building, and he didn't stop until he got to a locked door at the end of the hallway. Stier rapped knuckles on the door.

From inside, a voice. "Go away."

By now, Grigg had caught up to him and said, "It's all right. It's not essential that we—"

Stier knocked harder. Again, the voice, a low croak from inside the room.

"Busy."

Grigg grabbed him by the arm. "Don't worry, man. We can—"

The rage that had pooled in Falko Stier's gut now exploded at the point where his right shoulder met the door, splintering it at the hinges. He tumbled headlong into the room, where he found himself staring up at the Honorable J. Blasius Grimp.

Grimp said, "I don't believe we've met."

While Stier picked himself up off the bare wood floor, Grigg entered the room.

"B.H. Grigg, District Attorney, County of Northampton. And this is my associate—"

"Falko Stier, Bethlehem Police."

Grimp pursed his lips, took Stier's measure, then swung his gaze to Grigg.

"Bethlehem?"

Stier said, "That's right. Why?"

Grimp sucked his teeth. "Well, you can have Bethlehem pay for that door. Or better yet, pay it yourself."

"Eat shit."

Grimp said to Grigg, "Get him the fuck out of here."

"Your honor, if I may—"

"You may not."

A woman's voice said, "Now, now, boys. Play nice."

Grigg and Stier turned to look at the back corner of Grimp's chambers, where Adams sat in a chair.

Grigg said, "Your honor, this woman is responsible for the murder of W.W. Kamp."

"Nickel Glock was wanted," Adams purred, "dead or alive."

"And furthermore, your honor, this woman has been stalking me for the past two months. She's made multiple attempts on my own life."

Grimp raised his eyebrows. "And yet, here you are."

"That's not the point, your honor. This woman is a menace, an assassin."

Grimp took out his tin of Turtle Island Tobacco Bits and put a pinch inside his lower lip. "What did you say your name was?"

"Grigg. And this is—"

"Mr. Grigg. You're telling me you're afraid of this woman, this beautiful woman, who stands not even five feet tall and who, I might add, is missing a limb. You're telling me that she's a cold-blooded killer?"

Falko Stier said, "Judge, you seen what she did to Duny Kunkle, and then to Kamp."

"You'll be held to account, too, Judge. You can't just let a murderer walk free."

"Who said I'm letting her walk free?" Grimp motioned to Adams' wrist, which was chained to the radiator. "And as for holding me to account, well, you're deluded."

Grigg said, "If you're not charging her with a crime, why is she shackled?"

Before he could answer, Adams said, "He wants the reward for Kamp. He doesn't want me to get it."

"Bullshit," Stier said.

Grigg looked at Adams, whose gaze shifted from Grimp to Stier and then to him. *She's weighing her options*, he thought. *There's something else she wants to say.*

Grigg said to her, "If all he wanted was the reward, you would've already acquiesced and been set free. There's something else he wants, isn't there? Something he wants you to tell him."

The Honorable J. Blasius Grimp said in a flat tone, "It's time for you to leave, gentlemen."

Neither Grigg nor Stier moved.

Grigg said to Adams, "What does he want to know about? The lies about Nickel Glock?"

Adams' expression didn't change.

Grimp said, "It can only get worse from here, gentlemen, I assure you."

Grigg sensed that he was close to the core of the mystery, that Adams knew the whole story. He leaned toward her.

"What does he want to know?"

She drew in a deep breath then said, "He wants to know about how Black Feather is connected to the Fraternal Order of the Raven and their plan for the mine. They're getting ready to—"

The sound of the gun blast ruptured one of Falko Stier's eardrums, and before he and Grigg could react, Adams' brain had splattered against the back wall of Grimp's chambers.

By the time Stier looked at Grimp, the Judge had already trained the Colt revolver on him. Stier rolled to the side as Grimp fired, catching him in the right shoulder. Grigg hooked Stier under the armpits and dragged him out of the room as the Honorable J. Blasius Grimp kept firing.

When he emptied the Colt, Grimp called out, "There's been a shooting. I've been attacked!"

WYLES AND PICKLER DIDN'T BOTHER getting a hotel room. She intended to finish her business well before sun up, and Pickler wanted to leave town much sooner than that.

He trailed a few steps behind her as she made the walk from Joe's cabin and toward the mansion on the mountainside.

"Miss Wyles? Ma'am?"

She ignored him and kept walking, her long braid swinging behind her like a metronome.

"Miss Wyles, I have to go. I have to get back to the store."

Still, she paid no attention to him but kept marching between the trees and then picking her way across a stream by stepping from one dry rock to another.

Pickler tried to follow her steps, but he teetered off the first rock, splashing one foot and then the other into the water and getting soaked to his knees.

When he reached the far side, he slipped on the bank, pitching forward onto his knees, glasses falling into the mud.

Pickler balled his fists and said, "Miss Wyles, I'm not going with you."

Now she stopped and turned to face him. "Yes. You are."

Still on his knees, Pickler pulled a clean, silk handkerchief from his vest pocket and wiped the splatters from his glasses.

"No, I'm not."

"We don't have time for this."

Pickler stood up, put his glasses on and said, "I listened to you, against my better judgment, I listened, darn it. And now I've nearly been killed. I've nearly been killed, and I've been party to your, your..."

"My what?"

"Your madness. You've been seduced, seduced by what I know not. But, madam, you are under a spell. And I must say it, I must. Mr. Kamp was, too!"

Wyles set down the medicine bag and slapped Pickler hard across the face.

"As for madness, you're entangled in a variety of insanities, the fearful symmetry of which you can't even begin to fathom. And Kamp was my friend."

She picked up her medicine bag again, turned and started walking. Tears welled in Pickler's eyes as he watched her go.

GRIGG AND STIER FLED at a full sprint. The hundred-yard head start they got was enough to allow them to slip down a side street where two horses and a carriage stood unattended.

Grigg helped Stier into the carriage, then clambered up to the driver's seat. He snapped the reins and said, "Hya."

Apart from a few curious stares, Grigg attracted little attention as he piloted the carriage across the bridge and out of town. For an hour or more, neither man spoke, and Grigg didn't feel safe easing up until he reached the bridge at Treichlers.

He said to Grigg, "Are you all right back there?"

"Yah, yah," Stier said. "We're fine?"

"We're?"

"It's not just me back here. Looks like we stole the meat wagon."

Grigg slowed the horses and pulled them to a stop on the bridge. He climbed down from the driver's seat, opened the carriage door and looked at Stier.

"Say again?"

"Bodies back here. That sheriff, and Kamp."

"Christ." He looked in both directions and saw no one on the road. The sun had begun to set, and they heard nothing, save crickets and a solitary crow. "Which one's the sheriff?"

Stier peeked under a winding sheet.

"This guy."

Grigg slid his hands under the sheriff's back and tried to lift him.

"Help me."

Together, they removed the corpse from the carriage and dragged it to the side of the bridge.

"One, two, three."

They watched it splash in the river, then bob to the surface and start its lonely journey down the Lehigh.

43

Night had fallen by the time Emma Wyles reached the mansion on the mountainside. Candles burned on every floor, but all the curtains were drawn, and she couldn't see in any of the windows.

She'd cleaned up as best she could, changing into a clean white blouse and putting her hair in a fresh braid. She heard talking inside, and for an hour or so, men would appear on the veranda to smoke. She heard English and German, all in hushed tones.

At one point, Wyles saw the hunter who'd talked to her in the forest earlier in the day. He stood looking out over the valley and smoking a pipe.

From her hiding place in the woods, Wyles scanned the outside of the building and noted an armed man at each corner. She peered up into the bell tower and saw the cherry of a cigarette, winking like an ominous red star.

She waited and watched until all the men, save the guards, went inside. Minutes later, one last carriage, a fine black-lacquered brougham arrived. A man she recognized stepped down from the carriage and went in the back door. The Big Judge Tate Cain was here.

And now, every man responsible for the degradation of her life and the destruction of Kamp's was inside. She would confront them and have her say.

She pulled in a deep breath, picked up her medicine bag, and marched toward the front door. Before she reached it, Wyles heard the pump action of a shotgun and then a man's voice.

"Stop there."

She didn't recognize the man who emerged from the shadows.

"I need to go inside," she said.

"Party's closed. No visitors."

Wyles held up the medicine bag. "I'm a doctor. I've been summoned by the owner."

"What's the owner's name?"

She spoke slowly. "They didn't say. Now step aside."

"First I heard of it."

The man tightened his grip on the gun.

"Then someone should have told you," she said.

Wyles walked past him and up the stairs to the front door, where she encountered the next guard.

She said, "I need to be let in at once. I must—"

The first guard came up behind her, grabbed her by the wrists and said, "I don't know that no one called for no mouthy bitch doctor."

"Me neither."

The second guard yanked the medicine bag from her hand and began riffling through it.

She said, "Stop this instant."

The second guard looked up at her and brushed her cheek with the back of his hand. Then he unbuttoned the top button of her blouse.

"Or else what?"

NYX HOPED ALL OF THEM—Angus, Joe, Shaw and Wyles—had left hours ago and that no one else would get hurt. No one else she cared about, anyway.

And yet here was Emma Wyles, not only in the way but directly at the center of a conflict that could derail Nyx's plan.

Through the scope on the rifle, she'd watched Wyles emerge from the darkness and in her typical style, march straight to the front door.

If the situation deteriorated further, Nyx knew she'd have to abort her carefully laid plan and effect a rescue. She stiffened in her hiding place, ready to burst out. She saw one of the men at the front door grab Wyles and saw the other one touch her as well.

Nyx stood and raised the Sharps, sighting the first guard in the scope and curling her finger around the trigger.

THE GUARDS HEARD FOOTFALLS coming up the drive and then a man hustled up the steps. Before they could turn their attention from Wyles, he'd reached them.

He said, "Oh, you're here."

Nyx took her finger off the trigger.

The second guard took his hands off Wyles and said, "Who are you?"

The man adjusted his glasses and said, "Uwe Wedekind Eu—"

"No visit—"

He cleared his voice and spoke louder, "Uwe Wedekind Eugen Schiffhorn, the Third."

"Well, Uwe—"

"But you can call me Pickler."

"Yah well, Pickler, you can just turn around and go back down the drive."

Pickler said to Wyles, "Thank heaven you're here, doctor." Then he turned to the guards and said, "And thank you, gentlemen, for receiving the doctor so graciously. Now, if you'll pardon us."

Pickler tried to push past the guards, who blocked his path. The second guard gave him a shove.

"We don't know you, little fella, and nobody called no doctor."

Pickler looked at the first guard's face and then the second.

"I'll have you know that I'm the chief pharmacist at Native Plants and Medicines, Bethlehem, Pennsylvania. My employer is Black Feather Consolidated. My supervisor, and my supervisor's supervisor are inside this very building."

He pointed at the front door for emphasis.

The first guard looked at the ground and said, "Well, ya don't have to be so—"

"And as to whether they called for medical assistance, yes, they darned well did. Now come along, doctor."

As soon as they were inside, Pickler turned to Wyles and said, "Okay, now what?"

THE FACT THAT Wyles was in the mansion greatly interfered with what Nyx intended to do, and if Wyles didn't emerge of her own accord, and soon, Nyx knew she'd have to go in and get her. She picked up her burlap sack and the rifle and crept down the mountainside.

WYLES SCANNED THE DOWNSTAIRS and listened. Through a set of closed double doors, she heard talking. She and Pickler stepped to the doors, and Wyles put her eye to the crack between the doors. She saw a great room and costumed figures, maybe a dozen, seated around a long table.

At the head of the table was a high-backed chair on a platform. Wyles couldn't see the face of the person in the chair. She pressed her ear to the crack, and now she could hear what they were saying.

She felt a hand at her elbow.

Wyles snapped her head around and saw the face of the hunter to whom she'd spoken earlier the day.

"Yes?"

The man studied her face and said, "I thought you said you weren't a doctor."

Pickler spoke up. "That's correct, sir. She is not a licensed medical doctor."

"Well, then, I'm afraid you're going to have to—"

"But she is a most excellent physician."

The man turned to Wyles.

"Is that so?"

She looked the man in the eye and said, "Where's the patient?"

NYX FELT HER BREATHING SLOW, and she felt no fear in spite of the armed men who guarded the perimeter of the house. The throbbing in her back where the bullet had broken one of her ribs receded and then disappeared.

She crept in silence to the stone patio and looked in the windows at the back of the house. In the dim light of a candelabra on a table in the foyer, Nyx saw Wyles and Pickler talking to a man she'd never seen before. Then they followed him up the stairs.

BEADS OF SWEAT FLOWED from Joachim S. Thaler's blond hair as he thrashed in his bed.

Wyles pulled up a chair and sat beside Thaler.

"Let me see it," she said.

"*Wer ist es?*"

"*Der Arzt.* I'm here to help you. Let me see your arm."

Thaler rolled onto his back and held out his left arm, which was wrapped in a crude bandage. Blood had soaked through it at the elbow.

Wyles gently unwrapped the bandage and saw the jagged, exposed ends of broken bones amidst the tangle of ruined ligaments and flesh at what used to be his elbow.

The man said, "How bad is it?"

"How do you know this man?"

"He's my brother."

"Your brother is going to die—"

"For god's sake, help him."

"Unless I amputate."

Thaler's brother shook his head. "There must be some other—"

"Tell me your name."

"Barend."

"Barend, get me hot water and clean towels."

He said, "Fine, fine" and left the room.

Wyles looked at Joachim S. Thaler and saw desperation and terror in his eyes.

He said, "You're not here to help me at all, are you?"

NYX CAME IN through an unlocked window. She saw no one in the downstairs hallway and heard no sounds on the ground floor. She tiptoed down the hallway and reached the double doors of the great room.

Nyx wanted to see all of the men in that room and to hear clearly what they were saying. But she couldn't see or hear enough without opening the doors. Perhaps she could get the access she wanted from above. She turned and headed up the stairs and encountered no one on the second floor.

She heard footsteps coming in her direction, so she ducked into a room and closed the door just as the man she'd seen talking to Wyles went rushing past.

Nyx waited a few moments and then explored the second floor until she found a balcony overlooking the great room. She crawled on hands and knees until she could see all the men, who were arrayed in their bizarre and fantastic outfits.

E. WYLES APPLIED THE SPIRAL TOURNIQUET to Joachim S. Thaler's arm, cranking the large brass screw until the blood flow stopped. Then she inspected the limb and looked for the precise spot to start her work.

She said to Pickler, "Come over here and get ready."

"Get ready?"

"You must hold him down when I begin."

Pickler positioned himself as Wyles reached into the medicine bag, removed a large ringed syringe, then produced a green bottle labeled with a skull and crossbones.

Barend Thaler said, "What in god's name?"

"Laudanum. For pain," she said, dipping the needle in the bottle and filling the barrel. She secured a leather belt around Thaler's good arm and found a suitable vein.

Wyles inserted the needle, looked at Barend and said, "Listen carefully. Half of this dose is sufficient for your brother."

"Good."

"The full dose will kill him."

"Say again?"

"If all of my demands are met, he will live."

"You're out of your mind." Barend Thaler started across the room.

Wyles shook her head gently and pressed the plunger, injecting half the dose.

"Stop right there," she said, "and lower your voice."

NYX LAY ON HER STOMACH and peered down through the balusters at a ceremony, the likes of which she'd never seen.

Nine of the eleven men seated around the table wore formal attire in the Victorian fashion. The tenth wore an elaborate army uniform and one wore a black robe. And each wore an elaborate mask depicting a different animal. Stag, bear, turtle, ram, and so on.

The last man, seated in the ornate chair at the head of the table wore a black robe and the most elaborate mask, a raven's head with eyes that blazed sapphire.

The raven spoke in a low growl and in a language that Nyx didn't recognize. When he became silent, two of the men, the goat and the lion left the room, and returned with a young woman between them.

She was nude, blindfolded with a black kerchief and bound at the wrists with a red silk ribbon. She offered no resistance. Nyx didn't recognize her.

The goat and the lion guided her to the front of the room and laid her supine on the table before the raven. From his vest pocket, he produced a dagger with a silver blade and set it on the table.

The raven said, "*Fais ce que tu voudras.*"

The men around the table stared straight ahead, and no one moved for several minutes until the ram stood up, walked to the front of the room and took the dagger in his hand.

44

When the laudanum began to take effect, the terror drained from Joachim S. Thaler's eyes and was replaced by stupor.

Barend Thaler stood motionless at the center of the room, a bead of sweat rolling down his cheek.

He said to Wyles, "What are your demands?"

"I need to speak to the man in charge. Immediately."

"You can't."

"Have it your way." She put her thumb back on the plunger of the syringe.

"You don't understand. There's a ceremony happening right now. I can't disturb it."

Wyles studied Barend's face, then looked at Joachim S. Thaler. His eyes rolled back in his head and then closed.

She said, "In other words you can't meet my demands?"

"Not that I can't get the man for you. I can't right now. For the sake of Christ, who are you, and what do you want?"

"My name is Emma Wyles. And I want—"

Joachim S. Thaler vomited and began thrashing in the bed.

Barend Thaler said, "God damn it. *Please*."

Wyles turned to Pickler and said, "Saw."

Pickler retrieved the instrument and put in in her hand. Without hesitation she went to work above the elbow, cutting deep.

Joachim S. Thaler's eyes shot open.

Wyles said, "Pickler, put your hand over his—"

Thaler let out a loud wail before Pickler could react. Seconds later, Thaler's mangled limb dropped to the floor.

"Get over here, Barend."

Barend Thaler stood stupefied, rooted to his spot on the floor and staring at the carnage.

Wyles called to him again. "Get over here and stanch the bleeding."

Now he moved to the bedside, picked up a clean towel and pressed it to the wound. Wyles retrieved the needle and thread from the medicine bag and began suturing.

THE MAN IN THE RAM MASK POSITIONED the blade at the young woman's throat. Still, she offered no resistance.

Nyx propped herself on her elbows and readied the Sharps, sighting the ram's head.

The raven raised the blade as she curled her index finger around the trigger. An instant before she squeezed it, Joachim S. Thaler let out his scream, and the ram lowered the blade. The three men closest to the door left the room and ran up the stairs.

In a single motion Nyx stood up and leapt over the railing. She landed square on the table, rifle in one hand, canvas sack in the other.

She shouted at the woman on the table, "Get going. Go!"

The woman didn't move.

Now two men, the bear and the turtle, advanced on Nyx. The raven held out his right hand, and they stopped.

Nyx could feel all eyes on her. Her heart, which had been pounding, slowed, and she stared directly at the raven.

A minute passed, and no one moved or spoke until the raven said, "We've been waiting for you."

"Why's that?"

"So you can participate."

The raven held the dagger across his open palms and held it out to Nyx.

"Liberate her, he said.

The woman on the table tilted her head back.

Nyx said, "What?"

The raven set a small gold box on the table, opened it and removed four silver, eight-sided coins.

"We know you have no concern for yourself. So, these are for Agnes Kamp, Joe Six Killer."

"Fuck you."

"And the last one is for Kamp's daughter. Each of these coins will be delivered to its intended recipient."

"Unless I—"

"Once you've completed our ceremony—and certainly you're not squeamish about blood—once you're finished, your debt is paid. We won't deliver these coins. Your choice."

"You're telling me I can leave then?"

"No, not at all."

"Then what?"

"You'll remain with us. In a sense you're already one of us. It's a very great honor."

The raven motioned to an empty chair at his right. She laid the rifle on the table and removed a skull from the canvas sack.

Nyx said, "This was Hugh Arndt, the man you sent to murder Rachel and Jonas Bauer, two good and upright people, my parents. You sent this son of a bitch to kill them in order to hide your crimes. And that led to the deaths of Danny Knecht, and now, Kamp. And it started with this son of a bitch right here!"

With both hands, Nyx raised the skull above her head and slammed it down on the table, smashing the jaw, sending the teeth flying.

She took the dagger from the ram's hands and plunged it into his neck. Then she picked up the rifle, aimed for the raven and shot him through the left eye of his mask.

The force of the shot knocked him backward, and he tumbled out of the ornate chair.

Nyx grabbed the woman by the wrist and yanked her off the table. She hurried the woman out of the room, while all the men watched her leave. She guided the woman down the front hallway, opened the door and shoved her onto the porch.

"Run."

The woman disappeared down the stairs and into the darkness.

"OPEN THIS DOOR!"

The shouting and pounding on the door barely registered on E. Wyles, who continued sewing Joachim Thaler's wound.

"Uh, Miss Wyles," Pickler said. "Ma'am?"

"I know, I know. Almost finished."

"It would be best to get quit of this situ—"

Something heavy slammed into the door.

She looked at Barend, "Tell them to back off."

"Gentlemen, wait."

From the other side of the door, a voice. "What?"

"Wait!" Barend Thaler turned to Wyles. "What do I do?"

"Keep this wound clean, hear me? And in eight hours, give him the rest of the laudanum. Now, Barend?"

"Yes?"

"How do we get out of here?"

He pointed to the closet.

She left her medicine bag on the floor, shoved Pickler and followed him into the closet. The last sound she heard was the bedroom door getting knocked off its hinges.

NYX RACED UP THE STAIRS, then stopped to reload. She moved down the hallway and saw a man sitting on a bed next to another man who lay there. She raised the rifle and walked slowly toward them.

Barend Thaler could do nothing to protect himself from Nyx.

He said, "I don't know what you want, and I can't help you. I've been instructed to—"

Nyx pressed the tip of the barrel to his forehead.

"Where are they?"

"Attic."

She went to the closet and saw that a ladder had been pulled down from an attic door in the ceiling. At the base of the ladder were two of the masks she'd seen in the great room.

She listened for a moment, then slung the Sharps on her shoulder and began to climb, carefully and silently. When she reached the top rung, Nyx peered into the attic and saw one man and then the other climbing out a window and onto the roof.

WYLES COULD HEAR THE FOOTFALLS of the men following them, though she dared not look back. She and Pickler headed for the only place that might offer some protection, the bell tower rising before them on the western side of the building.

As soon as she reached its base, Wyles found handholds between the bricks, and then began to climb with Pickler alongside her. They were aware of the men right behind them. What neither she nor Pickler saw, though, was the guard in the bell tower who'd extinguished his cigarette and waited, pistol drawn.

FROM HER VANTAGE POINT, Nyx saw Wyles and Pickler making their way up the outside of the tower, as well as the guard who stood inside the tower waiting for them.

She thought about calling out to them but realized that it would do no good. They couldn't climb down, nor could they stay where they were.

When she saw the guard in the tower point his pistol at Wyles, Nyx raised the rifle and fired. The bullet whanged off the bell.

The sound sent the men on the roof scrambling for cover behind one of the chimneys, and the man in the tower ducked low.

Nyx hurried to reload and aim once more, but by the time she did, the guard in the tower had begun shooting at Wyles and Pickler. The first two rounds missed, but when he shot a third time, Nyx heard Pickler let out a low moan. He did not, however, fall from the side of the tower.

Nyx drew in a long breath, and on the exhale she squeezed the trigger. The bullet connected and sent the guard toppling backward out of the bell tower and crashing to the ground. She reached in her pocket for another cartridge. Empty.

The two men who'd taken cover behind the chimney now emerged. One ran for the tower, the other for Nyx.

WYLES CLIMBED INTO the bell tower and then pulled Pickler over the ledge as well. They crouched there, both breathing hard, and by the moonlight she saw blood on Pickler's shoulder.

He said, "I'll be fine."

Wyles knew they were defenseless in the tower. She peered over the side and saw the man scaling up the outside of the tower. She kicked off her boots, then stepped onto the ledge and reached for its roof. Once she'd gotten a good grip, she swung her foot onto the roof of the tower and then climbed onto it.

Now she stood in an even more precarious position atop the tiny roof, which slanted at an extreme angle.

But she found what she needed there. Wyles grabbed the iron weathervane, adorned with a flying raven, and worked it back and forth until it snapped at its base.

She said, "Here," and handed it to Pickler. Then she slithered back into the bell tower just as a guard appeared at the ledge.

Wyles took the weathervane from Pickler and with one thrust buried the pointed end in the man's chest, sending him tumbling off the side.

THE OTHER MAN SAID NOTHING as he approached Nyx, and she said nothing, either. She flipped the rifle around so that she held it by the barrel, and when the man reached her, she raised it over her head and brought it down on his skull.

The man swayed but didn't fall. Nyx raised the rifle and brought it down again with enough force to splinter the stock.

Now the man collapsed. Nyx dropped the broken Sharps and ran to the tower, scaling it the way Wyles had. By the time she climbed into the bell tower, armed men swarmed onto the roof.

Nyx turned to Wyles and said, "Where now?"

She pointed to a tall maple tree, growing beside the building.

Pickler said, "No."

They lifted him onto the ledge of the bell tower.

Wyles said, "Jump," even though she could tell he wouldn't be able to cross the chasm.

"I can't!"

A bullet hit the tower, and the ricochet nicked Pickler's ear. He steadied his feet, bent his knees and balled his fists.

At the instant Pickler made his leap, Wyles gave him a hard shove, launching him into the branches that bent and snapped as he descended through them.

Without hesitation, Nyx followed suit, hurling herself into the tree and catching a sturdy bough. Then Wyles felt her bare feet on the slate ledge, spread her arms, bent her knees and propelled herself through the darkness into the waiting branches.

45

G rigg and Stier arrived in Bethlehem well ahead of the news that Black Feather's mansion in Mauch Chunk, Pennsylvania had been attacked, it was later said, by a "nefarious element."

When the pair reached the city limit, Grigg pulled back on the reins and brought the horses to a stop.

He called back to Stier and woke him from a deep slumber.

"Where do we put him?"

"Who?"

"Can't take him to the morgue."

"Gotta take him home."

Grigg started the horses again and guided them in the direction of Kamp's small farm. He began imagining what he'd say to the imposters who occupied

Kamp's home. While Grigg was eager to avoid further trouble, he was resolute in his intention to bury
the man properly. And he was sure that Stier
wouldn't hesitate to impose his will on the imposter,
if the need arose.

But when they reached Kamp's small farm, no
candle burned in the window, and when they went
to the front door, they found it locked.

Stier circled the house and seeing no signs of the
inhabitants, broke in through the back door. He
walked through the upstairs and then back down the
stairs.

He opened the front door and said to Grigg,
"Whoever they were, they're gone."

ON THE SOUTH SIDE OF BETHLEHEM, the Royal Traveling Company packed its caravan and prepared to
leave town. The company had gotten word from a
representative of their patron, Black Feather Consolidated, that they were to start a run of shows in Philadelphia the next night.

One of the members of the Company, the man
who'd been playing the part of Kamp, was instructed
to vacate Kamp's house immediately along with the
woman who'd been playing Shaw.

Black Feather didn't give the man the additional
compensation they'd promised, and as he stood

waiting for his fellow players to finish packing, he felt a flicker of resentment. *They owe me.*

He knew he wouldn't get his recompense from Black Feather, though perhaps he could score another way.

He remembered that the district attorney B. H. Grigg lived close by and that no one had seen him in weeks. His house would be unoccupied, unguarded, maybe even unlocked.

The man ran down the block, up the stairs to Grigg's front door and turned the knob. It opened.

In his haste the man didn't think about the wire he nearly tripped over on his way in. Nor did he pay attention to the hissing noise before the explosion that blasted his corpse back out onto the street.

GRIGG DIDN'T HEAR THE SOUND of his house exploding. When it happened, he was five miles away and three feet deep in the hole he and Stier were digging with spade shovels. At the base of a maple tree near the top of the mountain behind Kamp's house, the two men worked in tandem.

Having talked to Kamp at this very spot the year before, Grigg knew its significance and knew that the grave would never be found or disturbed. When the hole reached the requisite size and depth, Grigg climbed out and wiped the sweat from his brow with the back of his hand. Both men looked down at the grave and then at Kamp's body wrapped in its winding sheet. Neither man was religious, and no prayer was said. There was nothing left to do but bury him, but neither man wanted it to be finished.

A blackbird whirled overhead, and Stier said, "It's time." He bent down to take hold of the body.

"Wait," Grigg said, as he knelt down, unwrapped the winding sheet and said, "Personal effects."

Grigg went through the pockets in Kamp's shirt, found nothing and then checked his pants pockets as well. Grigg pulled out a piece of paper, folded small and nearly falling apart at the creases. He unfolded it gently.

It was a child's pencil drawing, showing a simple house with two smiling faces, one in each upstairs window. In one downstairs window was a candle, and in the other window, a Christmas tree. Across the top of the picture were the words "WEEL MISS YOU DANNY!" Across the bottom, it read, "LOVE MERCY."

Grigg folded it back up, returned it to Kamp's pocket and wrapped him again in the winding sheet.

They lifted Kamp's body and lowered it as best they could before letting it fall to the bottom.

NYX PARTED WAYS WITH WYLES AND PICKLER at the turnoff to Long Run Road. She'd decided to go back to the burned cabin where she'd lived with Angus to see if anything could be salvaged.

Wyles and Pickler started the walk back to Bethlehem, moving along the roadside in silence and wondering what awaited them upon their return.

46

Nyx found nothing worth saving in the charred ruins of Angus's cabin, except for a set of double triggers. As night gave way to dawn, she realized she had nowhere to lay her head.

Instinctively, her feet began moving in the direction of the mine, and soon she fell into the line of miners headed there as well. When she entered the company store, no one gave her a second look, not even the clerk who handed over her Gezähe in his typical officious way.

On her way into the mine mouth, Nyx felt numb. The throbbing from where she'd been shot had receded, and she wanted nothing more now than to return to a routine, isolated and in the dark.

The first sign that that wouldn't happen came when Nyx reached the large wooden door and waited for the trapper kid to swing it open. A different person, a wizened little Irishman yelled, "Hold your horses, I'm coming" when she knocked.

Nyx said, "What happened to the kid?"

"Who?"

"There's usually a kid here."

"Is that so?" he said and closed the door behind her.

She kept her head down as she made her way to the back room at the bottom of the mine, her only refuge.

Memories of Aodh flooded her consciousness, and she stood still for a long moment, waiting for the emotion to pass. When it did, she took her pick in hand and began to hew the seam. Nyx let the memories and feelings recede and let her body take over.

B.H. GRIGG STARED AT THE REMAINS of his home from a distance, because he still dared not let his presence be known. Instead of trying to pick through the wreckage for any semblance of his former life, Grigg resolved to go straight to the Big Judge Tate Cain, come what may.

Emma Wyles walked to town that morning in a similar state of mind. Considering what she'd risked in order to make her case directly before the Order of the Raven, she believed she had a right to demand that the Judge rectify all of the skullduggery that led to the loss of her livelihood.

Grigg and Wyles converged on the courthouse before the first county employees arrived for the day. They'd both decided they'd wait as long as necessary for the Big Judge to appear so that they could make their demands known to the only authority in Bethlehem who held real power.

When they met at the front door, Grigg said, "Here to see the Judge?"

Wyles nodded and turned to the front door, which was ajar. She looked to Grigg, who raised his eyebrows. She gave the door a gentle push, and it swung open.

Wyles called into the lobby, "Hello?" and got no response.

They walked in slowly, listening to their footfalls echoing on the marble floor. The doors of the Judge's courtroom were closed but unlocked.

When Grigg opened the door, he and Wyles witnessed the grim spectacle.

The corpse hung by a heavy chain, wrapped around a bare white ankle. The chain had been thrown over a rafter and fastened by a railroad spike hammered into the floor. Shards of orange early morning sun lit the room through tall windows, and the only sound was the dripping of blood that pooled on the floor.

Wyles and Grigg walked to the body and inspected it. The cut had been made after the body had been turned upside down, and the instrument had entered below the navel and stopped just below the chin. The genitals had been removed.

The long white beard obscured the corpse's face, and when Wyles pushed it aside, she saw a bullet hole where the right eye had been. In the open mouth, she found a penis and testicles. No scrotum.

The handle of the gavel had been pounded into the left ear so that only its head protruded.

Grigg stepped back once again to take in the scene. On the back wall of the courtroom the letters "HOR" were written in blood.

He scanned the room and saw no cutting tools. They looked at the body once more and at the blue silk dress that hung from the corpse, a tattered death shroud.

Wyles and Grigg began to contemplate the questions, the causes and the massive implications of the scene, knowing that there would be great upheaval and confusion. One thing was certain, though.

The Big Judge Tate Cain was dead.

NYX FELL INTO A WORKING RHYTHM, her muscles remembering how to move without her having to think. She didn't care that she'd never make seven cars for the day. Nyx only wanted solitude, but then she sensed she wasn't alone.

At the back corner of the room in which she'd been hewing, Nyx discerned the outline of a figure in the darkness.

She heard the sound of a match being struck and then a man's voice.

"I don't see that you're no diff'rent," he said.

"What?"

"No one gets out till they've paid the last penny. And you'll earn yer addlings today. Tha's certain."

Nyx recognized the voice. She'd known all along he'd come after her, and now the moment had arrived.

The man moved toward her.

"Stop. Don't."

She heard him unbuckling his belt.

Nyx turned to face him and saw that he was tall with a wide chest, broad shoulders and forearms thick with muscle that twitched when he squeezed his fists. Sweat poured down his face from the powerful heat in the chamber.

Nyx took off her coat.

"Tha's better. Now we can enjoy ourselves."

She said, "You're Dis Padgett."

He smiled. "That I am. But I'm much, much more than that. This world belongs to me. And after we're finished, I'll be your lord and protector. I'll be your daddy."

"Why did you do it to him?"

"Who?"

"Aodh."

"Tha's for later. No questions now."

"Tell me now."

"He was a good man, but he always wanted what was mine."

"Bullshit."

"They told me Nef Bahr was feisty. I do like my boys feisty. I can give you more than Blackall ever imagined. Now, let's get to it."

Nyx unbuttoned her wool shirt, exposing the bandage wrapped tightly around her torso. She unwrapped it, letting her breasts fall free.

Padgett's eyes grew wide, and he said, "Sweet Jaysus."

She said, "Now you take off your shirt."

"Gladly."

When Dis Padgett reached for the first button, she pulled the pepperbox pistol from her boot with her right hand and held it to his forehead.

Dis Padgett said, "Fire that gun in here and you're killed too. Damp will explode. And even if it don't, all my boys'll come runnin'."

"Maybe."

"There's more trouble in this than you know."

She cocked the pistol and held it steady.

He held out his hands, palms up.

"I can give you anything you want. Tell me. tell me what you want."

Without shifting her gaze, she hefted the coal axe with her three fingers and thumb.

She saw a flicker of recognition cross the man's face.

He said, "I know who you are. After what's about to happen this very day, you and me, the two of us, we could start—"

Nyx swung the coal axe, penetrating Dis Padgett's skull at the left temple. He let out a low groan and went down hard.

She didn't feel triumphant or even satisfied, and she knew that her life in the mine was over. On her way out, she caught sight of another figure in the room, someone sitting in dark.

She gripped the coal ax tighter and stepped across the room so that her head lamp lit the corner.

It was Short Pinky, seated on the floor, skin blue, eyes open, dead.

He had a purple lump at his left temple, the site of the killing blow. In each of his hands they'd placed a stick of dynamite. One last sick joke. Both sticks were connected to a fuse that led out of the room. Now Nyx discerned a faint hissing that grew louder.

THE FIRST EXPLOSION SHOOK THE GROUND beneath Nyx's feet, the walls beside her and the ceiling above. The next one caused large chunks of coal to fall to the floor and forced the timbers to bow.

She remembered that Aodh had told her of an iron ladder in an air vent that ran from the mine mouth to the very bottom. She'd never looked for it before, but she had a good idea where it was and started in that direction. The next series of explosions—Nyx counted six—brought more rocks down on her helmet and extinguished the candle.

She crawled on hands and knees in complete darkness and found her way, in part, by following the shouts of men also looking for the ladder. As she neared their voices, Nyx felt a breeze of fresh air on her cheeks.

When she came within ten feet of the base of the ladder, a cave-in blocked her path. Men clawed at the rocks that kept them from reaching the ladder, to no avail.

Nyx, though, was able to slide through a crease barely wide enough for her narrow frame.

She called back to the trapped men, "I'll send help," and she began to climb.

The explosions came in waves as long fuses set off each line of charges. She climbed steadily, hands raw and naked torso scraped and bleeding. The wound in her side throbbed and her head ached. One tumbling rock would finish her.

After more than an hour of climbing, Nyx looked up and saw a disc of blue sky. She pulled in a deep breath. After twenty more rungs, Nyx made it out, clawing her way to the surface, rolling onto her back and taking great gulps of fresh air.

Men gathered to see the spectacle of a woman, nude from the waist up, bloodied and bruised.

A fire captain with a bushy red moustache leaned over her face and said, "This is no place to rest."

"You have to help them. There's many more down there. Trapped. Go get them."

The fire captain gave a sad shake of his head. "All's lost," he said. "The damp."

"They did it on purpose," Nyx said, although the fire captain had already moved on.

Two firemen picked her up by wrists and ankles and carried her to safety. They set her down behind a fire wagon and wrapped her in a wool blanket.

One of them said, "Doctor'll be here directly."

But Nyx knew that soon someone would recognize her and that she'd be arrested, or worse. She stood up, pulled the blanket tight around her and ran down the back of the mountain.

47

Nyx spent the next three weeks at Joe's cabin letting her wounds heal and awaiting the return of Angus, Joe, Shaw and Autumn. But they never came.

Instead, an odd letter carrier arrived one cold winter day with a letter, written in Angus's scrawl that read, "Gnaddenhutten."

She knew that meant they weren't coming back, not soon anyway, and that she could find them in Ohio, if she wished.

Nyx had no plans to join them, though, no plans to do anything at all, really, except perhaps to find Aodh.

She assumed she was still wanted for a variety of reasons: the original bounty on her head, killing the sheriff, the raid on the mansion, Dis Padgett. And so, Nyx resolved to remain hidden.

But her need to find Aodh won out. In the pre-dawn she made the familiar march to the mine mouth. She suspected that after the previous batch of miners had been slaughtered and their deaths ruled an accident, a new crop would have been sent in at lower pay. And she was right.

As she approached the summit of Sleeping Bear Mountain, she heard all the familiar sounds that signaled the start of the day. Someone would know Aodh's whereabouts.

Nyx quizzed a half a dozen men, all of whom spoke Hungarian and none of whom recognized Aodh's name.

She found an old German woman at the base of the spoil heap and said, "Where's Aodh Blackall?"

The woman gave her a long look and then pointed halfway up.

Nyx recognized Aodh there, or rather, recognized the sad facsimile of the man she'd known. He was hunched, scuttling along the side of the slag, searching for shards of coal.

When she climbed to where he was and took him by the arm, he looked up, mouth hanging open. He stared at her and showed no flash of recognition. Then he shook her hand off his arm.

Nyx trudged back to Joe's cabin, head down. When she walked in, at first she didn't notice the smell of coffee or the man seated at the table. Nor did she see another man, who held a shotgun and stood behind the door.

The man seated at the table said, "I've made enough for both of us."

He spoke with a refined German accent, and now Nyx noticed his wavy blonde hair, lightly oiled and combed straight back. Joachim S. Thaler.

Nyx looked at the man with the shotgun, and Thaler said to him, "Wait outside."

The man went out the front door and closed it behind him.

Thaler gestured to the empty chair at the table and said to Nyx, "Have a seat."

He took a sip of coffee from the mug she always used. Nyx stood motionless. She'd been running for the past two years, and finally she'd been well and truly caught.

"Whatever you're going to do to me, just do it."

"I'm not here to do anything to you. That time has passed."

"Then leave."

The anger and sorrow had drained from Nyx. There was nothing left.

Thaler shifted in his chair. "I do need to speak with you briefly. Please, sit."

Nyx sat down and stared past Thaler, out the back window.

He said, "I need you to understand something."

"Really."

"Our revels are now ended, Nadine. You're not to press the matter any further."

She looked at him now. "The matter?"

"Indeed. And I'll speak in plain terms here—"

"Good."

Thaler leaned toward Nyx and looked straight in her eyes.

"Your claim against Black Feather, a legitimate claim, has been settled. Or should I say, you've settled it in a most spectacular way."

"What about Kamp? I guess you settled your claim with him, too. Is that it? Why couldn't you just leave him alone?"

Thaler shifted in his seat, but his gaze didn't leave Nyx.

"He got caught up in something. He learned information he shouldn't have known. And he committed horrific crimes. He wasn't well, Nadine, even before he was injured in the war. You should know that."

"You're insane. All of you."

"You were drawn into this matter as an unintended consequence, as were your parents. It couldn't be helped."

"What about the Fraternal Order of the Raven and your dumb fucking coins?"

Thaler looked out the window, then said, "I assure you there's no such thing as a Fraternal Order of the Raven."

"Of course there is."

"As far as Black Feather Consolidated is concerned, you're free to go and no harm will come to you or those about whom you care."

"Why?"

"I thought that would be welcome news to you."

Nyx felt the flames of anger burst to life at the base of her skull.

"What about what you did to Aodh Blackall? You ruined him. And all the people you killed in the mine just so you could get other guys who'd work for less. What about all of them?"

"Nadine, it's beyond your understanding."

"Like hell it is."

"The money must move. Those men in the mine, including your friend, needed to be replaced. Expeditiously."

"Fuck you!"

All the rage and grief Nyx had held inside since her parents were killed and some from even before that burst forth now. She slapped Joachim S. Thaler with one hand and then the other. And when that didn't do enough damage, she balled her fists and punched him again and again in the face.

Thaler offered no resistance, and soon a welt formed under each eye and blood flowed from both his nostrils. He pulled a silk handkerchief from his pocket, wiped away the blood and then combed his hair back with his fingers.

"Nadine, you've done the same as we have. And you know it."

"Only because—"

"We live in the same world, alas. It's the cost of doing business. And now the business is done."

Nyx looked up. "Why would it be over now?"

Thaler laid his hand on the table, palm up. "Give me your hand," he said.

"I'm not—"

"The injured one."

Nyx reached out her hand and let him touch it. He caressed it and ran his fingers along the places where her missing fingers had been cut off. She felt the pulse in his fingertips.

He leaned forward and said, "It was never intended for you to be hurt. We wanted to help you. I wanted to help you."

"Jesus Christ."

"It's true. That's why I returned your father's pistol to you."

Nyx pulled her hand away.

"Your friend Wyles has settled her claim as well. She saved my life, and no harm will come to her. She is free to pursue her livelihood without interference."

Nyx said, "I still don't see why I—"

"You won the game, Nadine. You killed the raven."

Joachim S. Thaler stood up, put on his hat, tipped it to Nyx, and left.

EPILOGUE

The *Bethlehem Daily Times* reported the following items:

"**James Shelter**, 52, Chairman and Chief Executive of Black Feather Consolidated, perished unexpectedly on the evening of August 31, 1873 in the town of Mauch Chunk, Pennsylvania. A devoted husband, father and accomplished industrialist, he is survived by his loving wife, Elyse, and their two boys.

The **Honorable Tate Cain**, 64, longstanding adjudicator and benefactor to the County of Northampton, died peacefully in his sleep after a brief illness. His contributions to the people of Northampton County cannot be overstated, and he will be greatly missed.

Bartholemew H. Grigg, 33, Northampton County District Attorney, is hereby the Acting Judge until such time as a new judge is elected.

Joachim S. Thaler, 46, former head of Black Feather Extraction, has been named Chairman and Chief Executive of the Black Feather Consolidated Industries of Bethlehem, Pennsylvania.

The murderer Nickel Glock was killed by the Honorable **J. Blasius Grimp** of Mauch Chunk, Pennsylvania. Judge Grimp donated the entire reward in the amount of one thousand dollars for the founding of an Indian Industrial School at Carlisle, Pennsylvania.

Captain Wendell W. Kamp, 28, member of the 1st United States Sharpshooters, veteran of the Second Battle of Bull Run and the Battles of Antietam and Frdericksburg and former Detective, Bethlehem Police Department, succumbed at his home to complications related to injuries received during the War Between the States. He is preceded in death by his father, Horace G. Kamp, his mother, Alice B. Kamp (née Erzähler) and his brothers Wilhelm, Johannes, and Matthias.

May he rest in eternal peace.

www.ingramcontent.com/pod-product-compliance
Lightning Source LLC
Chambersburg PA
CBHW051535250626
47157CB00001B/57

* 9 7 8 0 6 9 2 7 8 9 6 6 7 *